The Invisible Woman

ANNA WINSON

Never fear reinventing yourself.

-Anna.

CONTENTS

Chapter 1   1

Chapter 2   8
Chapter 3   21
Chapter 4   29
Chapter 5   42
Chapter 6   58
Chapter 7   64
Chapter 8   74
Chapter 9   94
Chapter 10   126
Chapter 11   153
Chapter 12   196
Chapter 13   220
Chapter 14   238
Chapter 15   251
Chapter 16   273
Chapter 17   293

ACKNOWLEDGMENTS

Thank you to my friends and family who have supported my venture into writing. I cannot thank you enough for your patience, kindness, guidance, and love.

And to my readers who have supported this independent writer in her dream of becoming an author.

1

The sun streamed through the glass as I revelled in my happy place. I bought this chalet because I fell in love with this very window. The first thing I noticed as I walked into the inspection was a bench seat, nestled in front of an open fireplace looking out into the wintry landscape beyond. I ignored the places where the fabric had worn through and the foam beneath peeked out, or that the exterior of the property was in desperate need of a new coat of paint - forest green, like all the other chalets that surrounded it. None of that mattered because I had found the one place I wanted to exist. Right here. In front of this fireplace reading a book with a glass of red wine. I'd be lying if I said the name of the Chalet hadn't also ensnared me. Arendelle; the kingdom from Disney's Frozen.

Taking a deep breath, I turned and checked the clock on the stone mantel. 8.30 am. Time for work. Grabbing my coat and scarf off the hook in the drying room, I zippered up and headed out into the morning.

The Alpine Ski School doesn't open until 9 am, which makes it the most perfect place to work on the mountain. I get to sleep in and spend the day playing in the snow. What else could a girl ask for?

I walked down the recently ploughed lane, smiling and waving good morning to neighbours as I pass.

I have a number of seasonal jobs, one of which is assisting with the day to day running at the Alpine Ski School. Located on the mountainside, the ski school is for 'little skis', aka children.

As someone who was born with no natural grace or balance, skiing has never been my forte. I do not pretend to hide my awe when watching 5 and 6-year-old children take to the snow like a duck to water.

I must admit, I do enjoy seeing their faces and hearing their giggles and squeals of delight as they bolt down the mountainside.

"Morning Ava!" Zak's exclamation breaks my reverie as I step onto the landing.

"Morning Zak, full day again today?" I ask, picking up the registration clipboard to see two full pages of names. I look up to see Zak eyeing me.

"What? Oh, god do I have something in my teeth?" I turn to the nearest reflective surface just inside the front door to check my smile.

"No, there's just something about you today. Something different."

"Oh, my new beanie? My mum knitted it and sent it up for me, she has decided she'll send me a new one each season!" I touch the emerald green fabric perched atop my ginger locks. She said she picked the colour because it matched my eyes.

"Yeah, that must be it,' Zak sputtered awkwardly, "looks like we have 2 allergy flags for the morning session. Do you mind double-checking that the catering from the kitchen caught them?"

"Sure thing,' I reply, looking up to Zak's retreating back.

How odd.

Setting off into the snow once more, I notice more adults clambering out of their chalets, heading toward the ski lifts at the bottom of the town. Dinner Plain is most popular for families and beginner skiers, but it also draws large crowds of cross-country skiers. I have never understood the appeal of flying at breakneck speed down a flat, straight, unimpeded hill. What on earth would possess someone to want to do the same thing whilst dodging trees, rocks and other people is beyond me?

Smiling at a group of tourists, I head across the street and back toward the main village to the Mountain Kitchen restaurant. With the snow crunching underfoot and the scent of the log fires burning inside the chalets all the way up the mountain, I am reminded of just how lucky I am to live in such a beautiful part of the world.

The timber and stone facade of the Mountain Kitchen never ceases to make me smile. It encapsulates alpine architecture so beautifully. Opening the door to the clang of a cowbell, I look toward the chalkboards crammed full of the day's specials. Unable to resist the lure of fresh espresso this early in the morning, I wander to the counter wallet in hand.

"Good Morning Ivan,' I say to the face hidden amongst a tray piled high with muffins. Placing the tray down on the countertop, a head of long grey hair appeared.

"Ava, my lassie! How good to see you!" A wide smile breaking across his face, crinkling like a well-worn leather glove, "an espresso shot to start the morn'?" Cranking up the coffee machine, already knowing my answer.

"Please! I also came to check on the order for the Ski school this morning. There were two allergy flags, I wanted to be sure we got you that information,' I pulled the list up on my mobile phone, "the peanuts and the crustaceans".

"Aye, sounds like a terrible Broadway musical!" Ivan chuckled to himself from behind the machine. Steam crackling, beans grinding, Ivan hums to himself what I can only imagine is the show tune for the imaginary musical he is now envisioning.

"Any plans for the weekend young lass?" Ivan asks, placing the hot espresso glass on the counter.

"I think I'll probably go for a hike and spend it writing mostly." I'd been working on a story for many, many years and since arriving in Dinner Plain, have finally found the inspiration to finish it.

"Ah, when ca' we get a peek at this story! We've been kept waiting too long!" Ivan chuckled, reminding me suddenly of Albus Dumbledore.

"Not until it is ready! You can't rush genius. What about yourself? Are you and Marianne doing anything special?" I pick up the shot and down it in one go, relishing the heat as it hits my throat.

"Marianne, my old ball and chain. She said she wants to do something 'interesting and different' this weekend. What is there tha' is interesting or different to do in this town! We've lived here for over 30 years!" He exclaimed, throwing his crumpled tea towel on the counter.

I couldn't help but laugh. The town's longest permanent residents, Ivan and Marianne's relationship is the stuff of legends.

"Ivan, if I could only love someone as you love Marianne, my writing would have much happier endings!" I giggle, imagining what it must be like to love another being as much as they love one another.

"Ah, pish posh. There's a gent out there for you my dear, you just ha'n't found him yet. I 'spect he might need a map or a sherpa to find you hiding away up here, mind." Ivan's accent from old Scotland occasionally surfaces, making me smile.

"I can always count on you to bring a smile to my day, Ivan! Why don't I come across on Sunday to have tea with Marianne? The two of you can continue your attempts to teach me to play checkers." I grinned across at him whilst dragging my bank card out of my wallet, "surely that counts as interesting?"

Eyes twinkling, Ivan nodded, "Aye, I'd say that might cover it. I'll check with her ladyship when I ge' home tonight and I shall let you know."

Digging a box of packed lunches from the cold room to my left, Ivan mumbled to himself through the doorway.

"There you go my dear, peanuts and crustaceans accounted for." Handing over the box, Ivan studied me closely.

"If I were but 40 years younger and not already marrit to my soul mate..." He shook his head, the cheeky grin evident on his face.

Box in hand, I exited the restaurant and found myself smiling all the way back to the school.

With the final session of the day coming to an end, I fill a giant silver thermos with chocolate powder, boiling water and milk, mashing up the lumps with a whisk.

One of my favourite parts of the day is watching the kids come off the slopes, flushed cheeks and hoarse from squealing. They file in, exhausted and elated, grab a mug of hot chocolate with marshmallows and flop down on the couches in the rec room. Sometimes in the adult batch I add flavouring to the milk, today we have peppermint candy canes. It tastes like Christmas.

45 minutes later, the last parents have collected their children and the school is blessedly quiet. I hear Zak flip the sign on the front porch, dusting the snow from it.

Gathering the final mugs from the recreation room, I head into the kitchen to finish stacking the dishwasher.

"Well, I'm officially buggered, I'm so glad it is Friday,' Zak humphed as he slumped into a chair at the dining table.

"You coming for afternoon beers up at the hotel?" I glance at him sideways. Friday afternoons are when staff finishing the week gather and 'pass the torch' to the winter casuals who work the weekends on the slopes.

"Nah, Hayley wants to head up to Hotham to try and catch the nightlife,' Zak rolled his eyes, "speaking of, I'd better get up to the bus if I value my life!"

Donning his ski jacket, Zak juggled his scarf and bag in his arms, looking around aimlessly.

"Go, I'll lock up." I laugh at him, wondering what he would do if his head weren't attached to his body.

After locking the door to the school, I turn and smile fondly at the sign on the porch, "School's Out", proudly carved into the timber. The flip side reads "Snow Day".

Sighing contentedly, I step into the evening snowfall, the flakes catching on my scarf and eyelashes. Meandering up the street toward my chalet, I soak up the sounds of the village. Crunching footsteps, laughter, music, crackling fires and returned skiers stomping the ice out of their boots, hanging various skis and boards on racks in drying rooms.

A scent catches my attention, stopping me in my tracks. Someone is baking fresh bread.

"Ava!" I turn to the direction the call comes from, spotting a stout little woman carrying a German beer stein.

"Mrs Norris,' I smile back, encircling her in a warm embrace when she nears. "I promised Ivan I'd come and have tea with you both on Sunday, if that's okay with you?"

"Of course my dear! We would be honoured to welcome you into our home. I'll be sure to put on some scones for us tomorrow." Her chin wobbled slightly as her head bobbed.

"I see you are coming well prepared for Danny's discounted ale?" I laugh, pointing to the stein.

"When you are as old as I am my dear, you don't let a little thing like embarrassment stop you from a bargain or a good time."

I trundled up the path in the wake of her riotous laughter hoping I might have half her pizazz when I reach that age.

2

The next morning broke to fresh powder piled high on my windowsill. Checking the snow report whilst my coffee brewed, I noted only 10cm reportedly fell overnight. I peered out the window, eyeing my drive dubiously.

Throwing some bacon into the cast iron pan on the gas, I duck into the bathroom to shower quickly, conscious of my footprint. Ensconced in my cookie monster robe, I pull on my ugg boots and settle at the kitchen counter.

By 9 am I am dressed, fed and ready to drag out my shovel to commence the morning task of shovelling and salting my drive and walkway.

Turning the corner from my garage, obnoxiously large shovel in hand, I notice a gentleman standing in my front yard staring off into the distance.

Now, one could be forgiven for not recognising they were standing in 'my yard'. Part of the alpine appeal is the open spaces and lack of fences dividing properties. But something about his presence felt uneasy.

He was standing too straight, his posture too perfect, oddly still in the bustling morning surrounding him.

"Good Morning Sir,' I call as I stumble my way through the snow toward him, "can I help you?"

He turns toward me as I near, his almond eyes a reflection of the sky above.

"I am sorry to disturb your morning,' His baritone rang out, heavily accented. "I was enjoying a hike at sunrise when I lost my way."

I look around confused. He's standing in the centre of the village. There wasn't anyone with him nor did he carry a pack or ski gear.

"Sir, you are in Dinner Plain - are you staying here in the village?" Scrutinising him more closely I notice a graze on his hand, what looks like blood on his fingers. "Are you injured?" I close the distance between us, feeling his eyes settle on my face. I look closer, noticing a bump on his forehead, peeking out from under a salt and pepper fringe.

"Why don't you come and sit down and I'll get a first aid kit." I motion toward my porch, remembering I hadn't yet shovelled it. Scampering through the powder, 10cms my arse, I rake the shovel across the steps enough to clear a space for him to sit without getting a wet bum.

Returning from inside with a pair of gloves and a first aid kit, I squat down in front of him.

"Hi there, I'm Ava. What's your name?"

"Mr Huynh, but you may call me Winnie." He smiles down at me, flashing perfect rows of veneers.

"Well Winnie, what happened on your little adventure at sunrise?" I hold out my hand, inspecting his upturned palm. Scrapes and grazes suggest he tripped, stumbled or fell.

"I tripped over and bumped my head, but I am fine now." His fingers probing the darkening spot near his hairline. Wincing, he looks at me sheepishly.

"But you are fine now, huh?" I chuckle. "Do you know what day it is?"

"Monday,' He says confidently.

Uh-oh.

"Do you remember the name of your lodgings?" I try again.

"Tenaya, the most beautiful lodge in all of Yosemite."

"Winnie, I think you may have a concussion. We are not in the United States, but Australia."

Wide eyes turn to mine, shock registering on his aging face.

"I'm going to call you an ambulance and get you a blanket." Ducking inside I grab the comforter off the couch and punch '000' into my mobile phone.

As the ambulance crosses the town boundary, I chuckle at the village entry sign, "Dinner Plain; Population 142." The '2' had been painted over with rather a grotesque '3', in honour of my arrival just over a year ago.

"Ava,' the driver called from the front of the van. Ryan Murphy is a paramedic who works out of the Hotham Medical Centre. He's all smiles and beach boy hair, working the winter season at Mt Hotham and summers in the bustling city of Melbourne. We've seen each other frequently the past two seasons that I've been here; what with the minor bumps and breaks at the Ski School.

In such close proximity to the driver's seat, I'm intoxicated by his scent. Firewood, aftershave and my favourite Microshield medical-grade hand sanitiser.

"How are you, Ryan? I was wondering if I'd see you this week." I try to keep the giggle out of my voice. I frown at myself, am I giggling at him or is the adrenaline wearing off from discovering a bleeding man with head trauma on my porch?

"Been so busy at Hotham this week, what with the X-Trails on and..." There is something so very pleasant about Ryan's mouth when he speaks, even from this angle. I sit entranced at the sound of his voice, like caramel or coffee. A little bit spicy but warm and rich.

"Ava?" Ryan's chuckle breaks my reverie, "we're here."

Hell, how long was I daydreaming?

Feeling the heat of embarrassment creeping up my neck and into my cheeks, I pray the cold mountain air would save me from his teasing as I clamber out the back of the truck. I say truck because snow ambulances aren't quite as dainty and sleek as the standard ones in the city.

"Mr Winnie, I'm going to go and find some coffee while the doctors take a look at you."

"Don't be silly my dear, you have done more than enough for an old man already. You do not need to stay. Go and enjoy the sunshine." Mr Huynh grasps my hand, planting a kiss on the back of my fingers.

Rolling his eyes, Ryan laughs, pushing the stretcher down the corridor, "Okay now, 'Mr Romantic' let's get you into the CT machine and check out that noggin of yours."

After waiting several hours for a remote radiographer at the local hospital to double-check the CT scan, it was confirmed Mr Huynh had a concussion and was admitted to stay the night for observation.

"Is there anyone I can call? Were you travelling with anyone who will be looking for you?" I sit perched beside Winnie's bed, enjoying watching the snow floating outside the window.

"No thank you, my dear, there is no one to call. Unless you count my lawyer!" He chuckles to himself, a private joke.

A knock from the door has us both turning to see Ryan through the window. He beckons me, doughnut in hand.

"I'll be right back." I turn back to Mr Winnie, a knowing smile playing on his lips.

"Take your time,' he winks at me.

Feeling the heat rising in my cheeks again, I wander over to the door.

"You rang?" I enquire as the door closes behind me.

"I thought you might be hungry,' Ryan holds open the box of Krispy Creme doughnuts.

"Where did you get these!" I hadn't had glazed doughnuts since the last time I was in Melbourne.

"Listen, I've got to head back into the slopes, but if you'd like a lift back to Dinner Plain this evening I can swing past when I get off work? We could grab a beer at Danny's?"

"I'd be very grateful for a lift! It hadn't even occurred to me how I'd get back."

"You are so selfless and considerate,' it came out almost a sigh.

I look up at him startled, noticing the small freckles that dotted his tanned complexion.

"I think you have that the wrong way around, you're the paramedic. I just called '000' for a man who was bleeding on my porch."

Ryan chuckles, shaking his head, 'most people don't accompany their patients to the hospital."

"I guess I hadn't thought of it like that. I just know if I were injured and alone I would appreciate knowing someone was looking out for me." I shrug.

Ryan's partner hollers from down the hall, racing past with the stretcher.

"Probably should turn this back on,' toying with the dial on his shoulder-mounted radio, "so I'll see you when I finish? Should be around 6 pm?"

I smile up at him, nodding enthusiastically.

And then he was gone.

Feeling slightly bereft, but with no earthly reason why, I wander back into Mr Winnie's room.

"He seems like a kind young man." An observation. Rhetorical.

I sit down and busy myself with finishing Winnie's admission forms.

"Any allergies?" I query.

"Just hazelnuts,' he chuckles.

The door swings open following a quiet knock.

"Mr Huynh, we have received your blood results back from the lab. If I may have a moment, I'd like to discuss them with you." The doctor looks pointedly at me.

"I'll be outside,' I nod at Mr Huynh as I stand to leave.

"I'm an old man with no family and no loved ones. There is nothing you can say to me or about me that can't be said in front of this young woman." I freeze, shocked at his words. No family and no loved ones. *How is that possible?*

"Uh, okay then. Mr Huynh, you have high cholesterol. A man of your age really ought to be taking better care of himself. Do you have a doctor back home who monitors your health?" The doctor's face pinched and pouted like a pug.

"I will be sure to raise it with her when I return to Singapore."

I was still chewing over the 'man of your age' comment as the doctor departed, taking the forms with him. I know that Asian genes tend to lend themselves to aging extremely well but how old could Mr Huynh be?

Turning inquisitively back to the patient, I find his gaze scrutinising me.

"Tell me, my dear, how did you come to find yourself living in such isolation? Do not mistake me, I am very pleased to have stumbled upon your doorstep, but why is a beautiful young woman spending her day with an old man when she could be on the arm of a bright young suitor?" He wheezes, adjusting his oxygen mask.

"I fell in love with the idea of moving to the snow one hot Queensland summer. I'd been working in jobs chasing money and success and decided I wanted a change. Following a few weeks of googling, I had my heart set on buying a chalet in Dinner Plain and I worked my ass off for 2 years to get here. Oh, pardon my language."

"I now live here comfortably, working a couple of part-time jobs and enjoying the peace that comes with needing little and aspiring to a life full of things other than wealth." I look up to catch sight of Mr Huynh's face, that of a grandparent, appraising one's offspring.

"You do not aspire to wealth." His head cocks to the side, "tell me then, what is it you aspire to?"

"Happiness. Bringing joy to the world, and to others. I also try to give back where I can."

"A real philanthropist. Tell me, are you religious?"

"No sir."

"Have you ever known what it is like to 'have money'?" His scrutiny suddenly made the room feel heavy.

"No. But I have all I need - no more, no less and do not seek to be greedy."

"You do not wish to see the world from the perspective of how 'the other half' live?"

I laugh out loud at that, "I think you mean the 1%! And no, I do not. Wealth comes hand in hand with many, many other misfortunes. I couldn't imagine living my life unable to determine who my true friends are, or struggling to know the true value of something simply because I can afford not to worry about what it cost me.

'Don't get me wrong, I could certainly find a way to live 'with more', but I don't see how I could be happy sitting atop a mass of wealth, when so many others struggle to survive each day."

"You are most, unlike any other woman I have ever met Miss Ava. Someday I should like to welcome you to Singapore and show you the city I love so much." He beams across at me.

"I would be honoured, Mr Huynh."

We wiled away the day discussing all manner of things; politics, religion, fashion, cars, sport, literature, travel.

He noticed my ring that I had designed and set with an Australian Opal and asked me if I had a favourite designer. I nodded enthusiastically.

"Who doesn't love Harry Winston?" I giggled. Showing him a picture of the Winston Legacy Pink Diamond purchased at auction for $50m in 2018. We both agreed that $50m seemed a 'little' on the pricy side for a single piece of jewellery.

He wanted to know about me, growing up in Australia, my family, my education, professional background. He mentioned places he wanted me to see and experience, not only in Singapore but also around the world.

"When you are in Singapore I shall have to show you my library, I have spent a lifetime filling it with books that brought me joy. Many are in Mandarin but are beautiful to behold nonetheless."

He told me of how he grew up impoverished in China and spent the majority of his life working on the docks and in shipping. Moving to Singapore as a teenager to seek his fortune. He talked of precious items he holds most dear; a MontBlanc pen, an inherited oak desk thought to be from an ancient dynasty.

"Such rare treasures you have acquired during your lifetime. What a gift to live such a full and happy life."

We exchanged details; phone numbers, email addresses. He asked for my address so he could send me a small thank you. Despite my protestations, he reminded me that he could just get my address off the hospital forms I had completed for him. Begrudgingly, I included the details of my chalet.

A quiet knock came from the door.

Looking up I realise with a jolt that the sun had set. How had I managed to lose track of time so badly and how was it possible to have spent the entire day with a stranger who felt so easily like a long-lost friend?

Ryan sticks his head through the door.

"There you are, right where I left you." He smiles down at me.

"I had best let you two kids get on with your evening,' Mr Huyhn sighs from his bed.

"I'll be out in a second,' I hold up a finger to Ryan who disappears back through the door.

"Mr Huynh, it has been the greatest honour to meet you. I do hope we have the chance to meet again, in less dramatic circumstances next time,' I giggle.

Holding out his hand for mine, kissing my knuckles ever so gently. Such an ancient tenderness, from an era long forgotten.

"Miss Ava. It was my honour to have met you. You have given this silly old man a zest for life that had been long forgotten. For that and your extreme kindness, I can never repay you." I felt myself welling up as Mr Huynh blinks and clears his throat.

I bend over, placing a gentle kiss on his forehead.

"Until we meet again,' I smile down at him before turning to the door.

"Wǒ de tiānshǐ; my angel,' he whispers as I close the door behind me.

A silent tear burns down my cheek. What a beautiful, unexpected gentleman.

After washing my face in the bathroom, I straighten myself up, drag fingers through my hair and yank my beanie back on.

Ryan and I drove back to town in easy banter. It wasn't the first time we'd spent alone, but it had been a while.

The drive was peaceful, the snow drifting down in swathes and sprays on the windshield.

Danny's bar at the Hotel was an entirely different story. Saturday night saw even the most straight-laced parents from the ski school letting their hair down.

Drinks were flowing, pizzas baking in the wood fire ovens, laughter and music filled the space, flowing onto the alfresco terrace.

"Drink?" Ryan elbows his way into the throng of people at the bar.

"BBC Ale, in a pint please!" I holler, losing sight of him.

A wave of sudden exhaustion and melancholy washes over me. Digging out my phone I dial the medical centre to check up on Mr Huynh. The line was engaged. Hanging up, I pocket my phone.

I suppose we did only leave an hour ago. Probably best to leave them be for the night. I'll send him an email in the morning to ask how he's feeling. They'll discharge him tomorrow. He was returning straight to Melbourne for meetings on Monday anyway.

"Ah, my hero!" I elate, seeing Ryan appear, beers in hand, waitress in tow.

"Sorry it took so long, I wanted to order before things got really crazy in there,' Ryan chuckles.

Onto the table, the waitress places wedges, nachos, garlic bread and fried dim sims. It smelled mouthwatering. My stomach gurgles, reminding me that other than a doughnut, I hadn't eaten since breakfast.

"The pizzas will be out in 15-20,' the waitress saunters past Ryan, her barely-there skirt leaving little to the imagination.

"A toast, to saving lives and breaking hearts!" Ryan raises his glass toward mine.

"Breaking hearts? What on earth are you talking about?" I laugh, relaxing into the couch.

"Oh please, that old guy was making eyes at you all day. I bet he wanted to sweep you off to Singapore and make you his new wife." Ryan drank deeply, his face disappearing into his ale.

"If I didn't know any better, I'd say you sound jealous. All we did was talk." I laugh; men make no sense.

"Sounds like a marriage to me,' he scoffs back.

I decided to swiftly derail that conversation.

"What type of pizza did you order?" I ask, snuggling further into the couch, relishing the warmth of the hearth beside us.

"Your favourites; pepperoni on BBQ and Hawaiian with all the pineapple on one half." He makes a face. Ryan did not understand pineapple on pizza. He even has a shirt to prove it.

Pulling a classic male move, he scooted over further on the couch to put his arm around me while we ate.

Tracing my fingers over the Blizzard Brewing Company logo on my stein, I pondered how Mr Huynh could possibly have lived to his age without any family or loved ones to speak of.

"Penny for your thoughts?" Ryan was studying my face in the firelight.

"I wasn't paying much attention when I filled out his forms, how old was Mr Huynh?"

"Technically it isn't breaking confidentiality I suppose because you did see his D.O.B, you just didn't take any notice. He is 70 years old this year."

"70!" I spit what little beer I have left, all down my front and the arm Ryan had around my middle.

"Classy Ava!" Ryan jumped, shaking beer and spit off his sleeve.

"I'm so sorry!" I wailed, grabbing napkins and failing miserably to wipe down his arm.

70 years old. Wow.

"It's okay, you can make it up to me,' he simpers, wiggling his eyebrows suggestively.

Grabbing his face with both hands, I place a chaste kiss on his lips and turn back to the pizza.

"Uh, uh. You're not getting away that easily,' grabbing me by the waist, he lifts me easily to perch in his lap. Chuckling deeply, he nuzzles my neck. What a sexy sound. He smelled of wood chips, beer and alpine. It was heavenly.

"Ryan,' I breathe, "Ryan!"

He pulls back, his dark eyes ensnaring mine.

"I'm exhausted. I'm happy to make out, but then you're going to walk me to my door and kiss me goodnight before I fall into a coma."

Ever the gentleman, he nods his acquiescence and breathes, "I'll take what I can get,' before continuing his ministrations.

That night I fell into a deep sleep, drifting off I wondered; *How lucky am I? Could life be any more perfect?*

3

I smiled at the bartender as she shook up my third cocktail. I turned to watch the thunderstorm roll across the Singapore sky, feeling the atmosphere crackle, perched atop my bar stool high above the city.

"What made you pick Spago Bar for dinner tonight?" She leaned across the bar, placing a giant glass before me, expertly decanting the cocktail with a flourish.

I clapped applause and she bowed, both of us in fits of laughter.

"I just wanted to know what it felt like to be one of those people who were fancy enough to eat atop the Marina Bay Sands building. And I must say, it has been worth every penny."

I roll over in bed, the dream of my days in Singapore floating away like the distant memory they were. I was only there two years ago but it already feels like a lifetime has passed.

Checking my phone, I note Ryan texted last night to say he'd arrived back in Hotham safely. 10:35 pm. I was well and truly comatose by that point. I resolve to reply to him when I'm properly awake and caffeinated.

After downing a large bacon and egg roll to combat the very large beers we drank last night, I text Ryan back and then sit staring vagrantly at my laptop. Mr Huynh will be discharged shortly if he hasn't been already. I should write to him so he knows someone is thinking of him.

As I type, I am baffled once again at his admission to having no friends or family. How do you get to 70 years of age and not have a single friend or loved one?

Maybe he's in the mafia or a spy.

I shake the thought aside and start to type.

To: Huynh1@heh.com

Dear Mr Huynh,

I trust this email finds you well and you are safely on your return to Melbourne. It was a pleasure to meet you yesterday and I do hope to keep in touch, as unusual as that may sound.

Kind Regards,
Ava Elias

There, surely that's not too lame? What an odd email address. Huynh 1. I suppose Huynh is a rather common surname in Singapore and China. How many Huynh's are there at HEH? What is HEH?

Out of curiosity, I resolve to google it once I've sorted out my daily chores which once again include shovelling my drive, seeing as it did not magically shovel itself yesterday and it allegedly only snowed another 5cms overnight.

Standing in the middle of my half shovelled drive, I stare at the porch where 24 hours ago Winnie sat, bloodied and confused.

He only sat there for 20 minutes waiting for the ambulance and yet I will likely forever remember that as 'the spot where Winnie sat'.

After finishing up the morning with Ivan and Marianne playing checkers, I returned home and stretched out on the couch.

At 3 pm, right on schedule, the Vegetation van pulled into my freshly salted drive.

"I wasn't sure if that was salt or snow!" Gary hollers from his open window.

"I have a hate/hate relationship with black ice!" I laugh back, crunching my way down the drive.

"We couldn't get a couple of your requests in Miss Ava, so I added some substitutes free of charge."

"You didn't have to do that Gary, I'm happy to pay for them!"

"Sounds like you had quite the day yesterday, what with your visit to Hotham Medical and all,' He glanced sideways at me as he passed, as always clad in his khaki overalls. "The whole town is talking about it. Also heard you and Mr Murphy were getting snuggly last night at Danny's."

"News travels fast,' I blush.

"Now, it certainly isn't any of my business who you decide to hold hands with by the campfire but someone oughta warn you, that Murphy, he holds a lotta hands, if you catch my meaning." His embarrassed gaze anywhere but on me.

"Thanks for the warning Gary, I'll keep it in mind,' I smile at him, turning for the door.

"Well enjoy your week Miss Ava, I'll see you next Sunday."

I'm not sure which of us was more embarrassed by that conversation. I am always touched and caught a little off guard by how quickly the people of this town have come to look out for me.

Waving Gary's van down the road, my thoughts turned to Ryan.

Mmm Ryan. It's not possible for someone that attractive to be left alone. Even when we have been on dates together in the Hotham Village, women have hit on him in front of me.

I've never committed to anything too serious with him because he always returns to Melbourne the second the ice starts to melt.

And I've no doubt he has some pretty-little-thing sitting in some high-rise in the city eagerly awaiting his return. Pushing the thought aside, I trudge back inside.

Watching the yeast for my vegemite scrolls activating quietly beside the fireplace, frothy bubbles pluming, I hear the delicate 'ping' of a new email in my inbox.

Turning toward my laptop at the other end of the window seat, I feel my soul lighten.

1 new email from huynh1@heh.com

To: avaelias@outlook.com

Dear Miss Ava,

Thank you for your email. It was a most pleasant welcome to Melbourne to find this awaiting me.

I am much improved thank you. The staff took excellent care of me. Although, that Doctor did try to convince me once again that cholesterol is the devil!

I trust you had an enjoyable evening with Paramedic Murphy after you left?

Kind Regards,

Mr Huynh

I laugh out loud!

Cheeky Winnie! The audacity!

I am torn between immediately replying and chastising him lightly or leaving it a while before I reply and make him wait for it.

Wait, what am I thinking? He's not some teenage boy you have a crush on, he's not going to care if you seem 'too eager' by replying immediately.

To: Huynh1@heh.com

Dear Mr Huynh,

I must say! I am scandalised! Mr Murphy and I had dinner at Danny's hotel in Dinner Plain. He walked me home and returned to Hotham.

How is your head? Are you ready for your meetings tomorrow?

As for me, I will spend tomorrow on the slopes at the ski school. We've quite a bit of snow forecast overnight so it should make for a magical day.

Stay well,

Kind Regards,

Ava Elias

P.S It was a most enjoyable evening.

Giggling to myself, I hit send. Grabbing the bowl of yeast from the stone hearth, I skip into the kitchen with a smile on my face.

My cheesy vegemite scrolls resting on the countertop left the house smelling like freshly baked bread. I decided to indulge myself for my Sunday afternoon and take a bath.

Heading upstairs to the main bathroom I shut the venetians on the wrap-around-window, not wanting to give my neighbours a peep show. Leaning over the vast copper tub I turn on the water, my fingers sweeping through the cascade. Sprinkling droplets of Windella Farm essential oils into the water, the scent of bergamot, ylang ylang and patchouli wafts toward me.

Padding through to the master bedroom I pick up my book, cookie monster bathrobe and slippers. I loop the robe beside my towel on the heated rail. Shutting off the water when the tub is half full, I clamber in, careful not to bang my shins on the edge.

Gingerly leaning back into the edge of the tub, a shiver creeps up my spine as the icy copper touches my skin. Now safely in the tub, I reach across and re-open the shutters, watching the sun setting over the frosted mountains in the distance. Hues of pink and orange creep across the horizon, the mountains slowly enveloping the sun behind them.

Leaning over to light the shelf of candles beside the tub, I grab my book and settle in.

Later that evening once clean, dried and warming again by the fireplace, I grab my laptop. One new email.

I hurriedly open the mail program eager to see Mr Huynh's reply only to discover it is junk mail.

I lean back into the couch, feeling rather deflated and a little ridiculous.

I should probably stop thinking about him. This is getting a little nuts. *I spent one day with the guy and suddenly he feels like - what? Part of my life? Someone I want to get to know more? Why? I'm losing my mind. Why would he want to be friends with me anyway? Maybe I just feel sorry for him?*

I knew deep down that wasn't the case. I enjoyed the day we had spent together and learned so much about his culture, his life. The passion he lived with was inspiring and yet ensconced in this dark loneliness. His presence reminded me of the times I had spent with my grandparents. So much life lived and wisdom acquired.

Another ping from my laptop. 1 New Email. Knowing I was not going to win this internal battle, I immediately give in and open the email.

To: avaelias@outlook.com

Dear Miss Ava,

I am most pleased to hear you had an enjoyable evening. Thank you for indulging this old man in his curiosities, it has been a very long time since I, myself, have taken a lady to dinner.

I am prepared for my meetings. I reviewed the documentation this afternoon whilst dreaming of being anywhere but here. There is something about Profit and Loss, BAS and financial statements that dulls the soul. I am looking forward to Tuesday's meetings, I'll be down on the docks in Port of Melbourne. Back where I feel most comfortable.

On Friday I return to Singapore. I do not know how long it will be before I return to Australia. If I had realised how much I would like this country, I would have spent far more time here far sooner.

Enjoy your day on the slopes, Miss Ava,

Kind Regards,

Mr Huynh

I find such a strange sense of peace reading his emails. Similar to what I felt in his presence, I am again struck by his language and wisdom. I can only aspire to have that kind of an impact upon people in my world someday. Noticing the late hour on my laptop screen, I decide to turn in and reply to him in the morning.

4

Throughout spring as the ice began to melt and holiday makers deserted the town, Winnie and I wrote to each other every day, sometimes more. With Ryan's departure back to Melbourne and his communications rare, I found myself truly thankful for Winnie's friendship.

I would send him photos of the mountains and minor upgrades as my chalet received an (extremely expensive council-mandated) facelift. He would send me long lists of literature to read and travel destinations, often based on where he was on the globe at the time. Some of his recommendations came through in Mandarin. Google translate is now my best friend. Of a Saturday night, Winnie would always send me photos of incredible meals and beverages, no matter where in the world he was dining.

By the middle of Summer, it was a welcome distraction from our tiny town, where occasionally in the summer the routine became a little stifling. I spent my days assisting local businesses with bookkeeping, office management and general secretarial duties. Occasionally picking up a shift at the Mountain Kitchen with Ivan, keeping my barista skills sharp and taking the opportunity to catch up with the locals I hadn't seen in a few days.

One particularly warm Sunday afternoon, I sat outside on my deck soaking in the summer sun, my feet propped indelicately on the timber table, my toes kissed by the sunlight.

I had been reading my way through Winnie's recommended literature, ordering the books online and sometimes waiting weeks for them to arrive. On occasion I had to drive into Bright to pick them up because deliveries were delayed coming up the mountain.

Today I was in the middle of reading Dream of Ding Village by Yan Lianke. The translation of a harrowing tale of the Henan Province during the 1990s AIDS epidemic. A tad darker than my usual choice for an afternoon browse but I found myself completely enthralled.

So enthralled in fact that I barely noticed Gary from Vegetation peering around the corner of the house.

"Miss Ava!" he called. I nearly jumped out of my skin. Book clattering to the floor, knocking my 'dark and stormy' over in the process, sending rum soaking into the tabletop.

I really should re-varnish that next weekend.

"I'm so sorry, Miss Ava, I didn't mean to scare you!" Gary trundles across the lawn, box in hand.

"It's okay Gary, I was just reading a...uh...scary book,' I laugh.

"Would you like me to bring this inside Miss?" Gary held the box aloft.

"That would be great, thanks!" I indicated to the back door, propped open by a bulbous ceramic owl. Following him inside I collected a roll of paper towel and mopped up the spill outside.

Reappearing moments later, Gary bid me a pleasant afternoon and disappeared back around the corner of the house.

On my hands and knees wiping up overflow off the timber decking, I am once again startled by the sound of my name.

"Ava!" I bang my head on the underside of the table.

Ow.

"Oh, did you bump your wee noggin?" Ivan calls, approaching the deck. "What on earth are you doing under the table there?"

"I was mopping up my cocktail, I had a spill." I laugh, rubbing my head.

Taking Ivan's proffered hand I stood, dusting the grit and dirt from my bare knees.

"How are you this afternoon Ivan? Are you and Marianne enjoying the warmer weather this week?" I smile up at him.

"Well, Marianne hasn't been feeling too well these past days my dear. I hear there is something going around." Ivan's brow furrowed. Dinner Plain isn't always the easiest town to find medical assistance at short notice.

"Has she seen a Doctor?" I try to keep the concern out of my voice. Ivan and Marianne tend to be the 'she'll be right' type, often leaving things until the last minute.

"Aye, she has. We went to town yesterday. She's got some antibiotics and told to stay on bed rest." Ivan's voice catches as he hesitated. "Ah, Miss Ava, I was wondering if I could ask ye a wee favour?"

"Of course Ivan, anything for you!"

He's starting to make me nervous.

"Would you possibly be able to help me out a few extra days in the diner this week? Just until Marianne is back on her feet again. I don't wan' ta leave her alone too much if I can help it." He looks at his feet, embarrassed at asking for help.

"Ivan, of course, I will! It is no problem at all. If you want, I'll pop by in the morning and pick up the spare key to open for you. Then you can come in whenever you are ready." I smile up at him, his long silver mane braided into loose pigtails today.

"Bless you, my dear. Where would we be without you?" He bent down to kiss my cheek and bid me farewell.

"I'll see you at 5 am!" I call to his departing figure, smiling to myself.

Ugh. 4.30 am wakeup; on the upside, I'll have free coffee to start the morning!

After setting an obnoxiously early alarm and washing my face, I lugged my laptop into my bedroom and mashed out an email to Winnie.

To: Huynh1@heh.com

Dear Mr Huynh,

I trust you are enjoying your suite in New York (ooh fancy!). Some day you will have to tell me what the secret is too convincing people to pay for such elaborate accommodations.

I must admit, your Chicago deep pan pizza from dinner yesterday looked divine. I have decided I will attempt to reproduce one next week after I've shopped for ingredients. I'll let you know how it works out!

In my literary update, I am most of the way through Dream of Ding Village. I am shocked by these people's stories. I had to google the history of the AIDS epidemic in the 1990s to check it was real.

I am realising the more I read from your recommendations, just how little I know about history and culture in Asia.

I hope you are keeping well,

Kind Regards,

Ava Elias

Turning out the light, I fell asleep dreaming of penthouses, pizza and New York City.

The week that followed was a complete disaster. 4.30 am starts to open the Mountain Kitchen, not closing until 6 pm; followed by immediately logging onto MYOB online to look at the multiple of local businesses I had been neglecting during the day. Tens of new emails from each of the businesses each day, all acknowledging that I wouldn't get their queries until I had finished assisting Ivan for the day and yet pushing their urgency nonetheless.

It wasn't until a lull at the cafe around lunchtime on Thursday that I realised I hadn't heard back from Winnie since his stay in New York.

It is unlike him to go days without a word. Even when he was holed up in a Tokyo hotel during a typhoon he sent a message to say that he was okay. What if he is angry with me? Did I say anything that could have been offensive in my last email?

Perhaps I missed a reply? I have been bone-tired these last couple of days, maybe I read it and don't remember.

When I got home that night I logged straight onto my laptop to check my emails.

No new messages.

A sense of unease grew in my stomach. I decided I didn't care how childish it might look, I opened a new email.

To: Huynh1@heh.com

Dear Mr Huynh,

I wrote to you on Sunday evening and have yet to receive a reply. I understand you must be extremely busy, jet setting across the globe. As silly as it sounds, would you please let me know you're okay?

Kind Regards,
Ava Elias

I didn't sleep that night. I spent hours staring at the ceiling listening out for that 'ping' from my laptop. It never came.

The next morning I dragged myself out of bed, thanking the gods it was Friday. I had the kitchen open before the sun was up, the first customers sleepily entering in dribs and drabs. Not the smell of the espresso nor the freshly baked cinnamon scrolls could pull me out of this funk. The customers started to notice it too.

"Are you okay today Ava? You seem a bit distracted?" Danny, of Danny's Bar in the hotel, stands in front of me, arms piled high with purchases waiting to make payment.

"I'm so sorry Danny. How long have you been standing there waiting for me?" I laugh, it sounded hollow.

"Not long! It was the fact that you made me a hot chocolate and not a chai latte that made me ask,' he looks down at the cup on the counter.

"I am not myself today I'm afraid. Why don't you head back to the hotel, I'll bring you a new cup."

After ringing up his purchases, Danny departs for the hotel.

Ivan arrived to relieve me a few minutes later, giving me the opportunity to take Danny his corrected beverage.

Spotting him crouched at the far side of the hotel lobby stacking firewood into the large open fireplace, I took a moment to drink in the grandiosity that is the hotel. From the cabin style timber beams to the large plush leather couches scattered around or the floor to ceiling stone fireplace Danny currently tended to. This building is a masterpiece. A sudden pang of guilt washed over me.

I really should spend more time in here. It is beautiful.

"Danny,' I call as I near, "I am so sorry for this morning. I put in two extra marshmallows as an apology. Don't tell Ivan,' I whisper.

Brushing his hands off on his jeans, Danny took the cup and smiles at me.

"It is no problem, Ava. We all have off days. I had a guy turn up here yesterday for a room we had him booked into for next weekend. We managed to fix it, thank god, but we all have our moments,' he chuckles.

"You wanna tell me what's on your mind?" He indicates toward the couch nearest the fireplace.

Perching on the edge of the seat I realise I felt like I hadn't really stopped all week.

"I've just had a manic week and I haven't heard word back from a friend I am a little worried about,' I sigh. Explaining it like that just didn't seem to express the weight of what I was feeling.

"Have you tried calling them?" Danny turns to look at me, one eyebrow raised.

I sit there dumbfounded.

Why on earth has that not occurred to me? I have his phone number, I've just never used it. International dialling is SO expensive.

"You know, I haven't. Ha! Thanks, Danny." With that, I felt some small relief as I left the hotel to finish the day up with Ivan.

I got home and checked what time it would be in Singapore. Melbourne is 3 hours ahead of Singapore which means a phone call now would not be discourteous. It has also been almost 24 hours since my last email.

Digging out my laptop, I double-check I hadn't heard anything back. No new messages.

Taking a deep breath, I dial his number.

Why am I so nervous? It isn't unreasonable to want to be sure he is okay.

The phone beeped in my hand and disconnected.

Odd.

Oh, the international dialling code.

Duh.

Dialling 00-11 and then his number, I tried again.

It beeped as the international extension connected.

"该号码已断开连接。Gāi hàomǎ yǐ duàn kāi liánjiē." A woman's voice on a -prerecorded message in Mandarin.

What the hell does that mean?! There was no 'beep' for an answering machine, the call just disconnected.

Firing up google translate on my laptop, I dial the number again and use the dictation tool to record the woman's message. Hitting the 'translate' button. My stomach dropped.

Five little words.

"This number has been disconnected."

Okay, maybe I just have his number wrong in my phone? Or he lost his phone. Or all of Singapore is currently without telecommunications because of a freak storm?

Okay, that one was grasping a little.

I decide to send Winnie another email for little other reason than because it was all I felt I could.

To: Huynh1@heh.com

Hi Winnie,

I know how ridiculous this is, but I have an unsettling feeling and I need to know you are okay. Please call me or email me back to let me know you are alright.

-Ava

Launching myself away from the computer I run to the bathroom and jump in a scalding shower. I don't know how long I spend standing under the spray, my scattered thoughts headed in every direction.

Do I get on a plane to Singapore and track him down like in the movies?

What if I offended him somehow and he's angry with me?

What if he decided he doesn't want to be friends anymore and he's tired of talking to me?

What if something really bad happened to him?

How will I ever find out what happened?

What if he is unwell somewhere with no friends or family to care for him?

Is it reasonable for me to be thinking these things?

Do I have any right to be this upset about losing contact with him?

How do you determine who is and isn't important in your life?

How long does someone have to be in your life to have a profound impact?

The image of Drew Dudley giving his Lollypop Moments TED talk pops into my mind.

A moment. A single moment is all it could take for someone to have a profound impact. One interaction, one phone call, one look, one smile.

Yes, I decide it is appropriate for me to feel the things I am feeling. I just couldn't figure out how to control them.

Wrapped in a fluffy bath sheet, I hedge my way back toward my laptop.

And there it was. 1 new message.

My heart stops.

To: avaelias@outlook.com

感谢您与Huynh Enterprises Holdings联系。

该电子邮件帐户不再有效。

对于所有紧急查询，请联系info@heh.com

Gǎnxiè nín yǔ Huynh Enterprises Holdings liánxì.

Gāi diànzǐ yóujiàn zhànghù bù zài yǒuxiào.Duìyú suǒyǒu jǐnjí cháxún, qǐng liánxì info@heh.Com

I don't understand. What is this?

Holy shit. It's an auto-reply.

Feeling as though I am going to vomit and pass out at the same time, I copy and paste the text into google translate.

"Thank you for contacting Huynh Enterprises Holdings.

The email account is no longer valid.

For all urgent inquiries, please contact info@heh.com".

A sudden urge to scream, cry and throw things overcomes me.

What the fuck is going on? Where is Mr Huynh?

In one final desperate attempt to gain some type of clarity I open Google and type into the search engine "Mr Huynh HEH Singapore". Sending a silent prayer to the gods I hit search.

Rows and rows of news articles and websites appear. I fall to my knees in front of the screen.

"CEO of Huynh Enterprises Holdings, dies age 70."

No, this can't be happening. This has to be a mistake.

I click on the link, confused as to why the article is referring to Winnie as 'the CEO'. He told me he worked in Shipping 'mostly on the docks'.

The page loaded, scalp crawlingly slowly. Then, there in vivid colour and high definition, was Mr Huynh smiling embraced in a handshake with another businessman.

"Mr Hyunh Li, CEO of Huynh Enterprises Holdings, has reportedly died in Singapore. A spokeswoman for HEH confirmed via press conference this morning."

The video began playing automatically.

A woman in her mid-thirties, dressed in a black pantsuit, pearls and french twist stood behind a large glass podium. HEH carved into the facade.

"It is with great sadness we confirm the passing of our founding CEO Mr Huynh Li, earlier this week following a short illness. He will be greatly missed. A memorial will be held at HEH at the conclusion of this week for staff and family. Thank you."

The pantsuit woman bowed, repeated the statement in Mandarin, bowed again and departed.

Hot, silent tears streamed down my face, tracing my fingers across the grinning veneers on the screen.

He died.

'After a short illness'.

He was sick. For how long?

Scrolling back up the article, I realise in horror it is dated 4 days ago.

He got sick after his last email and he died. He has been gone this whole week and I didn't even know. Why didn't anyone tell me! Why didn't anyone contact me! They could have seen we'd been in contact! His emails would have been on the company server.

White-hot rage burned through me. Even as I knelt there, I knew why no one had contacted me. Because I was no-one.

I didn't even know about the memorial. It would have happened in Singapore this afternoon.

What would I have done if I had known? What could I have done? I wasn't really in a position to drop everything and fly to Asia.

I knew in my heart that if I had known, I probably would have done everything in my power to get to him before he died.

I sink to the floor, the icy slate rising to meet my burning face; consumed with anger, sadness and grief. Hard angry sobs escape my throat, racking my whole body.

By the time my tears dried up, my body shook with cold, the fire having burnt out hours before. My head ached from exhaustion and hunger.

I slowly peeled myself from the floor, crawled to my bed and collapsed.

5

The woman staring at me looks somewhat familiar. But her messy bun, the dark circles and the vacant look in her eyes make her hard to place.

Blinking, I realise it is my reflection in the window of the post office.

I had to drag my sorry ass all the way to Omeo because I had a card left in my post box to say I had a delivery.

How does one end up with a card saying that there is a delivery and yet the delivery couldn't also make its way up the mountain?

The queue wrapped around the front facade of the building. I'd already been standing here for 20 minutes.

This is what they get for only opening for 2 hours on the weekend.

When I finally make it to the front of the queue I pass over the card to the unimpressed looking woman behind the counter.

"Do you have any ID on you?" She huffs.

I pass her my driver's license. She looks at it critically, eyeballing me. After an age, she passes it back and disappears through a doorway to find my package.

I am guessing this is the last book I ordered that Winnie recommended. Took its sweet ass time getting here.

Either that or it is something I ordered off an infomercial. I need to stop this new habit of drinking cocktails and internet shopping.

It had been two weeks since Winnie's passing. Slowly the news of one of Singapore's most wealthy businessmen started to trickle down through media across the world. It would seem that I had been living under a rock, as many people on the internet seemed to know exactly who he was.

I was emailing him for months, we even had ZOOM dinners a couple of times to catch up. How did I not notice or more to the point, how did he fail to mention, who he was?

Was he worried that I'd only be interested in getting to know him for his money?

Did he think I was expecting him to become my 'sugar daddy'?

Ms Unimpressed returns with a giant box wrapped in black plastic. Yellow 'QUARANTINE' tape doubled around the outside.

Well that explains why the delivery didn't come up the mountain.

I suddenly panic.

Did I accidentally order 100 copies of the book? Surely I would have noticed that on my bank statement. How much did I drink and order the other night on my little bender? It looks like it had a few issues getting through quarantine.

Lifting the box from the counter, I make my way awkwardly back to my Jeep. Struggling to get my keys out, I wedge the box between my hip and the car to give me two hands.

I think I'll wait until I get home to open it, otherwise I'll never get the box back out of the car.

I arrive home sometime later after stopping off at the supermarket and petrol station. Lugging my groceries in first and unpacking them took some time but eventually it is time to find out what is hiding in the giant box of surprise.

Staring at it suspiciously, I grab a pair of scissors and run them through the plastic on the top of the box.

After wrestling to get the sticky tape wrapped plastic off the outside, I eventually get the cardboard box cracked open.

What on earth is that?

Nestled in piles and piles of packing peanuts sat a beautiful walnut timber box. Gingerly easing it out of the static ridden peanuts, I place the box on the coffee table in front of the fireplace.

My heart skips a beat. On the lid of the box, carved in ornate gold calligraphy sat the initials HL. Huynh Li.

Suddenly finding it difficult to breathe, I crack open the kitchen window to let in the afternoon breeze.

Writing off any previous thoughts regarding reducing my recent drinking patterns, I pour myself two fingers of Whisky. Neat. I wash my hands and turn toward the box.

On second thought.

I grab the whole bottle and return to the living room.

The flawless timber box stares up at me. No latches or hinges can be seen from the exterior. About the size of a large shoebox, it takes up a fair proportion of my coffee table.

Okay then, Winnie (or someone he knows) has sent you a box. With his initials on it.

If it is his ashes I hope to god they are in a zip-locked bag in there.

Visions of opening the lid on this stunning vessel only to be bathed in a puff of Mr Huynh's ashes flash through my mind.

I take another big sip of my whisky. It burns on the way down.

Carefully grasping the front corners of the lid I gently ease it up until I see the hidden hinges appear and lock open.

The first thing I see is a gold parchment envelope, labelled 'Ava Elias' in flowing calligraphy. Turning the envelope over, I withdraw the letter written in the same hand on identical gold parchment.

Dearest Ava,

I send you this to thank-you for your kindness and compassion this week. Meeting you was a reminder for me that there is much life left to be lived and I am not ready to give up on mine just yet.

I cannot tell you what a joy it was to meet someone with such passion and enthusiasm for life. Not only for your own life, but the lives of those around you.

You reminded me that there is much to be thankful for, whether it is enjoying the peace of a sunrise or the scent of freshly baked bread; that little joys can be found all around us.

I had forgotten long ago why I do what I do and I believe fate intended us to meet that day.

This Montblanc pen is one of my most treasured possessions. When you come to Singapore I will tell you the story of how it came into my possession. It is one for the history books, I am certain!

Take this pen with you wherever you go and a part of me will always be with you.

I feel compelled to tell you, Miss Ava, I believe fate has great plans in store for us. I am certain that time will make clear what our respective paths are and how we shall be led back to each other.

With warmest regards,

Winnie.

P.S. I do not know how long this will take to arrive, so I will not mention it until you do, as not to spoil the surprise.

I duck my head to angle my falling teardrops away from the pristine parchment. He sent this the week we met but because of the timber in the box, it was held up in Quarantine at the border. Until now.

I'll never get to thank him for this.

Placing the letter back in the envelope, I peer into the box at the remaining contents. A sleek black box with a velvet edge catches my eye. Picking it up I crack it open to reveal a carbon fibre limited edition MontBlanc pen. My fingers shake as I lift the pen from its case turning it this way and that. A glint of sunlight catches my eye. I turn the pen to look at the signature MontBlanc star-emblazoned into the lid. This lid is unusual because the carbon fibre ends and a clear glass casing sits atop the lid, encasing a large star cut diamond.

Sitting in the top of the MontBlanc case is a letter of authenticity. Taking a quick look I note it indicates the age, origin and owner of the pen, as well as a GIA rating of the diamond ensconced in the lid. 2 carats, colourless and internally flawless, the diamond alone, is valued at $55,000.

Had I been sitting on a chair, I would have fallen off it.

I am holding $55,000 in my hands. I'm not sure I'm cut out for this kind of power.

My hands shake harder. I don't own a safe to put this in. Where am I meant to keep a $55k pen? What do you even use a $55k pen for?

I have a vision of whipping it out to sign the EFTPOS receipt at the supermarket.

I place it back in its velvety box, eager to refrain from touching it again.

Why would he send me this? It is an incredibly sweet gesture, but why would he send this to me only days after we met?

Does this mean he felt similarly to me? He said fate had a plan for us. Did Winnie also feel as though our meeting was more significant than just an afternoon of chatter?

Who was this man? What else don't I know?

Overwhelmed by a new wave of grief, I hurriedly close the timber box and carry it lovingly up to my bedroom. Placing it on the bedside table opposite mine, I grab my bathrobe and run myself a scalding bath.

I awaken in the darkness with an extreme sense of paranoia. I can't shake the feeling that the whole world suddenly knows I have a small fortune worth of pen in my home and that I'm going to be violently robbed in the middle of the night.

Rolling over to check the clock, I note it is just before 5.00 am. I decide to get up, shower and head into Bright to the bank in time for opening.

Feeling more in control now that I have a plan, I get on with my morning routine.

With freshly washed and blow-dried hair, I apply a little makeup and get dressed. Unable to bear opening the box again, I cover it with a handbag dust cover and stuff it into the biggest zippered bag I can find. A large Country Road canvas duffel bag.

Huh. Well, that looks like I've robbed a bank. I have nothing else to put it in, unless I put it back in the shipping box?

Looking over at the box and its static ridden peanuts threatening to spill out, I decide to stick with the duffel.

Bank robber it is then.

After signing every document ever written and selling my firstborn son, I am handed a key to a safety deposit box (one of only 20 in the whole town). Sitting in a claustrophobic room alone, I stroke the box and think fondly of Winnie. Taking the pen out for one final look, I feel the weight in my hands. Unscrewing the lid I realise the pen has a fountain tip.

This must be the pen Winnie wrote my letter with.

My eyes prickle once again as I say farewell to him and place his box in the hole in the wall.

The drive home felt longer than usual. These past two weeks I had really begun to get myself together again and this arrival knocked the wind out of my sails. Sighing heavily, I pull onto the slip road on which my chalet resides, squinting into the sun.

What the...?

A gargantuan SUV sits looking sinister in the middle of my drive. The black monstrosity blocking access to my garage, the tint so dark it was impossible to tell if anyone occupied it.

Do they know about the pen? Is someone ransacking my house as I sit here?

Parking on the street and unable to see anyone around I jump out, headed for the front door.

"Miss Ava Elias?" A man's voice, accented.

Spinning around I feel my heart jump into my throat. Clutching my bag by my side I immediately wish I was carrying a water bottle or a heavy book or something. The man standing before me reminded me very much of the black pantsuit woman from the news announcement. Clean, tidy, no fuss. His greying hair brushed back just-so.

"Miss Ava Elias?" He repeats eyeing me curiously.

I am so glad I put pants on today. And makeup. But mostly pants.

"Who's asking?" I counter.

Great Ava. Excellent comeback. Eye roll.

"My name is Zhang Wei Tony, but you can call me Mr Tony." He took a step toward me bowing minutely before extending his hand. He moved as quietly as the wind.

"What can I do for you, Mr Tony?" I ask, rudely ignoring his hand.

Why can't I shake the feeling that I shouldn't trust this guy? He's too, something. Too neat, too clean? Too...something.

"Winnie said you had spirit. I can see what he means about your determination."

"You knew Mr Huynh?" I sputter in shock. Taking another step closer to me I see him eyeing me curiously.

"Winnie and I were old friends. I am his General Counsel and longtime business associate."

Breathing a small sigh of relief, I step forward and offer my hand. Winnie had mentioned 'his lawyer' on a few occasions.

"I see. Pleased to meet you, Mr Tony." He takes my hand in a moderately firm grasp, seeming surprised that I shake it.

Ah, crap. I forgot that whole gentle lady fingers thing.

"Would you like to come inside? I can make us some tea." A cool breeze had whipped up leaving goosebumps on my arms.

"We'd be delighted." He turns to nod at the SUV.

We? Three large burly men, also Asian, also dressed in black, emerge from the vehicle.

Are they wearing black because they are in mourning or do they just know how intimidating it looks?

"Ah, yes. This way,' I hesitate, slowly turning toward the door.

Mr Tony passes me as he enters the drying room, in my ballet flats he and I are a similar height, I note curiously. His associates, on the other hand, were at least head or two taller than me. I suppress a shudder.

After inviting them to get comfortable in the living room I head to the kitchen to put the kettle on. Whipping out my phone I quickly text Ryan, Ivan and

Danny in a group message: UNEXPECTED VISITORS AT ARENDELLE. PLEASE CHECK-IN IF NO WORD IN 1 HOUR.

Switching my phone to vibrate, I slip it into my back pocket. Heading into the living room with the tea tray I try to remember what I learned of 'Chinese tea etiquette' watching Disney's Mulan. I assume as the female in the room I am expected to pour the tea.

"I have black, white, green, oolong, herbal..." I look about the room, four pairs of eyes resting on me. Three pair behind black anti-flash sunglasses.

That's not creepy or weird at all. Not in the slightest.

"Green Jasmine is fine Miss Elias,' Mr Tony states quietly.

I add the tea to the strainer in the pot, mixing in some cold water for green tea. I silently thank the gods that when I moved here I kept my T2 pot and saucer collection. Placing the cups and saucers on the table I use tongs to add an Afghan biscuit to each saucer whilst I wait for the tea to steep.

"Does anyone have any nut allergies?" I blurt out to no-one in general. The pecan glued to the top of the biscuit with chocolate ganache ought to give it away, but some people aren't that bright.

"No allergies, Miss Elias. Thank you,' replies Mr Tony quietly.

After a few minutes, I decant the tea into the cups and pass them around the table. The little vibrantly painted teacups looking satirical in the hulking hands of black-clad men.

"What can I do for you today Mr Tony?" I turn to face him, catching him with a biscuit midway to his mouth.

He looks at the biscuit awkwardly and places it back on his saucer.

"I have come to discuss the rather delicate matter of Mr Huynh's final Will and testament, Miss Elias." He reaches down to collect a dark brown leather briefcase from beside his chair. Rather a lot deeper than regular briefcases, it looked like the wheeled ones lawyers take into court, filled with reference papers and books. That would probably be an accurate assumption considering the man is a lawyer.

"With me?" I sputter, "but why?"

Digging around in the suitcase, Mr Tony hands me a gold envelope, a metallic wax seal on the back. It is the same parchment paper as the one Winnie sent with the pen. I wonder if Mr Tony knows about the pen? Might keep that one under my hat for the meantime.

I lift the seal away, careful not to crack it. The same beautiful calligraphy script stares up at me.

Dearest Ava,

I write to you today with deep sadness in my heart. I have become unwell these past days and I am afraid my body has decided it is time for my soul to leave this earth.

I have dreamed of the day I return to Dinner Plain to enjoy your company once again, in more pleasant circumstances than the last. I also had great plans to show you my Singapore when our long-discussed visit came to fruition. Alas, it seems fate has a different plan from the one I had hoped.

These past few weeks I have been updating my will and my company structure, in case something were to happen to me. It seems it was rather a foreboding decision, as merely days after putting everything in place, my health began to decline. I believe in the world of psychology they refer to it as a "self-fulfilling prophecy".

I am an old man who has lived a life weary before its time. I realised when I met you that I had many, many more plans for my life and began seeking out every opportunity to seize them.

I have never met someone with the same tenacity, zest for life and love that you show to those around you. You are an incredibly intelligent, kind, compassionate woman and for that reason I have made a decision.

I restructured my company Huynh Enterprises Holdings to ensure that a single individual could inherit and continue to maintain the company, just as I, myself, have done since its inception.

My team at HEH are good people and I have faith that they will support and honour my successor just as they have done for me.

Mr Tony has been a long time friend and business associate of mine. I have mentioned him previously on many an occasion, most often as 'my lawyer'.

He will walk you through what I am asking and assist you in making a decision.

Finally, I must thank you for reminding me of my purpose in life and bringing me such clarity. I truly feel, in these my final days, that I have achieved my purpose. You made an old man feel loved and cared for with no ulterior motive or incentive. That truly is, unconditional love.

I am sorry I could not deliver this to you in person Miss Ava. Always know that I have faith in you. I could not leave this earth with the future of my company and my people in the hands of anyone less worthy.

With Warmest Regards,

Your Winnie

P.S. Remember, a part of me will always be with you.

Blinking back tears, I excuse myself from the living room. After rinsing my face and fixing my running mascara, I returned to the table.

"Do you know what the letter says?" I ask the envelope in my hand.

"Winnie expressed his sentiments to me, I do not know the detail but yes, I know what he intended to explain in the letter,' Mr Tony eyes me wearily from across the table.

"What exactly is he saying?" I query, busying myself with topping up the teacups.

"I have a large amount of documentation here that I will require you to read regarding legislation and global business enterprises before we can get into the details-"

"In plain English, Mr Tony, if you please. What exactly does Mr Huynh want?" I cut him off, perhaps a little too sternly.

"Of course. Mr Huynh decreed in his final Will and testament, which we will need to 'officially read' for legal purposes-"

I clear my throat and stare at him pointedly.

"Ah, yes. Mr Huynh bequeathed you his sole heir and

recipient of his estate in full,' He sounded like he was parched, struggling to get the statement out.

"I beg your pardon?" I stutter. "But I read on the internet after he passed that Winnie was...he was..."

"Obscenely wealthy?" Mr Tony offers. His tone implying that I was feigning my naivety.

"I don't understand. Why would he leave everything to me? In the scheme of a life of 70 years, we barely knew each other." I drop my head into my hands.

What on earth is going on? Why would Winnie do this?

"Yes, well there have been many discussions amongst the directors at HEH regarding what this means for the company and many people are surprised and very anxious at the possibility of the company falling into the hands of an outsider. Of course, Mr Huynh's exact heir has yet to be disclosed to anyone but myself."

"I don't understand. Are you saying that currently, you and I are the only people on the planet who know Winnie left everything to me?" I look around at his three companions.

You and I; and these three hulks.

Suddenly it dawns on me that I may be in some kind of danger. Does Mr Tony have any ill will toward me, seeing as he was clearly very close with Mr Huynh for many years? Does he see it as a slap in the face that he was not left in charge? Did he bring these brutes with him to kill me? If I am dead and have not executed Mr Huynh's will then where does the money go?

"Thank you for coming by Mr Tony. If you wouldn't mind leaving the documentation here, I will review it and be in touch,' I stand and head toward the door, my hands shaking. I stuff them into my pockets.

"Miss Elias, it is not that simple. We must discuss the will, arrange a reading, establish what will happen to HEH. The company has been under temporary leadership for weeks now and needs stability."

I stare him straight in the face, reaching over to open the front door.

"If you leave me your card Mr Tony, as I said I will be in touch."

He doesn't budge an inch from where he stands, in shock I'd imagine at the audacity of a young woman to speak to a 'man of his standing' in such a way.

"If you please, Mr Tony,' I indicate toward the door once again. Slowly he and his three associates meander toward the door. Fishing a business card out of his pocket, Mr Tony held it out with another infinitesimal bow.

"We are staying at the Crown Hotel in Melbourne City. When you have made a decision, we can meet there to discuss the next steps. I will arrange a helicopter to collect you from Hotham Airport when you are ready." He took one last distasteful look around the inside of the chalet before descending the stairs.

Not moments after the SUV backed out of the drive, Ivan and Danny appeared, breathing heavily as they rush the chalet.

"Good...GOD...AVA! Who were those people!" Danny sputters sucking in breath. "They looked like goddamn Japanese mafia!"

"Singaporean/Chinese actually,' I exhale, a slightly hysterical giggle escaping my lips. Ivan stood before me, placing his hands on my shoulders and looking into my eyes.

"Are you okay lassie?" His brow furrowed.

"You guys wanna come in for tea?" I asked, hoping they'd say yes.

I don't know how I'll sleep here tonight knowing they are in Victoria. What if he is wrong, what if other people find out about me and come after me? I'm certain one of the pages I saw said Winnie was on the Forbes 500 list for the past decade. Ivan leads me inside and plonks me back on the couch, dragging up the comforter. Danny clears away the used teacups and brews a new pot of tea.

"What are these biscuits, Ava? They are divine,' Danny garbles around his fourth helping.

"Afghan Cookies,' I smile across at him. "Danny, do you have any rooms spare for me to crash tonight?"Danny and Ivan exchange a look.

"Miss Ava, are you in some kind of trouble?" Ivan probed gently.

"I have no idea. But I do know I need a lawyer. Either of you know any good ones?" The thought of paying the kind of fees that a lawyer of this calibre costs made my stomach churn. I have some savings, but not the tens of thousands of dollars it will cost to have someone examine these documents. Ivan and Danny's hoots of laughter drag my attention back to the present.

"What am I missing here?" I laugh.

Danny claps Ivan on the shoulder, beaming at me. "You are looking at one of Victoria's most respected QCs." I look from Danny to Ivan and back again.

"QC?"

"I, my dear, am a Queens Counsel. Sadly one of only a few left living these days." Ivan winks at me.

"You are a high calibre Barrister?" I ask incredulously. "Ivan, what on earth are you doing running a kitchen?"

"I could probably ask you the same about assisting at a children's ski school." He counters, "Marianne and I sought a quieter life after spending decades fighting the battles of the underbelly in Melbourne."

"Are you still a member of the Bar?"

"Until the day I die, my dear." He smiles proudly. "So, why don't we get you set up in a suite at Danny's and you can tell me all about this pickle you're in."

6

"There are two great places to see the evening light shows. One is down in the Gardens By the Bay where the Supertree Grove lights up. The other is Spectra, straight downstairs here in front of the Marina Bay Sands building. Get in early though, even on weeknights they fill up fast." Tarini smiled at me from across the bar.

"I'll keep that in mind. I am booked to see the Gardens tomorrow, so I'll see the light show then. I'll try to catch Spectra tonight before I head back to my hotel." I don't know if it is the cocktails or the holiday-high but in another life, I'm sure Tarini and I would have been great friends. Maybe she's just being nice to you, so you tip her well. I tamp down on my naysaying inner monologue and enjoy watching the sunset over Singapore.

"What made you decide to come to Singapore?" She asked, wiping out glasses with a pristinely white tea towel. The bar around us buzzed with people. A small wave of guilt washed over me, realising that she was possibly neglecting to assist some of the other staff to stay here and talk to me. Then delight bloomed inside me.

If only I were a lesbian my inner goddess sighed. I couldn't tell you if it was the way her white sleeves were rolled above her elbows displaying her tattoos or her black uniform vest, but this woman had charisma.

"*You're going to laugh because it is really lame.*" *I giggle at her.*

"*Try me.*"

"*I've always been interested in Singapore, but I fell in love watching Crazy Rich Asians and realised I had to come here ASAP. So I booked my trip to Europe and insisted on flying with Singapore Airlines so I could stop over here for a few days.*" *Tarini laughed hard, in a kind way rather than judgmentally.*

"*That's not lame at all! I love that movie! They really showed Singapore off. I've had plenty of people say that they came here because of that. The pool in the scene at the end of the movie - that's it right there.*" *She points to the infinity pool disappearing off the edge of the rooftop.*

"*No way!*" *I exclaim. I had never noticed that before and I've seen the movie about 10 times!*

"*Yup, the part with the synchronized swimmers!*"

"*I never really realised just how much money Singapore had as a nation, but then I get here and everything is in such pristine condition. Public transport, housing.*"

"*We are pretty lucky, I'll say that. But you know, the real money isn't in innovation or the real-estate markets like they suggest in the movie.*" *She smiles across at me.*

"*What do you mean? I thought your technology sector was the reason for Singapore's wealth?*" *I stared at her wide-eyed.*

Turning, she points toward the bay to the South-East. "*Look out there, what do you see?*"

I peer past her arm into the distance, thanking the gods I put my contacts in tonight.

"*The Bay?*"

"*Beyond that.*"

"The shipping lanes?" Row upon row of lights glowed on the water; what must have been tens of ships lined up awaiting the wharves to open in the morning.

"Exactly. Shipping is where the real money is in Singapore."

I awoke from what felt like the one-hundredth dream of my trip to Singapore in as many days. By now I'm quite certain I've spent more time dreaming about my trip than I spent there. I wonder where Tarini is now. I will always regret not going back there again to get her contact details, but I always thought it would seem kind of weird. Rolling over I spot a big glass of orange juice and a fresh bagel sitting on the coffee table in front of me. I'd fallen asleep on the couch for the afternoon whilst Ivan poured over the documents Mr Tony had left.

Downing the juice and nibbling the bagel, I find Ivan in the next room. Hunched deep in thought, he was a transformed man from the one I knew. Grey locks pulled up into a topknot. Lawer-ly looking-reading glasses perched on his nose.

"Any luck deciphering it?" I wander in and perch on a chair beside him.

"Well my dear, there is one thing I am quite certain of. You are now a very, very wealthy young woman." He chuckled. Waving his hands around in front of the pages he added, "It looks as though you've become 'eiress to a multi-national shipping conglomerate. This gent also owned many,' He stopped and looked at me, "many, high profile properties 'round the world."

"Residential or Corporate? Or Personal?" I ask peering over his shoulder curiously.

"The answer is D; All o' the above. Numerous personal dwellings, several corporate business towers and a large number of public housing facilities around the world, but mostly in Singapore." Ivan removed his glasses to peer at me curiously.

"You seem to be taking this rather well Miss Ava. Are you not in shock?"

"What am I supposed to do? Sit in the fetal position in the bottom of the shower denying any of this is happening? If Mr Huynh is who the internet says he is then I am facing a decision that may impact hundreds of lives."

"Uh, I'd say that estimate is closer to thousands. Tens of thousands in fact." Ivan pulls out something akin to a profit and loss statement and looks over the numbers.

"Okay fine, tens of thousands of people may not be able to pay their mortgages or put food on their tables if I don't get this right for them."

"What it boils down to is this. The Will lists you as heiress to the fortune, the company and the personal effects of Mr Huynh. In order to 'access' that ye will need to attend the official Will reading which will happ'n in Singapore at a time of your choosing. You must advise Mr Tony of when you'd like it done and ye will then officially inherit everything. From there, you will be able to make decisions about what you want to keep, sell and disassemble."

"And what do the financials boil down to? Am I going to inherit a money pit or did Mr Huynh do a good job of keeping his nose clean? Am I going to take this over and suddenly find that he owes hundreds of millions in debt around the world?"

"As with any investment or business venture of this size, there will always be debt. Without debt there can'y be growth. If I am interpreting this correctly, once all is said an' done, if you decided to sell everything and come home; ye would likely come out with approximately $500 million in the bank." I spit my orange juice down my front.

"Did you say $500 million?" Ivan nods sagely.

"If I decide I don't want to deal with any of this, I can just snap my fingers and walk away with $500 million? Is this some kind of sick joke?" I exclaim, running to the bathroom to find tissues to wipe up my dribble.

"I mean look at me, Ivan. Do I look like the kind of person who would know what to do with that much money?!" I shriek hysterically.

Ivan stands up slowly and wraps his arms around me in a warm embrace.

He is like a willow tree. Sturdy yet bowing gracefully in the breeze.

"I don't know if I can do this, Ivan. Why would Winnie leave this up to me?"

"Because 'e could see the strong, brave woman inside of ye. The one the people of this town were besotted by, the first day you arrived. You have a sense of peace and kindness that resonates with those around you. Your reaction says much about the type of woman ye are."

I pull back to look up into his face.

"I don't understand."

"Your first response is concern for the other people this will impact. Your second response is to reject the notion of such extreme wealth. Lassie, I've lived upon God's earth for many a year now an' it takes a rare person ta look such wealth in the eye and no' be caught up in its siren song."

"But it is such an enormous responsibility."

"I know my dear. What ye fail to see is that most people would already 'ave planned how to spend 'alf of it. Meanwhile here you are worried about employee mortgages and groceries."

"What are you saying?"

"I'm saying, Mr Huynh was an incredibly smart man. He made the right decision putting you in charge of his affairs. He ken you would care for his people, just as he did."

"Ivan, how on earth do I repay you for this? I'm sure a QC bills much more than a regular lawyer and I can't even afford one of those."

"Technically Miss Ava, you can afford anything you like now. But it is my pleasure to assist you without charge. I was due to find some pro-bono work for this year anyway."

"What would I do without you, Ivan? I guess I need to call Mr Tony now and organise to go to Singapore and find out the nitty-gritty?"

"Why don't you sleep o' it tonight Miss Ava and tomorrow we can call Mr Tony."

7

The next morning I called Mr Tony and booked the meeting. Ivan and I spent another few hours devising a game plan the night before. After packing a carry-on suitcase I met Ivan and Danny to drive to Hotham Airfield.

"And my plants need water Danny, remember that please?" I implore him as I drag a brush through my hair. The back seat had turned into my personal salon. Throwing on my hair and makeup within the short drive to the airport.

"Okay, now remember. You are in charge, Ava,' Ivan looks at me in the rearview mirror.

"Yes. I am in charge,' I tried to sound like I believed it myself.

Pulling up at the airport, there was not a person in sight.

"Did he say he was getting you a helicopter?" Danny asks, grabbing my suitcase and Tony's bag of papers from the tailgate of his Mercedes. Suddenly from the south, the sound of a rotor blade pierced the quiet growing louder as the helicopter approached. When it finally appeared over the tree line, the three of us gasped.

"Surely not,' Danny cries.

Approaching us was an enormous, sleek snow-white helicopter with black detailing. Pointy on the front, it looked like something off a warship. Three wheels suddenly sprouted from the bottom of the chopper, before it landed gracefully in front of us. The rotors had almost completely powered down before the three of us could speak.

"And I thought the ECO-Star I flew over the Grand Canyon in with my parents, was nuts,' I exhale.

Oh my god. My parents. Fuck.

I make a note to call my mum when I arrive in Melbourne and let her know I'm headed to Singapore for business. Technically it's not a lie. Although she will be disappointed I won't have time to stop by for dinner tonight. After what seemed like an age, two rather fetchingly uniformed pilots disembarked the helicopter and approached us.

"Miss Elias I presume?" The tall blonde one with beefy shoulders extends a hand.

"That is correct,' I reply, shaking his hand.

"I'm Danny, this is Ivan,' Danny interrupts, keen to be included.

After the formalities were over, the pilots explained that we'd be taking off in about 15 minutes.

A cool breeze sprung up, causing me to don my coat.

"Ivan, Danny. I don't know how to thank you both for your help. I don't even know where I would be without you." I clear my throat, blinking back tears.

"It is our pleasure, Miss Ava. Just look after yourself over there okay? Remember...?"

"I'm in charge,' I laugh, my nose starting to run. Ivan hands me a handkerchief and kisses my cheek.

"I called one of my colleagues in the city. He said if you need to find yourself a lawyer over there, this is your gal. She's known as 'the widow maker', because she eats businessmen for breakfast." Ivan hands me a business card with a grin; I stash it in my handbag. Danny gives me an awkward one-armed hug and then it is time for me to climb into the chopper for pre-flight checks.

The pilot and co-pilot, Brian and Evan, assisted me into the helicopter. The vast interior was all white, with plush leather seats, cushions and enough space to fit my entire family and then some.

"Is it just me?" I look around, the pilots laughing from the doorway.

"Yes, Miss Elias. Did you not see the side of the Helicopter? 'HEH'. This is a privately owned corporate vehicle." Evan, the co-pilot with the amazing arms chuckled. He assisted me in selecting a seat, fastening the belt and showed me where to find the chilled champagne, flutes and snacks as well as how to use the TV system. He also explained the basic safety briefing in case of an emergency and where to find my life jacket. After putting on my cans, the door shut and I heard them both greet me through the headphones.

"Miss Elias, welcome on board. Today you will be flying to Melbourne from Mt Hotham on behalf of Huynh Enterprises Holdings. Conditions are clear and we anticipate a flight time of 80 minutes. Should you have any questions at all, please do not hesitate to ask.

We are here to help. We hope you sit back, relax and enjoy the flight."

After digging out my laptop to work in aeroplane mode, I hit the button to 'release the champagne'. Out from nowhere, a bottle of Pink Domaine Chandon appears with two exquisite crystal glasses.

When in Rome?

Popping the bottle gently, uncertain as to how the altitude would affect the bubbles, I poured a rather overzealous glass and toasted thin air.

Here's to you, Mr Huynh. I truly hope you are getting a kick out of this. I pat my breast pocket whilst staring out into the vast valleys of the Victorian highlands.

The afternoon sun glinted off Melbourne city before me. Naïvely assuming we would be flying to Tullamarine airport, I was rather surprised when we commenced our descent in the middle of the city. Staring out the window I realise we are near the river in front of Crown Casino.

"Evan, where are we landing?" I ask through the microphone on the cans.

"The Melbourne City Helipad, Miss Elias." Came the crackling response. And with the tiniest of bumps we landed.

I can honestly say the Crowne Casino is one of the fanciest places I've ever set foot in my life. Clambering down from the big black SUV that had collected me from the helipad, which yes, was only 800 metres from the hotel, I looked around in wonder, hardly noticing the driver taking my tiny suitcase to the bellhop and tipping him. Marble tiles of ash and gold covered the floors. Plush wingback chairs scattered around a grand piano. The pianist executing a beautiful rendition of Ludovico Einaudi's Nuvole Bianche. As I stand on the precipice not only of the hotel, but of something much bigger, I take a deep breath and enter the abyss toward the lobby bar.

I spot Mr Tony almost immediately. Or more accurately, I spot Mr Tony's 'men' immediately. Dressed in almost identical outfits to yesterday with one notable exception. They had crisp white collared shirts on under their black suits. Although they were indoors and the sun was distinctly setting outside, the black anti-flash sunglasses remained.

Mr Tony was wearing a grey suit today. It matches his hair.

"Mr Tony, how good to see you again,' I tower over him in my 6-inch stilettos.

I can feel the eyes of people all around the hotel watching our exchange. I don't know if it is because of Tweedles big, bigger and huge here or if it is my emerald CUE dress and skyscraper pumps. Either way, I know I look great and I feel amazing. Bring it on.

Bowing significantly more prostrated than yesterday, Mr Tony appears to have discovered his sense of propriety overnight.

"Miss Elias, the pleasure is all mine,' he mewled, "Come. We have early dinner reservations at Nobu."

"Japanese; an excellent choice." I smile back.

Walking in silence through the casino, once again I become aware of people's eyes on us.

Is this what it will be like? Surely not always, not if I'm not parading around in public with a posse. Winnie was in Dinner Plain completely alone and anonymous.

The private dining room at Nobu was stunning. Soft lighting and beautiful timber decals.

The maitre'd seated me first, followed by Mr Tony. I found it surprising that Mr Tony's men did not join us, considering they all seemed joined at the hip.

"Anata no buka wa watashitachi ni kuwawatte imasen ka?" I enquire to Mr Tony. The maitre'd turning away awkwardly, catching my comment.

"You speak Japanese,' Mr Tony observes, "and no, my subordinates will not be joining us for dinner."

"As do you, it would seem,' I reply, praying he didn't ask me anything further. I'm a little rusty.

The waiter came by then to take our drink orders.

Normally I'd just order water but I assume that Tony will chargeback his bill to HEH for this meal so why not enjoy it. Mr Tony ordered a Monkey 47 G&T. I'll have to google that.

Oh crap it''s my turn to order.

"Whisky, two fingers neat. Thank you."

Phew. Managed to get the words out in one go.

"Which shelf Miss?"

Oh crap.

"Go ahead and treat yourself. She'll have something from the top shelf,' Mr Tony orders.

"Of course, Sir. We have a Dalmore 64 Trinitas if that is to your liking?" The waiter seemed rather perplexed about who to look to for a reply.

"Do you have anything by Sullivan's Cove? I'd prefer something home-grown." I level a look at Tony.

The waiter nods and departs hurriedly.

"Did you have a pleasant flight down. The ACH160 is my favourite of all the company aircraft." Mr Tony smiles sardonically at me over his gin and tonic.

"It was most enjoyable. Although I do have to wonder if the $18 million would have been better spent elsewhere?" Yes, that's right little man. I did my homework.

The fact that those were the single most incredible 80 minutes of my existence is a secret that will go with me to the grave. I incline my whisky toward him before taking a relished sip.

Mm. Worth every penny. I hope I get to see the bill after this. I'm betting this glass alone is costing him $150+. Hm, I suppose it is costing me $150+. I am not technically the heiress to HEH on paper just yet.

After the first two courses of sashimi and sushi, the heavier dishes started to appear. Beef Tataki like I've never tasted and Black Miso Cod that was to die for. Wiping his mouth delicately with a napkin, Mr Tony turned his attention to me.

"Tell me, Miss Elias, have you made a decision?" He eyes me speculatively. Taking a sip of my water I look across at him.

"I have. I have decided I will return to Singapore with you and hear the reading of the final Will and testament."

"Excellent. I will ensure preparations are made for us to depart tomorrow." He smiled tightly back at me.

Looking around the room awkwardly, Mr Tony is searching for an excuse to end the evening.

"Mr Tony, if you will excuse me. I am ready for a walk along the river before I turn in for the evening."

Ever the gentleman, Mr Tony stands, the waiter rushing over to grab my chair as I stand to depart.

"I will send a messenger to your door with instructions for our departure by 10 am. You may enjoy room service for breakfast or dine in the hotel and chargeback to your room." Mr Tony bowed and, at that, I departed.

By 9.30 am I had received word from Mr Tony regarding our flight to Singapore. At 11 am I met him downstairs with my carry-on suitcase and Tony's bag of papers in tow.

"Good Morning Mr Tony,' I smile, "how did you sleep?"

"Very well Miss Elias, thank you. Did you find a way to occupy your morning?" He smiles back.

"I did. I went for a walk along the river at sunrise, had breakfast at Bowery To Williamsburg with an old friend, had a massage at the spa and now here I am."

We walk out to the SUV together, one of the bellhops racing across to open the door for me. I thank him and get in, placing my case at my feet.

"You know these vehicles have designated spaces for luggage,' Mr Tony observes.

I smile across at him, letting the comment pass.

As we approach the airport the driver detoured off the main highway.

"Uh, aren't we going to the airport?" I ask, peering out the window at the vacant looking industrial space surrounding us.

"Oh dear. I forgot you are not used to this life yet. Your naivety is so endearing. We are not flying commercially." Tony spat the final sentence as though flying with other people was for peasants.

The car turned onto a drive passing a security booth, coming to a stop in front of a large metallic building.

Melbourne Jet Base.

Of course, how silly of me. We are going to the private airstrip where the company jet is parked.

Ugh. I hate how snobby this guy is. Most people have never SEEN a private jet in their lives, let alone flown on one. Or owned one.

That final thought really started to dawn on me. In a matter of days, I could say 'My jet is parked at the Melbourne Jet Base.' Why do I find it so hard to reconcile that? And why do I feel so uneasy about it?

After having my single bag scanned at the security booth where Tony and I were the only passengers, we walked through to a lounge area where we used the restrooms before boarding. Our luggage was taken to the aircraft by the staff.

"Is there anything you would like to do before boarding? We could have a meal or a glass of champagne before we depart?" Mr Tony offers.

"No thank you, I'd rather not delay."

We walk down a set of stairs and there before me, in a vast metal hangar stood a neat row of private jets. All shapes and sizes some with jet engines, others twin props. Glistening under the bright hangar lights they looked like something out of a 'billionaires' magazine.

Last night after discovering the cost of the helicopter during my flight I decided to further investigate some of the aircraft listed in the HEH dossier. I noted that HEH was supposedly the owner of more than 20 different aircraft on the planet. Helicopters and jets on each continent, covered their yearly expenses whilst also earning a healthy profit as rentals out of a subsidiary company. The gross capital expenditure on acquiring these aircraft stood at close to 1.2 billion dollars. I had to hand it to Winnie, he really did treat the world like his own monopoly board. Collecting businesses, properties and possessions as he played around the world.

There was one aircraft that caught my attention on the list and I prayed all night that I would see it turn up at the airport. The Gulfstream-650.

Following a lush red carpet toward the hangar door, I held my breath.

There it was sitting on the tarmac in all its glory. Crisp white with swept wings and two giant Rolls-Royce engines perched astride the tail. This jet cost HEH 62 million dollars and is the most commonly used jet in Winnie's collection. It was nicknamed "Screaming Eagle" in the register.

Catching me staring, Mr Tony leans in a little closer. "This was Winnie's favourite,' he chuckles smugly as he passes by me, shaking hands with the pilot and cabin crew. I smile to myself. I'm sure it was.

The interior of the jet was like a dream. The photographs on the internet did not do it justice. Cream leather upholstery with timber accents, large recliners and flat-screen TVs. An enormous bathroom and galley kitchen, plus the ability for myself, Mr Tony and his three hulks to sleep comfortably in lay-flat beds.

After enjoying my second Singapore Sling- I couldn't resist! I used the bathroom, noting with a giggle that it was about the same size as the bathroom in my chalet.

And much fancier!

Then I was ready for a movie and settled in to enjoy the remainder of the flight in pure luxury.

8

Singapore was just as I remembered it. Humid, busy and beautiful. It didn't take long to get into the city from the airport. Last time I arrived here I took the train and that was simple, efficient and cost me about S$1.90. I am quite certain this is costing HEH a little more than that.

I peered at the city from inside yet another monstrous vehicle - some kind of Suburban with tinted windows you could barely see out of.

Once I had checked into the hotel, the evening went rather similar to the one before. Mr Tony and I ate dinner, he told me there would be someone here to pick me up at 9 am for the 10 am will reading and then he departed. I presume to wherever he lives in the city.

It was no coincidence that I requested a room at the Marina Bay Sands. I needed a friend in this city and I could only pray that Tarini still worked at the bar upstairs.

What if she doesn't remember me? She must meet so many people in her job. Well, Ava it's now or never.

Adjusting my cocktail dress and stepping into my heels, I head for the elevator. Catching my reflection in the mirrored interior I saw my ginger tresses curled and piled high; my green eyes brought out by my dress. The elevator only had to travel 10 floors to the roof.

I guess that's what happens when you're staying on one of the top floors. I take a deep breath and head for the bar.

After checking in at the front desk, I was led toward the spectacular space that is Spago. It was as if nothing had changed since last I was here. Except everything had changed.

I can order whatever I like. If I wanted to eat, I could order full meals, not just entrée sizes because I couldn't afford to pay for them back then.

I looked toward the city, back over the infinity pool dropping away into the abyss. The sun was setting and the city began to light up.

"What can I get you miss?" I jump a little, my reverie is broken. I turn to see a tall man in the bartending uniform smiling across at me.

"Whiskey sour please,' I smile back.

"Coming right up,' he disappears to the other side of the centre island in the bar.

Looking around I wonder if Tarini is even working tonight.

I lean back, my elbows resting on the bar behind me. Nursing my cocktail, I stare out over the city wondering if I am on a wild goose chase.

What if I misremembered her name? Oh god that would be just typical.

I began to wonder if I should show the bartender her picture to see if she still works here. I took a photo of a cocktail and she happened to be standing in front of me at the time, that's not creepy, right?

"Are you eating tonight Madam?" My head snaps around. Turning slowly around I see the short black hair, rolled white sleeves, slender arms adorned with tattoos and a black vest. Tarini was even wearing the same black studs I remember from that night.

"Tar-ini?" I stammer.

"Wait, I remember you. You are that Aussie who came through here a couple years back!" A wide grin breaks out on her face. She immediately runs out from behind the bar to envelop me in a hug.

"Ava, yes! It is so good to see you! I am so sorry I couldn't come back again on my first visit Tarini!" I cry.

"Don't be silly, it's so great to see you too! And please, call me Tari. How long are you in town this time?" She beamed at me.

"Uh...I'm not sure exactly."

After returning to the bar, she must have seen my face fall.

"Hey, what's going on? You don't have the same holiday glow you did last time. Although you look smoking!" She states pointedly.

"It is a very, very long story and I'm exhausted. I'm not going to lie, I ordered a drink as an excuse to look for you. Are you working tomorrow?"

"I sure am. Don't have a day off until next week now, working through the weekend,' she beams at me.

"Is it weird if I give you my number? I don't have a Singaporean one but I use WhatsApp and Viber. Come to think of it, I guess I need to get a Singaporean number now. Oh, there's just so much to think about."

I put my head in my hands. The flight, the sleeplessness and the cocktail were all going to my head.

"I know what you need. Have you had dessert yet?" Tari quizzed. I shake my head staring at the countertop.

"One of my personal favourites- coming right up,' she pats my hand and disappears to enter the order into the computer.

I sit in awe watching her serve a few other customers around the central bar. Mostly young couples looking sickeningly in love, a smattering of businessmen and several Australian accents sat nearby.

Returning to her post in front of me, just as she did two years ago, Tari places down a napkin in front of me, followed by a stunning crystal glass filled to overflowing with cubes of sago, coconut, mango, puffed black rice and condensed milk.

"Voila!" She announced as she hands me a spoon.

"You are my guardian angel,' I whisper marvelling at the creation in front of me.

"Now, why don't you tell me 'Part I' of this 'very, very' long story."

"I guess I can start at the beginning?"

"Just like a fairytale." She rolls her eyes.

"Ha. I'm not so sure this one is a fairytale. It feels more like a nightmare."

The feeling of elation at sipping champagne in the helicopter resurfaced.

Okay, not entirely a nightmare.

"A few months ago, a gentleman appeared on my front lawn. He had fallen over and hurt himself so I called an ambulance and went to the hospital with him."

"Okay, that is definitely not how I was expecting this story to start!" Tari leaned in on her elbows, chin in hand.

"I spent the day sitting with him and we talked. Turned out he was from Singapore."

I suddenly wonder how much I should tell her. I wasn't intending on revealing too many details but now I'm wondering if I should be telling her anything before the Will reading tomorrow.

It's not like Tony made me sign a Non Disclosure Agreement. I can talk to whomever I like. Although, I have only spoken to Ivan about it 'as my lawyer', even Danny doesn't know exactly what is going on.

"Haha, earth to Ava?" Tari stands flapping her tea towel in front of me. "Did you have a stroke?"

"Sorry. Uh, we became friends and kept in touch for months and then he died."

"Oh Ava, I'm sorry. So you're here to pay your respects to his family?" Tari pats my hand gently.

"Something like that,' I sigh. I looked down at my half-eaten dessert.

"This is delicious. Do you think they'd mind if I took it with me?"

"Sorry babe but yeah, probably. They don't like glasses and cutlery leaving the hotel."

"Oh, I'm staying downstairs. I uh, managed to swing a good deal."

Not entirely a lie.

"In that case, feel free. Room service will just bring it back up whenever they clean the room."

We exchanged phone numbers and I note down her roster for the rest of the week.

"I'll book a seat at the bar for dinner tomorrow." I smile sleepily across at her.

"Off to bed now! I'll see you tomorrow." Tari shoos me way before turning to assist the honeymooners on the other side of the bar.

I smile all the way back to my hotel room. Maybe, just maybe, things will turn out okay.

The will reading was to be held in Winnie's office at HEH head office. The tower stood tall amongst its fellow skyscrapers in the Financial District. I'd been to this area once before on my last trip. Level33 was a microbrewery that was touted to have the best view of the Marina Bay Sands building at night as well as the best craft beers in the city and boy it did not disappoint.

Yet another BBSUV (big black SUV) collected me from the hotel to drive the short distance to HEH. Mr Tony met me at the front doors. His welcoming bow was more prostrate than ever before. Probably because he has an audience. Audience was an understatement. There must have been 20 people standing there with him, lined up in perfect rows on either side of the entry.

I am suddenly reminded of the episodes of Downton Abbey when important guests arrived and the entire household was expected to stand outside in welcome.

"Miss Elias, welcome to Huynh Enterprises Holdings head office,' Mr Tony beams.

After introducing me to half a dozen or so of the bystanders he whisked me into an elevator up to the top floor.

"I trust you had a pleasant evening Mr Tony. Are you enjoying being home?" I enquire politely.

"Very much so Miss Elias. Although I will sleep much better once these matters are settled." I ignore his comment and follow him into what appears to be another lobby space.

Huh, is it weird that this floor has its own lobby and reception?

Walking past lounges and an ostentatious reception desk, Mr Tony approached a large frosted glass wall. Upon approach, the wall shifted back and disappeared into a cavity revealing a vast space surrounded by floor to ceiling windows looking over the bay and the Marina Bay Sands. The space was minimally decorated but full of personal touches. In the centre of the room, facing toward the windows, sat the ancient oak desk Winnie had mentioned was one of his prized possessions.

I tiptoed over to it, my heels clacking on the marble floors. Reaching out I caressed the desk with my fingertips. I could feel his presence in the room.

"Shall I take your coat, Miss Elias?" Mr Tony indicates toward an open panel in the wall displaying a hidden coat rack.

"No thank you, Mr Tony, I am feeling a slight chill." I nod, turning away and subtly patting down my coat pockets, checking I hadn't dropped anything.

I place my handbag on a mahogany leather armchair that reminded me of a speakeasy bar. The whisky decanters neatly arranged on the beverage trolley adding to the charm. Looking around the room I can see Winnie in the space; writing letters, holding meetings, taking calls as he stands by the window staring out across the city. Drinking whiskey from his crystal glasses, with his socked feet up on his leather couches. I smile at the imagery.

A phone buzzing on the desk breaks the silence, making me jump. Mr Tony picks up the handset.

"Yes, see them in. We will take coffee during the meeting." He replaced the handset a little forcefully, if you ask me.

"The lawyers have arrived to read the will. What would you like to drink? Sasha will be in to take orders shortly."

Odd. I don't know why I assumed Mr Tony as 'Winnie's lawyer' would be officially reading the will. As he already seemed to know what it contained.

The men who entered the office were cookie-cutter businessmen, like Mr Tony. The three of them standing side by side wore near-identical suits, their hair swept back in similar styles with the same frameless glasses perched on their faces. After bowing, they reached for my hand revealing they all wore eerily similar Rolex watches.

What is with the matching outfits? Clearly, I missed the 'wear all grey, have grey hair and own a Rolex' memo.

I look down self consciously at my outfit like an ad for Mastercard; black and cream pencil dress $60 (on sale), Basque blazer $100, black patent stilettos $50, clutch bag $0 (gifted from my boss from Queensland). Feeling like you 'fit' in the meeting in which you're about to become an heiress, priceless. Perhaps I need to update my wardrobe. I don't want to be labelled a joke. Labels.

Why does it always come down to labels?

The meeting did not take long. After Sasha, a young woman of about 25 years, returned with coffees from the in-house cafe, I'd taken two sips before the meeting was called to a close. As far as I could tell there were no big surprises. The lawyers read out Winnie's last Will and testament which stated I would inherit everything. There was only one note I didn't quite understand, a reference to an external company to look after Winnie's body after death.

Ironight? No that wasn't it. Anyway, for all I know, it is some cryogenic suspension company and Winnie is not dead but frozen in suspended animation set to be defrosted 100 years from now. It suddenly dawned on me.

Winnie's body is gone. He isn't even buried somewhere I can go and visit him; talk to him.

I suppose I should be grateful that I'm not going to stumble into a room someday to discover an urn with his ashes in it. I've never understood what people see in having their ashes sit in a pot on a shelf for all eternity, until eventually no one can remember who was even in the jar in the first place.

It would have been nice to talk to him, all the same. He did say 'I will always be with you'. I guess his soul or spirit or whatever is floating around watching all of this unfold.

I look around and smile. Yes, I think he is quite enjoying his front-row seat to this; popcorn in hand.

"Miss Elias?" One of the gentleman's thrice was staring at me.

"I beg your pardon, what were you saying?" I reply trying not to be too offensive that I hadn't been paying attention.

"We need you to sign these forms, confirming your intention to take Mr Huynh's place as CEO and commence transferring the business and his title deeds into your name." I look down at the forms.

"Sir, half of these documents are untranslated. I am sure you have been made aware that I do not speak nor read Mandarin,' I state bluntly, levelling my gaze at him.

"Ah, well. All the same, we require your signature or we cannot proceed. There are some rather time-sensitive issues at hand here." He spluttered as he reached into his jacket pocket to withdraw a pen. Offering up the pen toward me, I felt the intense stares of the other men in the room. I sit there for what feels like an age.

The man's hand continued to wave the pen in my face, reaching across the coffee table between us. Every moment I delay, I feel the other men inching closer like vultures circling a corpse from the sky.

Looking down at the hundreds of pages stacked in neatly bound piles I hear Ivan's voice in my head. "You are in charge."

"If I do not sign immediately, what happens?" I ask.

"Um...well...I suppose...", Pen guy stutters, "technically the will has been read so you are officially the recipient of Mr Huynh's property and possessions..."

"Does that mean that these documents are simply a 'formality'?" I eyeball him.

"Yes."

"Now you have read the Will, I can direct you to transfer the properties and titles on Mr Huynh's accounts without signing anything?"

He stares dumbfounded. Mouth slightly agape, it took a moment for him to recover, his hand dropping to the table; pen and all.

I look down through the documents and select the execution of the Will. The entire document is in English and as I had to sit here and listen to the entire document reading, I am confident I know what it contains. Other than the bit about where his body went. But does that really affect me if that is what he wanted to do with his remains? Maybe it's a medical school or 'donation to science' thing.

Reaching into my blazer pocket, I withdraw a pen. I see Mr Tony's eyes widen, a vein popping out on his forehead as I slowly uncap Mr Huynh's diamond MontBlanc pen. Reaching down, I sign my name with a flourish on the appropriate line. I turn the page to face Pen Man to sign the witness line.

With the will officially executed, I decide to make use of my newfound power.

"If you will excuse me, gentlemen. I'd like to get acquainted with my new office." I smile sweetly. The men all stayed rooted to the spot.

"But Miss Elias, the other papers..."

"I will have my lawyer review them. For now gentlemen, good day." I stand, confidently extending my hand to shake each one in turn. Standing over the documents to ensure not a single one went missing, I watch as the men file out resentfully, Mr Tony in tow.

Once the door closes I slowly sink into the mahogany couch.

Holy shit.

The room suddenly feeling hot, I drag off my blazer, placing Monty the pen, lovingly on top. I begin pacing back and forth in front of the vast window, taking in the vista.

What the fuck do I do now?

A timid knock came from the door. I turn to look and see Sasha, the young woman who had brought in our coffee standing on the threshold.

"Can I get you anything, Miss Elias?" She asks.

"Oh, Sasha. May I please have a jug of water. Tap, room temperature."

She offers a slight bow and hastily disappears.

A minute or two later Sasha returns, an exquisite crystal jug and matching glass in hand. She places both on the coffee table on large coasters and turns to depart.

"Sorry, Sasha - can I ask another favour please?" I turn to look at her. Noticing for the first time today just how beautiful she is. Heart-shaped face, framed by flowing brown hair. Hazel eyes like a Disney character, almost too big for her face.

"Yes, Miss Elias?"

I walk back to my purse sitting on the leather chair. Sasha began scribbling notes into an iPad.

Where did she pull that from?

"Can you please contact this woman, tell her I need an urgent meeting with her. She was recommended to me by a dear friend." I look down at the crisp black card Ivan gave me. Chang, Jia-Xin Senior Counsel, Allen & Gledhill. I haven't even had time to google her.

Here goes nothing.

I take a quick photograph of the card with my phone before handing it over. Just in case I miss transposed her number into my phone.

Sasha disappears through the door. I like that she doesn't hover.

I wander aimlessly around the room, taking in the space. My heels keeping a steady rhythm on the marble. Click, clack. Stop. Click, clack. Stop. My stomach garbles.

Hm, I forgot about lunch. I don't have anything planned. I'll ask Sasha what she recommends nearby when she comes back.

Not 15 minutes later Sasha returns, this time carrying a large box.

"You have a meeting with Miss Chang at 2.30 pm today. I've arranged a car to be here at 2.15 pm. You can decide when the meeting concludes if you want to return here or to the penthouse. Mr Xi, your driver is familiar with both."

I stand staring at her with my mouth open.

'Catching flies' as one of my 7th-grade teachers used to say.

"If I may, Miss Elias?" Sasha inclines the box.

"Oh, god, yes of course. Please uh, put it on the coffee table."

Another box. What is it with these people and boxes??

"Sasha, sorry. May I ask another favour?"

"Miss Elias, I am employed by HEH as the Personal Assistant to the CEO. It is my job, it is no favour at all." She smiles across at me.

"You're my PA?" I find it hard to get the words out.

"Yes, Miss. And Olivia is your Executive Assistant, she will assist you with higher-level business matters. She is currently on leave. If you don't mind my saying Miss, she took the loss of Mr Huynh rather hard. She had been with him for the last 5 years."

"How long have you worked here?"

"2 years Miss Elias." She looks toward the floor.

"Would you mind compiling the CVs of the people I will see most commonly from HEH? I'd like to have some idea about who everyone is before I get too far." I ask, looking up to see her eyes widen in horror.

"I have no intention of changing a thing, Sasha. I trusted Mr Huynh and want to surround myself with the same people he did. I'd like to know their backgrounds and strengths to ensure I am not overlooking any special skills. When I was an assistant back home, my biggest pet hate was inheriting new directors who had no idea what I was capable of." I tried to smile reassuringly at her.

"Do you know what this box contains?" I ask her, changing tactic.

"Yes, Miss. Mr Huynh was insistent on having his affairs in order before he passed."

"Please, sit. We can go through the contents together." I incline toward the chair opposite me. As I take the lid off the box I ask her if there is somewhere nearby she recommends for lunch.

"We usually get lunch from the cafe downstairs. Mr Huynh had meals included in staff salary packages. I can show you through if you like?"

"I'd like that very much." I smile across at her.

Peering into the box, the first thing I notice is another gold envelope.

"You can read that one in private Miss, if you like,' Sasha whispers.

"I think that might be a good idea." I feel my throat tighten.

The box was filled with little compartments. One section was filled with keys, others documents and notebooks.

What caught my eye was a leather compendium. I ran my fingers over its cover, noting HL embossed in gold into the bottom corner.

"Mr Huynh's compendium. He used to take it to meetings with him. Mostly to hold his papers. He never really took any notes."

Picking up an envelope stamped 'DBS Bank', I looked up at Sasha quizzically.

"A company credit card Miss. For your expenses. Mr Huynh used to bill everything to the HEH accounts and chargeback anything considered 'personal'. Pretty much everything you do from now on will be considered of a 'business' nature Miss. Meetings, travel, dining, shopping. Everything you do as the CEO of HEH is essentially a business expense because you work 24/7. Unless you decide to renovate the penthouse. But that was only re-done a year or so ago."

"Penthouse, yes you mentioned that before?" I withdraw the letter from the envelope. There, stuck to the bottom of the page sat a Black Amex card. 'Ava Elias' embossed in silver capitals, stared back at me. Pulling it away from the letter, the card weighed heavily in my hand.

Literally and metaphorically. *Good lord, what is this thing made out of?*

"Yes, Miss. Mr Huynh's penthouse apartment." Leaning over, she lifts a shiny silver keyring from the box of keys. Hanging from the keyring were multiple glimmering keys and a large silver heart. Turning the heart over in my fingers it read 'PLEASE RETURN TO TIFFANY & CO. NYC.'

"He thought you'd like it." Sasha smiles across at me. A wave of sadness washes over me.

"He knew that I'd end up here. And he'd be...gone. But he didn't pick up the phone and call or email to tell me."

"Oh no, Miss!" Sasha implored, eyes impossibly wider than before. "Mr Huynh had a list of requests written up 'in case of emergency'. I'll show you one day. He told me he was expecting to have 'a visitor' from out of town in the next 12 months and that he might need these things ready for then. I think, Miss Ava, that he intended to tell you he wanted you to take over HEH. He just didn't get to tell you himself and so the emergency list was enacted."

"So you put all this together after he passed?"

Sasha nodded.

"But he wrote me the gold letters?"

"From his hospital bed, Miss Ava. As far as I know, this is the last one." She looks down at the gold parchment envelope, 'He gave it to me the last time I saw him."

We sat in silence. I don't know for how long. My stomach garbled again, loud enough to cause Sasha to jump.

"Miss Elias, why don't I show you to the cafe? Then it'll be time for you to meet Miss Chang. We can go through the rest of this tomorrow. Unless you'd like to stay in the penthouse tonight?" She looks over at me.

"I think I'll stay one more night at the hotel. I'll pack my belongings in the morning."

"You will be needing these Miss Elias." Sasha digs a slim phone case out of the box. Black leather, AE embossed in gold. The iPhone was larger than many of my evening clutches. "It has a Singaporean number pre-loaded as well as your HEH email address." She hands me the phone and a small note card with details of the device and my HEH login details. As I examine it, Sasha walks across to Winnie's desk and pulls a stunning leather laptop bag from the bottom drawer. Again, monogrammed.

Good lord. Do we have stocks in a monogramming company?

"I suppose I was a bit of a foregone conclusion,' I state rhetorically staring at all the personalised stationery.

"Mr Huynh always said to commence as you intend to go on. It was his wish to see you succeed him here."

After placing the phone and stacks of papers in the laptop bag, I gathered my purse and followed Sasha out of the office. She stopped by her desk to pick up her staff ID and phone and we walked through the lobby to the elevators.

"The Cafe is where staff meet for lunch, although it is open 24/7 so staff can collect snacks and beverages at any time of day."

We ride the lift down a handful of floors and exit.

The entire floor stood open before me. Staring around, I had an almost 360-degree view of the city through floor to ceiling windows. Booths, tables and chairs were smattered around the space. Linen tablecloths, water glasses and silverware adorned every surface.

Cafe my arse. This is a full-blown restaurant.

"Sasha, great see you. Table for two?" An impeccably dressed woman greets us.

We have a seating attendant. In our 'in house restaurant'.

"Hi Lou, yes, please. May I introduce Miss Ava Elias."

Lou's eyes widened.

"Welcome Miss Elias,' she bowed. "Please allow me to show you to Mr Huynh's favourite booth."

After being seated, Sasha and I are handed menus. The waitress brought us each a glass of still and sparkling water and offered to return in a few minutes to take our orders.

"It is quite something isn't it?" Sasha looked across at me.

"This is incredible. Was this Winnie's idea? To feed the staff? How many people can they seat in here?" I look around at the tables.

"He said that staff who are encouraged to take regular breaks work more efficiently. No one works well with a hungry stomach. Some of the lower-income staff collect leftovers to take home at night. Staff can also order lunch boxes if they are working off-site for the day. On a busy day there can be up to 200 people in here at a time."

"How many people do we employ in the building?"

"HEH owns the building and uses every inch of it, so everyone who works within it is employed by HEH. Last I checked we had about 3,000 people on staff here."

"Where do they all go in a fire evacuation?" I look toward the window, trying to recall the streets below.

"We'll go through all that in the safety induction. I've got a big week ahead for you next week. I thought I'd give you a little settling in time to finish up this week in peace." She grinned across at me.

"You did all this in anticipation of me saying 'yes' to taking on HEH?" I look at her in awe. "How could you be so sure I'd do it?"

"Mr Huynh was certain of it,' she smiles back.

After eating our meals, which could easily have come from a 5-star restaurant, Sasha and I indulged in hot fudge brownies and coffee.

"Have you lived your whole life in Singapore?" I ask, making conversation.

"Yes, I grew up on the outskirts of the city and moved in when I finished school. I wanted to work in an office."

"Where did you work before you came here?"

"A technology manufacturer, in that building there. I was an administrative assistant." She laughs, pointing out the window to another of the towers in the district.

"What made you come here?" I ask, genuinely curious. Clearly, Winnie took care of his staff but are the perks the only reason people want to work here?

"HEH is one of the most sought-after employers in the country. In Asia. Mr Huynh was renowned for looking after his staff, offering equal pay and encouraging continued education for his people. I'm currently finishing a degree in Business which is being subsidised by HEH." I sit back contemplatively.

Winnie. You really were a man of the people.

I started to feel a little less guilty at the thought of the helicopters and jets. He is feeding his staff as well as helping educate them. I suppose it isn't so bad if the company can afford luxuries on top of all the good it is doing.

"We had better get you washed up for your meeting Miss Elias. The Executive Bathroom is through that door." Sasha pointed toward an ornate white door behind me.

Pushing the door open I am once again astounded by the beauty of this building. The room opened into a large powder room complete with chaise lounges and floor to ceiling mirrors. Soft lighting and gold accents made the woman staring at me in the mirror look like a princess in a castle.

Toward the back of the room were individual bathroom cubicles each with their own sinks, fabric hand towels, moisturisers and assorted hygiene items; packets of breath mints, perfumes and aftershaves sat in silver trays on the counters.

After drying my hands on a plush towel and dropping it into the laundry basket beside the sink, I dispense some moisturiser onto my hand. It smells heavenly; of flowers and citrus. Grabbing a packet of breath mints, I head toward the door. Unwrapping the packet, I place a mint on my tongue. Dropping the plastic wrap into a bin, I place the packet into my purse.

With one final look in the mirror, double-checking my lipstick, I head back to find Sasha.

9

"Here we are Miss Elias,' Mr Xi, my driver calls from the front seat as he climbs out.

I laugh out loud. "You're kidding right?"

I had quite literally climbed into the BBSUV, we drove around the block and parked in the drive of the building opposite HEH.

I may as well have climbed in one door and out the other. That would have made just as much sense. I can SEE the door I just walked out from.

"Why didn't we just walk across the street?" I ask incredulously.

"Because that is not how it is done, Miss." Mr Xi smiles at me, holding my door open and offering me his hand.

Hm. That is the most stupid thing I've ever heard.

"How much do your shoes cost, Miss Elias?" I look over at Xi quizzically.

"Uh, pardon?"

"If your shoes are worth what most young heiress' shoes are worth, you won't want to walk a single step further than you need to,' he winks at me.

Ah. If I had paid $2000 for Christian Louboutins, I suppose I could understand what he is saying.

I look down at my $50 patent stilettos. I tap the heels together playfully and smile up at Xi.

I gotta hand it to Allen and Gledhill, whoever they are. They sure do know how to convince you the money is well spent. I sat in a vast lobby space, the ceilings three-story high with long glass hanging pendant lights. The space had a very Swedish feel to it. Lots of natural light and bleached timber accents. In front of me sat an iPad for 'perusing while I waited' as well as a glass of orange juice, sparkling water and a latte in a takeaway cup. If I drink all of this I will need to pee again before Jia-Xin shows up.

Midway through sculling my organic OJ, I look up to spot a woman striding toward me. Woman is the wrong word. Supermodel. She must be over 5'8. Look at that hair. I'm officially developing a girl crush. Oh god please don't let her be my lawyer.

"Miss Ava Elias?" She had the voice of a newscaster.

"Miss Chang?" I held out my hand in greeting. A strong grip met mine.

"Jia is fine. Please come with me." She turns swiftly and at an impossibly fast pace for such towering heels she sashays toward the elevators.

How does she move so quickly? Because she has such long legs. She's a little scary. I wonder where she got her lipstick?

About halfway up the elevator ride, I realise I'm staring. I look down at my feet. I feel like a potato standing here next to her. And I'm usually a fairly body-confident woman. She even smells amazing.

One of my girlfriends once told me that the potato was her favourite vegetable so it's okay to feel like a potato because they are amazing and so versatile. I smile at the memory. That life feels so far away from the one I currently find myself in.

I struggle to keep up with Jia as she makes her way toward a row of offices. We pass door after door to fancy glass-walled cubicles. Finally, she stops at a door in a dark forgotten looking corner of the floor.

Uh. This is odd. I thought she was Senior Counsel. Do all those other offices we passed belong to partners?

Oh wow. Am I being an office snob?

Until 5 hours ago I'd never had an office in my life.

"Please sit,' Jia indicates a chair sitting wedged between the door and a desk. Shuffling her way around her desk, she takes a seat opposite me. I feel as though I am in a satire, looking around at the tall neat piles of books and papers suffocating the space.

"What can I do for you today?" She asks pointedly.

From the laptop bag, I dig out the documents left by the grey suits this morning.

"I'm not sure where to begin. Perhaps if you take a look over these..." I hand her the documents.

"I do not have time for games Miss Elias. I agreed to this meeting because the girl on the phone said she was calling from the Executive Suite of Huynh Enterprises Holdings. My superiors would have my head if I turned down a meeting with a prospective client like that." She looks across at me, dubiously eyeing my outfit.

"Sasha is the PA to the CEO at Huynh-,' Jia holds up one perfectly slender, perfectly manicured finger to silence me. Flipping hurriedly through the pages of the documents, Jia begins to slow when she reaches the executed will. Silently, her mouth pops open. Her ruby lips shape into a little 'O'. Her long black lashes flash up and suddenly she is glaring me in the face.

"Is this some kind of joke?" She rages from across the table.

"No. Mr Huynh left everything to me,' I state quietly, wishing the chair sat further back from the desk. "I'd like to hire you as my personal lawyer."

"What? Why?" She stares at me dubiously.

"Because I heard you 'Eat Businessmen for breakfast'". I state, looking around the office wondering if I had the right woman.

"So it was a personal reference?" She simmered down.

"Yes, Ivan Norris, QC. His colleague from Melbourne recommended you."

"I've heard of QC Norris. Never met the man. Rumoured to have done a lot of work related to the Underbelly Gangs in Australia."

"Sounds about right." I hesitate. "You don't have to take me on as a personal client. I just need to find someone who can interpret these documents for me in confidence and tell me what I'm signing. I'm not entirely sure I can trust HEH In House Counsel." For the first time, Jia appeared to be smiling.

"Zhang Wei Tony?"

"Yes."

"What makes you say that? Have you known him long?" She tilts her head at me curiously. Like a raven with something shiny.

"I have spent a few days with him. Call it a gut instinct." I shrug.

"How old are you Miss Elias?"

She certainly doesn't mince her words.

"31."

She suddenly lets out a laugh, a beaming smile dawning on her face.

"I'll take you on. But I have to warn you, A&G charge an arm and a leg. This meeting alone just cost you S$400." I look down at my watch. I've been here less than 12 minutes.

"You bill in $200 increments?" My eyes nearly boggle out of my head.

"I can assure you, Miss Elias, as the CEO of HEH, you will be charging a lot more than that when you're in full swing." I stare at her.

"Seriously?"

"Oh, pet. You have no idea what you've gotten yourself into here, have you? Business is a man's world. But you've not only walked into Business, you've walked into Business in Asia. An heiress to an Asian Shipping Conglomerate."

Oh fuck.

"You'd better get yourself a strong network of business associates ASAP or these men are going to make you wish you'd never been born." She stares at me deadpan.

"Any suggestions on where I might start?"

"Outside HEH. Find other women in business. They will have advice on how they have navigated this world of men."

"Do they hang out in bars like businessmen?" I look around aimlessly, my focus coming to rest on Jia's immaculate eyebrows. "Or spas maybe?"

"You're sharper than you look, Miss Elias. I'll give you that. Why don't you leave these with me? I'll give you a call in a day or so when I'm done, and we can meet somewhere to talk." She drums her fingers on the documents and looks critically around her cramped office.

"I'd like that,' I smile at her and show her the card Sasha gave me, to copy down my Singaporean phone number and HEH email address.

Xi dropped me back at the hotel around 3.15 pm. He bid me farewell, reminding me he would be downstairs at 9 am to take me to the office.

Dead on my feet, I decide I'll take a nap before I head up to Spago for dinner. After showering and putting on a little makeup, I don a navy blue wrap dress and latticed ballet flats.

My skirt fluttered about my knees on the rooftop, the wind smelling of rain. I make my way to the bar to my favourite seat and pick up the menu. After having such a large lunch with Sasha, I wasn't particularly hungry.

"I was wondering if I'd dreamt it or if you were going to disappear again without so much as a glass slipper?"

Tari smiles at me from across the bar. The breeze whipped around us, she smelled like lime and mint.

"Hi,' I smiled back at her.

"Was your day any better than yesterday? You look like a weight has been lifted." She eyes me critically.

"Really? I'm not sure I feel it,' I laugh.

"What are you drinking tonight?"

"I think I'll lay off tonight. Soda water and bitters please."

"Jet lag been getting to you?" She expertly gathers a glass, filled the bottom with bitters, fresh orange and lime.

"Maybe? Honestly, I'm not sure if I'm exhausted because I'm not sleeping or because of everything that is going on." I watch as she gracefully mashes the fruit with a glass pummel before topping it with ice and soda water. She places a sprig of mint on top and finishes the performance with a curtsey.

I applaud her with giggle and golf clap.

"What on earth is that?" She laughs, imitating my clapping.

"It's a golf clap."

"What the fuck is a golf clap?" She whispers, in absolute stitches now.

"You know, when you're watching the golf on TV - I mean, I don't watch it on TV, but when I've seen it on TV, this is how they clap when a player hits the ball."

She bends over, hands on knees, gasping for air.

"Shut up! It's a real thing!" I squeal at her, leaning over to peer at her from my chair.

A rather surly looking couple pass our exchange, turning up their noses as they head toward the pool in their bathrobes.

"Miserable sods,' Tari mutters to me under her breath, watching them pass, "I'd better get to it."

Once again, I find myself sitting at the bar, staring out over the bay contemplatively. I decide to relocate to a lounger, overlooking the Gardens by the Bay. I watch as the lights twinkle on the supertrees" way down below. From this height, they just look like little glowing circles on the ground. I look up to catch Tari's eye, so she sees where I moved to. She comes out from behind the bar to offer me a top-up.

"Tari, where should I go to buy new clothes? I think I need to invest in some statement pieces."

"What's wrong with your clothes now?" She looks at me appraisingly.

"I've got a couple of big meetings coming up and I think I'm going to need to spruce up a bit for them."

"I have an afternoon off next week. Do you want me to show you Orchard road? Just make sure you wear your walking shoes. And bring your credit card,' she laughs and stops suddenly. "Does this mean you're staying in town for a little while?"

I look up at her, frowning. "You know what, I suppose I am?" She beams down at me and skips off to serve another customer.

9 am seemed to race around the next morning. I was standing down at the entry to the hotel when Xi drove in.

"Good Morning Miss Elias, how are you this morning?" He smiles warmly at me. I notice for the first time a small scar running up the centre of his chin.

"I am very well thank you, Xi, how are you?" He opens the door for me and offers me his hand as I clamber in.

"I am most grateful it is Friday, Miss Ava. I have tickets to the Night Zoo for my daughter's birthday."

"How lovely! I've heard it is magical. How old is your daughter?"

"She is eight, Miss. We go every year."

"Well do wish her a happy birthday. If you need to finish up early, please don't worry about me. I can catch a cab."

"I wouldn't dream of leaving you driver-less Miss Elias. You will meet two other drivers this afternoon who can always assist you on weekends and in emergencies."

Upon arrival at HEH, Sasha presented herself at the car door.

Has she been standing here waiting for us to arrive?

"Good Morning Miss Elias, how are you today?" She takes my laptop bag and hands me a glass enviro-cup.

"It's a latte, Miss,' she inclines toward the cup. "You are going to need it, we have quite a few things to get through this morning."

I do as I am told and start sipping the coffee as Sasha leads me toward the ground floor security station. There I have my photograph taken for the system and am given my ID tag and building swipe access.

"Miss Elias, it is very important that you understand this. If you lose this swipe, you must call us immediately. Sooner if possible."

"Sooner than immediately?" I smile, "I'll do my best."

"Miss, if you lose this card, every single HEH owned building in the world is at risk."

Holy fuck.

"Don't lose the card. Got it,' I swallow.

We departed the security station and headed toward the elevator bay.

"Oh, Miss Elias. This way." Sasha turned and veered to her left. There, behind a strategically placed water feature, sat another elevator.

"What's this?" I ask with intrigue.

"This is the Executive Elevator. It is faster than the others and goes directly to our floor. It requires special swipe access to get in and to make it move."

Of course it does. Bless you, Winnie.

Sasha returned to her desk, allowing me some time to enter Winnie's office and get myself settled in. Approaching the glass door, I swipe my card against the access panel. Once again, I am caught off guard by the beauty and simplicity of the space. As I hang my coat in cloak nook, I notice a couple of other doors beside it. The cloak nook was wide enough to fit the majority of my wardrobe, including racks for spare shoes, ties and a wall-mounted jewellery case.

Peering curiously at the other doors, I hold my breath as I gently open the first one. A bar fridge and wine cellar, inside a space similarly sized to a walk-in robe. Hanging inside the door on an intricate rack were rows and rows of crystal glasses. Red, White, Champagne, Prosecco. Wandering into the 'cupboard', I check out the wine cellar.

I have no idea what any of this is, but I am sure it is all incredibly expensive. I close the cupboard gently and turn to the next door.

And behind door number two! I giggle quietly to myself.

A much more standard looking door this time. Beyond it sat a powder room not dissimilar to the one in the restaurant. Only slightly smaller than the one downstairs, and with only two 'cubicle' doors at the end of the room. Edging my way into the space, feeling somewhat like I am entering Narnia, I notice subtle details; fresh flowers sit on the low table beside the chaise lounge, velvet cushions. Opening the first cubicle I see a similar toilet/basin combination as was upstairs. In the second cubicle, I am surprised to find a full shower, complete with a multi-directional rain shower and hose.

What a great idea. If you are going out to dinner after a long day, you can shower and change here without having to go home first. Reluctant to leave the beautiful space, I close the door behind me and turn to the final door in the sequence.

What could be in here? A safe perhaps? I've seen that in a lot of movies. Opening the door I am faced with a big black, nothing.

What? It's just empty.

About a meter square, the door opened into a space that contained nothing. No shelves, no racks. How bizarre. Maybe it's a secret passage!I laugh at myself, but walk into the space and close the door behind me nonetheless.

I probably should have checked if I can open it from the inside before doing that.

The second the door was shut, the room began to glow. I hear a gentle whirring sound and ever so slowly, the wall in the back of the closet begins to disappear.

It is a secret passage! Winnie, you are by far the coolest human to walk this earth.

In front of me, lit up like the aisle on an aeroplane, was a narrow staircase leading up into the roof.

Should I go tell Sasha that I'm in here? Does Sasha know this exists?!

I decide to throw caution to the wind and begin to climb the stairs toward a dimly lit doorway above.

Reaching the top of the stairs, I stop. With shaking hands, I open the door. I stood in a glass room on the precipice of a helipad, the highest point on the HEH building. I can see from where I stand that there is an elevator on the other side of the helipad. I guess that is the elevator guests ride down when they come to visit HEH. But this door, protected from the wind inside this little glass room, is the one Winnie would use to get straight to his office. Finding myself smiling once again, I descend the stairs and think about the day ahead.

Back in the office, I stand staring at Winnie's desk. I haven't yet brought myself to sit in his chair. I've been standing here for 10 minutes. I've set up my laptop, plugged in my phone to charge. Pulled out the compendium and placed Monty lovingly in the pen holder adorning the desk.

I'm about to lap the room for a third time when Sasha knocks on the door.

"Come in,' I call, releasing a breath I didn't realise I was holding.

"Ah, good you're getting settled in,' Sasha observes. She motions for me to join her on the leather couches.

"For the remainder of your schedule today; I have your PS Officer here to meet you, I hope you don't mind that I picked one out with our head of security; Mr Tony wants a meeting to discuss philanthropic funding and announcing your arrival at HEH, and then I have organised for Xi's weekend cover to take you to the apartment to get settled in before the weekend. Any questions?" She smiles across at me.

"What's a PS Officer?" I feel my forehead furrow.

"Private Security Miss Elias."

"Please call me Ava. Private Security for what?"

"For you, Miss El- uh, Ava. It is standard protocol for you to have a PS with you during the day and when you are at home in the penthouse, there is 24/7 security on-site in the building."

"What happens when I am travelling?" I query.

"The PS will travel with you."

"Okay, let"s pretend I'm okay with this. Who have you picked for me?"

Sasha holds up her iPad with a smile. Staring back at me is a clean-shaven, very well-built man in his mid-30s, looking like a MIB character; in a crisp suit and black sunglasses.

Is he posing?? Well, I suppose if I am forced to spend my days with a shadow, he's certainly not bad to look at.

"Sure, he's not unappealing Sasha but is he good at um, security--ing. That's not a word. Is he good at his job?"

What does a private security officer even do? Is this guy meant to just keep people away from me, like crowd control or is he expected to shield me from violence?

"He's a Chinese-American Ex-Navy Seal,' she beams across at me.

I laugh at her expression, "Okay, well if you like him so much you can have first dibs." Sasha giggles and claps her hands. I'm really enjoying having her around. Plus, she is all over this. There is not one thing I've needed yet that she hasn't already thought of. She is a gold class assistant.

"I have morning tea ready, unless you'd like to go to the Cafe?"

"I'm happy to take it in here. Did you say Mr Navy Seal is here to meet me?"

"I did, he is waiting in the lounge."

"Right, well I'd best go introduce myself." Before Sasha can stop me, I straighten my skirt and cotton blouse and march out the door.

He stands with his back to me.

And my, it is a nice back. Great shoulders. I give him the once over, my gaze catching at his hips.

Is that what I think it is?

"Are you carrying a gun?" I exclaim staring at the holster on his belt.

Turning slowly to face me, Mr Navy Seal takes off his sunglasses, his eyes raking their way up from my stilettos to my face.

"I am, in fact, carrying two ma'am." He unbuttons his jacket to reveal a holster under his arm on his left side. I find myself trying to place his accent. Boston maybe?

"Sasha!" I call.

Materialising beside me, Sasha smiles up at Mr Navy Seal.

"Sasha, was Mr Huynh ever shot at?" Sasha stares at me, wide-eyed. She shakes her head.

"Was he ever stabbed?" I wave my hand in reference to the clearly defined stab-vest under Mr Seal's tight button-down shirt. She shakes her head again.

"Was there ever a time that Mr Huynh was in physical danger, requiring assistance from his PSO during his time as CEO of HEH?"

"No, Ava,' She whispers.

"Then can someone please explain to me why I need a babysitter with TWO guns?"

Mr Tony's voice makes us both jump, "Because when some people find out that you inherited HEH after little more than an interlude with Mr Huynh, there will be more than a few ruffled feathers."

"Mr Tony, are you implying that my new heiress status may lead people to wish me harm?" I stare incredulously at him. Would people really go to those lengths simply because they don't like me in this position?

"It wouldn't be the first time people have done immoral things for the sake of protecting their businesses. Or their personal interests,' he saunters closer, eliciting a shiver down my spine. He's like an insect. He gives me the heeby-jeebies.

"With respect Sir, please take a step back from the lady." Mr Navy Seal steps forward, his arm reaching between me and the ever-encroaching Mr Tony.

"Excuse me?" Tony splutters.

"The nature of your speech comes across as rather threatening, Sir. Please keep your distance." Boston, definitely Boston. Oh man, he smells good. What is that? David Beckham? I catch sight of Sasha out the corner of my eye. She is swooning.

"Do you know who I am son?? How exactly am I meant to hold a meeting with Miss Elias, if I am unable to be in the same room as her?" Tony's eyes were blazing now.

You know what, maybe I will keep Mr Navy Seal. I like the effect he has on Tony.

"Sasha was about to have morning tea brought in. Let's all sit down and we can have the meeting right here." I sigh and sit myself down in one of the cream leather wingback chairs right there in the lobby.

"Here? You want to hold a confidential meeting, here?" A large vein on Tony's forehead looked like it was about to explode.

"I've an idea. If anyone walks in, we can just stop talking." I roll my eyes and wave him into the seat opposite me.

Sasha has disappeared, presumably to collect the supplies for tea. Mr Navy Seal stands beside the two of us, eyeing the lifts for new arrivals.

"This is most unorthodox,' Tony continues to splutter, parking himself in a chair and pulling paperwork from a briefcase.

"Have you had a chance to sign the documents we left with you yesterday?"

"They are being reviewed by my lawyer. I will let you know when I am ready to discuss them.' Tony blanches a little at that statement.

"Very well. The next point for discussion is the philanthropic ball. Winnie always hosted an evening in honour of an important local cause. It is an annual gala and the date is fast approaching."

"When is this ball?"

"July 1st."

"We have plenty of time. I'll get Sasha to set a meeting with the team in charge. What else?" I state brusquely.

"Uh, as you wish. We need to discuss announcing your takeover of HEH. Media, publicity, etcetera."

"Let's avoid using the word 'takeover' shall we? I would like to take some more time before meeting the public. I assume HEH has a spokesperson?"

"We can arrange an Executive Spokesperson to behave as a mouthpiece specifically for your office. Until you are comfortable facing the media yourself."

"Excellent. I should only need a few weeks. I will speak with the Public Relations team regarding a statement."

"Is there anything else Mr Tony?" I stare him down.

"No, Miss Elias. That covers it for today." He packs his papers and stands.

"And in future Mr Tony,' he turns to look at me, 'be sure to have the appropriate teams contact Sasha regarding these matters in future. I am sure as General Counsel for HEH, you must have much more important issues at hand than what philanthropic endeavour the HEH ball will honour." He nods stiffly and stalks to the elevators.

"I have never heard anyone put Mr Tony in his place like that. He was forever pushing Mr Huynh around but no one ever seemed to notice how out of bounds he was." Sasha observes quietly as the elevator departs.

"I want to see his employment record. Christ knows we're probably paying him a fortune. And to do what? To threaten my PSOs and throw his weight around?"

"I am sorry to interrupt Miss Elias, but does that mean you are hiring my services?" Mr Navy Seal steps forward.

"Who knows, maybe someday I'll need you to shoot Mr Tony for me." I wink at him, turn on my heel and head back into my office.

That afternoon I ask Sasha to book me meetings with the Executive Directors of each of the departments. Next week I wanted to know who was in charge of what, and what HEH owned. Already one step ahead of me, Sasha went through the schedule for the next week which included these meetings as well as briefings from the teams on project status.

Sasha should be in charge around here! I don't trust Tony. I want the information to come straight from the people who are in charge. His interjections are so strange for someone who is supposed to be a Lawyer. It's like he thinks he's running the show.

Sasha's comment came back to me, "He was forever pushing Mr Huynh around."

Maybe that is his beef. He wanted to be the big kahuna.

After getting plans for the following week sorted, Sasha tells me it is time to grab some lunch and head out to the penthouse.

"Do you have any plans this weekend?" I ask Sasha as I pull my coat off its hanger.

"My boyfriend and I are repainting our apartment. So we will probably be consumed with that. What about you?"

I stare at her. I hadn't even thought about it. What am I going to do this weekend? I suppose I'll move into Winnie's penthouse? That won't take long- I only have one suitcase. I guess I should call my parents.

"I haven't quite decided yet. I'll probably go to the Gardens by the Bay. Make the most of the sunshine, and my anonymity whilst I still have it." I laugh. I grab the box Sasha gave me with the keys and other assorted items. May as well go through this over the weekend too.

As I double tap my swipe to lock the door to the office, I notice Sasha sitting at her desk.

"Are you coming with us?" I peer at her over the desk, waving in the general direction of Mr Navy Seal.

She looks up at me, stunned. "You want me to come with you? To see Mr Huynh's penthouse?"

"Sure! Why not? Unless you have too much to do before the weekend. I don't want to put you out." Within 30 seconds she was standing beside her desk, purse in hand and a cardigan draped over her arm.

Downstairs at the BBSUV Xi introduced me to the two alternate drivers. Sasha appeared with our packed lunches in a basket and we all piled in. Seal in the front with Xi and Sasha and I in the back.

Pulling into a private driveway to an underground car park, I really began to have an out of body experience.

"Where are we?" I ask, peering out at the grey concrete garage surrounding us.

"The underground carpark of the Concourse Skyline residential tower, Miss,' Xi smiled into the rear-view mirror.

We drove through one archway and reached a gated section of the garage. The gate retracted allowing us to drive into a large carpark. There must be 20 cars here.

Holy shit. These are all muscle cars.

Rows of shiny Mustangs, Ferrari, Lamborghini, Bugatti; sat sparkling under the fluorescent lighting. There were also several more BBSUVs- all of different make and model.

"Whose car park is this?" I hesitate.

"Yours, Miss,' Xi replies.

Mr Navy Seal made a choking sound from the front seat.

"Mr Huynh owns all of these vehicles?" Now I sounded like I was the one choking.

"If you don't mind my saying Miss, Mr Huynh liked things that go fast,' he laughs, "he was also an avid collector."

"Of cars?" I stare at what must have been millions of dollars worth of motor vehicles as I clambered out of the SUV, not waiting for Xi to open my door.

"Of many things Miss Elias,' Xi smiles at me, a twinkle in his eye.

"Sasha!" I call, having lost sight of her in the SUV. She appeared out the other side of the car. Her face mirrored mine, I'm sure.

"Did you know about this?"

"I mean, kind of. But it"s very different looking at them all in person."

I catch sight of Seal smirking. Seems none of us are immune to the overwhelm caused by such opulent wealth.

"Ah, well then. Should we take a look inside?" I ask to no one in general, reaching for my suitcase.

"Allow me Miss,' Xi beat me to it.

Standing in the awkward silence of the elevator I ask Sasha to give us the rundown on what she knows of the penthouse.

"Oh, where to begin! Winnie got me to go through the manual and let him know what he needed to know immediately. From what I recall it has 5 bedrooms, 5 and two half baths plus the Master Suite which takes up most of the top floor. A huge kitchen with a Maid's quarters and a butler's pantry. Five large balconies and a huge terrace with lap pool and jacuzzi. Steam room, study..." She gains enthusiasm the further she gets.

"Okay, we get it. There are a lot of rooms,' Seal grumbles from the back corner.

The elevator comes to a stop in a dark hallway. Black as far as the eye can see. Walls, carpet, ceiling.

That isn't depressing at all.

We walk to the end of the hallway through a barely visible door opening into a light airy room filled with artwork. A large violet and blue painting of abstract colour adorns most of one wall. The others are covered in similarly exquisite pieces. We wander from this room to that, in awe of the sheer size and swankiness of the space.

"I believe each of these rooms have names, Miss Ava,' Sasha whispers in awe.

"Names?" I frown at her in confusion.

"Oh yes, it isn't enough for the study to be called a study or the entry to be called the entry. There is a large manual that the housekeeper will give you in the morning. It explains everything."

The study space contains floor to ceiling timber shelves set behind a large timber desk, a long lounge running beside the window. Similarly, the library houses shelves from floor to ceiling on all sides except for one where a sandy-colored rug hung from the wall.

"The Forbidden City." Seal comments, looking up at the odd square and rectangular bumps on the carpet. I stare at him quizzically.

"I am not as uncultured as you might think Miss Elias,' he sniffs.

A long brown room opens out into what is presumably the 'lounge' with large sofas a dining table and piano sit.

"I believe there is a massage room and an atelier on this floor too, Miss Ava,' Sasha looks around us.

"Atelier?" I quiz.

"For suit fittings with a private tailor."

Ah, but of course!

Behind what appears to be a secret panel in the wall, a large gold powder room beckons.

We proceed up the stairwell, deciding against all climbing into the elevator to the second floor.

"Good lord, how big is this place?" Seal grumbles, stepping out into a space that could only be described as another art gallery.

On this floor we find 'closets' for him and her. Full rooms larger than the living room at the chalet. Filled with clothes racks and shoe displays similar to top-end designer stores. "Armoire" Sasha proudly advises us these rooms are known as.

The master bedroom is all muted grey timber shiplap walls and crisp white accessories, with a central California king bed and floor to ceiling windows. The master bath ensconced once again by floor to ceiling windows, covered in white and grey marble with black accents. A large black freestanding bathtub proudly placed in the centre of the window.

That seems private. Large windows looking straight into the giant black bathtub.

I note with relief that there are large grey block out blinds at the top of the windows.

The entire second floor stood wrapped around in a large balcony complete with lounges, barbecue area, bar, lap pool and spa overlooking the Marina Bay Sands and Singapore flyer.

Finally, we return downstairs at the kitchen, all muted greys and blues. Two ovens and a timber and marble benchtop that waterfalls down into a large island for breakfast.

I reach without seeing, into the fridge door and grab the first bottle that looks like bubbles. I realise as I shut the door that a large wine fridge sits immediately adjacent to the regular fridge.

Sasha joins me at the bench, opening cupboards here and there in search of champagne flutes.

"This would be much easier if we read the manual first,' she laughs, nodding toward a giant binder on the marble bench.

"That's tomorrow Ava's problem!" I laugh back, dragging the wrapping and cage off the bottle. We both walk out onto the terrace and hand around the glasses. I take my thumb off the cork and pop the bottle.

"Oooh!" I exclaim. Seal and Xi look at me curiously. "It isn't a real bubble popping if someone doesn't day 'Ooh!"

I pour everyone a half glass and place the bottle on the bench.

"Here's to Winnie. May he rest in peace. Or wreak havoc wherever he is. To Winnie!" I raise my glass and feel the tears prickle. Looking around at these people who have essentially become my instant family I wonder if that is inappropriate considering they are technically my staff.

As we watched the sun dip toward the horizon, Xi sighs; "As much as I have enjoyed the company, it is about time I take you two home respectively and we leave Miss Elias to settle in."

"Don't forget the housekeeper will be here in the morning to go through what's what okay? And Xi will be here to pick you up at 8.30 am on Monday." Sasha beams at me as we say goodbye.

After saying my farewells and watching the others disappear into the elevator, I felt suddenly weary.

I realised too that I had forgotten to tell Tari that I wouldn't be staying at the hotel tonight.

Darn, Xi has just left too. He could have dropped me at the hotel for dinner. I could always drive...hm better not.

I decide to SMS Tari instead.

> Found some new digs.
> Won't make it to Spago tonight.
> Will tell you all about it when I see you.
> Xx A

She must be almost ready to start work. Uh, what am I going to eat for dinner?

I wander back into the kitchen and look over toward the 'bible' sitting on the counter. Apparently, I can call down to the concierge and have them order me something. It is like living in a hotel. And a museum. And an art gallery. Who wants to bet they'd come up and run me a bath if I asked them to?

Hm, a bath sounds like just the ticket. On second thought...

I look out the giant window toward the Singapore Flyer, my focus coming to land on the jacuzzi built into the rooftop deck.

Did I pack swimwear? That would be a 'no.'

Wait, it's my apartment – does it matter?

After deciding it doesn't, I head to the guest bedroom where I find a fluffy robe hanging freshly laundered inside the ensuite. I drag my skirt and blouse off and wrap myself in the robe. Heading back toward the balcony, I hear my phone ping.

> Can't wait.
> Get some food for your fridge.
> Tx

Returning to the kitchen, phone in hand, I grab my Prosecco glass only to realise it is empty.

Well that won't do.

I open the fridge to dig the bottle back out and stare suddenly.

Was that always there? Or was I just too focussed on finding booze that I didn't notice the food in here? The fridge contained bowls of fresh fruit, vegetables, meats and cheeses. I pull out the deli meats, some grapes and the bowl of paper wrapped cheeses and decide to have a charcuterie board for dinner.

Placing the board down beside the spa, I de-robe down to my bra and lace underwear and slide into the bubbles. As I sit there admiring the city as the sun sets behind me, I watch the lights twinkle on the Singapore flier and atop the Marina Bay Sands building.

I cannot believe I am here right now. I raise my glass to the sky in a silent toast to Winnie.

Here's to you, Winnie. I pray you made the right choice by putting your faith in me. I guess only time will tell.

I realise with a start that I hadn't read Winnie's letter from the box with the keys and compendium. Jumping from the spa I wrap a towel around myself and find my handbag. Digging out the letter, I carefully lift the seal.

Dearest Ava,

I hope you will make yourself comfortable in my old office as well as in the Beach Street Penthouse. Take this as a symbol of my 'passing the baton' to you, my dear.

-Winnie

The next morning, I awake to the sound of a vacuum cleaner.

What the fuck is that?

I suddenly remember I am no longer in the hotel anymore. Jumping out of bed I grab the robe I stole last night and tiptoe to the door of the Master Suite. Peering around the door, I suddenly wonder to myself why I am hiding. I hear the vacuum stop.

Straightening up, I walk in what I hope appears to be a confident manner, downstairs to the kitchen.

Oh, okay, not in here.

I try the living room. Not in here either. Where the hell was that coming from. I eventually hear the Housekeeper in the study.

"Hello?" I call, pushing the door open.

A woman in her mid-50s stops to look at me. She bows deeply and smiles.

"Miss Elias! I had been hoping to meet you this morning. Come, I shall make you some breakfast. What would you like?"

I follow in her wake toward the kitchen. Suddenly I am hit with the paradox of choice.

What do I want for breakfast? Eggs? Bacon? Pancakes? French Toast? Omelette?

Wait, were there even eggs in the fridge? I feel my brain begin to liquify from the pressure. I enter the kitchen; the woman stops and turns to look at me.

"Uh hi, I'm Ava,' I say, holding out my hand, "What's your name?"

"I am Gladys Wong. You may call me Gladys. I live downstairs in the building; Mr Huynh covered my rent and I spent my days cleaning and keeping his house."

"I am more than happy to uphold Winnie's previous arrangement. I am not sure there are many groceries for breakfast I'm afraid. I just arrived here last night." I frown, looking around the kitchen. It looks different in the daylight.

"Oh, that is no matter. I take care of the groceries, cleaning, shopping. Pantry full now. What would you like for breakfast? Coffee? Tea? Juice?" She smiles across at me.

"Coffee would be an amazing start." I glance around as she busies herself in the kitchen. At a loss as to what else to do with myself, I perch on a bar stool and watch her work.

With a perfectly foamed latte in front of me, she asks me once again what I want to eat. After my small dinner last night I realise I am starving.

"Um, French toast and bacon please?" I hesitate. Is that appropriate to ask for?

"Of course, Miss Ava. It will be ready in about 20 minutes. Why don't you go take a shower? When you've eaten, we can discuss what you'd like to eat for the week." She smiles once again and busies herself in the kitchen.

Hm. A shower sounds fabulous.

Caffeinated, washed and dressed, I lazily make my way back toward the kitchen. It smells heavenly!

I turn the corner to see a plate of French toast topped with fresh strawberries, maple syrup, bacon and what appeared to be mascarpone.

I couldn't have afforded to eat like this every weekend in my old life. These ingredients alone would have taken up my whole grocery budget. Mascarpone mixed with fresh vanilla bean! I stand staring at the food, in absolute awe.

"Sit, sit! Eat,' Gladys waves a fork in my face. I smile at her and take a seat.

"Apple or Orange?" She looks across at me from the fridge.

"Juice? Orange please." She pours me a large glass and disappears, leaving me to enjoy my scrumptious breakfast in peace.

I decide to take it out onto the balcony and enjoy the fresh breeze coming up off the beach.

The rest of Saturday passed in a blur. I spent most of it going through the plan for the apartment with Gladys. She also went through how things work in the building and the penthouse. In the afternoon, whilst she grocery shopped, I took a walk around the neighbourhood.

On Sunday I slept in, feeling like I had finally begun adjusting to the time zone. When I finally made my way to the kitchen, I found Gladys awaiting my arrival. I sat the counter and smiled at her.

"Good Morning."

"Good Morning Miss Ava. Coffee?" She asks as she collects a large mug from the cupboard.

"Please and an orange juice?"

I thank her as she places the juice in front of me. The coffee machine grinding away.

"French Toast again for breakfast?"

"I was thinking perhaps something lighter. Fruit Salad? And Greek yoghurt?"

"You can't eat just that Miss, you'll waste away!"

I look at the clock. 9.30 am. By the time I've eaten and figured out what I'm going to do for the day, it'll be lunchtime.

"Why don't you pack me a lunch and I promise to eat it at midday."

"Are you going somewhere, Miss?" Gladys began pulling fresh fruit from the fridge. Pineapple, strawberries, passionfruit, watermelon.

"I was thinking about taking a walk around the Gardens by the Bay."

"Do you want me to call your weekend guy?"

"Weekend guy?"

"Yes, Miss, the one who drives you around and looks after you on the weekends. Did Sasha or Xi not give you his number?"

"Ah, yes. That guy. They did, I thought maybe I'd just walk."

"Walk to the gardens! But Miss it is such a long way!"

"Okay, okay. Sure, if it's no hassle. I'd appreciate the lift."

And so I spent Sunday walking around the Gardens By the Bay. Just as beautiful as I remembered them. My 'weekend guy', like a Hugo Boss-suited shadow, following along behind me. His justification was that he had to drive me home again, so it didn't matter.

Much to the displeasure of my Shadow, I decided to drop in and see Tari on the way home. The hotel was after all only a 15 minute or so walk from the gardens.

Standing there, no makeup, sun-kissed skin from the day outside, the skirt on my sundress billowing around me in the wind. I smile across at Tari as I approach the bar. My Shadow made the smart decision to distance himself from me, as to avoid people thinking we were there together.

Another bartender beats her to me.

"What can I get for you, Miss?" He smiles approvingly across at me.

"Something alcoholic with passionfruit. Light and spritzy."

"Coming right up,' he barely seemed to take his eyes off me as he gathered the ingredients and unnecessarily flamboyantly mixed me a summery cocktail. Mint, pineapple, passionfruit. Perfect.

When he finally finished and placed the drink in front of me, I could almost feel Tari's seething jealousy from across the bar. I thank the guy and watch him depart to assist another customer.

"I think that was some kind of record,' Tari appears, a bowl of spicy potato chips in hand. I look at her quizzically as she places them in front of me.

"What do you mean? Oh, are these for me?"

"He's never taken that long to produce a cocktail, in his life,' she rolls her eyes.

"I was starting to wonder if he needed re-setting,' I laugh back quietly. I watch as the jealousy fades from her face.

"Did you come to see me?" She asked, her face lighting up. She looks around and picks up a glass and crisp tea towel to 'dry it' with.

"Maybe. Or maybe I just wanted to eat the food and buy the cocktails."

"Is this place anywhere near your new digs?"

"Not really. I guess. It's over on Beach Road?"

"Fancy. I didn't realise you were looking for somewhere to live. I thought you were just here temporarily."

"I'm not quite sure what I'm doing to be completely honest. I'll explain it more when we go shopping this week. What afternoon did you say you have free?"

"Wednesday!"

"Wednesday it is."

We sit there in peaceful chatter, Tari occasionally disappearing to assist other customers before returning.

A rather rowdy group of businessmen appeared and broke the peaceful vibe that Spago had going on. They all sat at a high table not far from me, all facing each other and yahooing at one another. Stereotypical Western businessmen, they all donned suits without ties, top buttons open and jackets hanging from the backs of their chairs.

"Ugh,' Tari grumbles under her breath before moving across to wait on them.

A few minutes later she returned, "Ugh." Was all she said again.

"Don't they tip well?" I ask peering at the table.

I mean, sure they are rowdy but is there any particular reason why she doesn't like them?

"Sexist bigots,' she huffs.

"Oh, they hit on female staff?"

"They think they're bigshot businessmen, but they run tiny little companies. Just like their micro-penises." I let out a howl of laughter.

"What are they being sexist about?" I whisper across at her. She leans in and replaces my cocktail with one of her specials.

She's going to get me tipsy. Ah, who am I kidding? I could use it.

"They are talking about a rumour that there's a new CEO who just arrived in town."

Oh crap.

"Apparently some foreigner has inherited the largest shipping conglomerate in Singapore, in fact, in all of Asia."

Oh shit.

"They're laughing because not only is it incredibly hard to break into the market in Singapore for foreigners, but because she's a woman."

Oh Fuck.

"Those pigs are taking bets on how long it will take a woman to single-handedly sink a conglomerate that has been an unshakable powerhouse for 50 years."

"And how long are they betting?" I swallow.

"One asshole said she'd tank it before he'd even finished his beer."

I feel my face fall. I knew this was going to be hard, but I hadn't expected it to be quite this vicious.

"Are they making judgements on her business savvy or simply because she's female?"

"Both, I guess. I'm not sure. It doesn't sound like they know much about this woman, like I said it's a just rumour. But they're upset that she's an outsider and…"

"Female,' I finish. Suddenly the joy of my day in the sunshine drains away.

What if I can't do this? What if I do sink a conglomerate that did so well in the hands of men before I got here? What about all the staff; their families? I'd be putting them all out of work if I mess this up for them. Tari catches sight of my face.

"Don't let my anger ruin your night! I for one, hope she kicks all their asses. Huynh Enterprises desperately needed a shake-up anyway. Why shouldn't a bright woman be the one to come in and show these men how it's done?"

"You really think so?" I look up at her, a glimmer of hope in my dark future.

"She's gonna have her work cut out for her, but someone willing to take on the Huynh legacy must have huge balls!" She laughs, winking at me before wandering off to assist another customer. I sit and sip my cocktail, deep in thought.

And tomorrow is Monday. Tomorrow I find out if I can do this, and if the people of HEH will trust and respect me to do right by them. The first thing I need to do is figure out Tony. And call Jia. I need to know what he had in those papers.

After fare welling Tari, I reconfirm that I'll meet her at Orchard road on Wednesday to shop. It wasn't until I got downstairs to the lobby that my Shadow caught up with me.

"Miss I am not supposed to lose sight of you." He exclaimed, his suit looking a little ruffled.

"And you found me!" I laugh, "come on, let's go home."

10

My first few days at HEH were insanely busy. I asked Sasha to clear Wednesday afternoon so I could shop with Tari. Then I met with the head of Security to discuss not only my security detail but also general security for staff, vessels and properties of HEH.

The marketing and publicity team were next. We discussed what the approach would be to 'launching' me as the new CEO and the charity for the upcoming ball. We ended up deciding on Winnie's favourite charity, and the first charity HEH ever supported. Singapore's "Public Housing" initiative. Concerning the CEO launch, the team told me they would get back to me and we would arrange to combine the two, announcing me as incoming CEO and announce the charity selection at the same time. The publicity team felt that would give some media outlets something to be distracted by.

Hah. Good luck with that.

By Wednesday lunchtime I was feeling rather good about where I sat. I'd met half the Executive Directors of HEH and had a general understanding of what their respective teams did. Real Estate, Aircraft, Shipping – Maintenance, Orders, Transportation and International relations.

I sat in the BBSUV as Xi drove toward Orchard road. I'd been there briefly only once before, last time I walked there. How times have changed.

"I will maintain a comfortable distance, Miss. You won't even know I'm there,' Navy Seal states confidently from the front passenger seat.

"We shall see about that,' I eye him dubiously from behind. I suppose at least suits are more common here than they are back home.

I walk into the restaurant Tari suggested for lunch and spot her almost immediately.

"Hi!" She jumps straight up and gives me a big hug.

I spot Seal out of the corner of my eye, taking a seat at a table within my line of sight. He pulls out a newspaper and settles in.

Oh my god, a newspaper. Why doesn't he just buy a t-shirt that says 'undercover spy' on it? Surely he could have brought an iPad or something to entertain himself.

Tari and I sat and chatted while we ate, catching up on how her week had been, she started telling me about her girlfriend troubles. I still hadn't brought myself to tell her about HEH yet. I wasn't quite sure how. Breaking through my thoughts she exclaimed from opposite me; "Oh well, I guess the rumours were wrong."

"What do you mean?" I look at her, a forkful of spaghetti in my hand. She points past me to a large wall-mounted TV screen.

There, in high definition stood Mr Tony behind the HEH podium. He was speaking in Mandarin. He turns and shakes hands with a young man, maybe mid to late 30s. Clean-shaven, suit and tie, silky black hair that sat around his shoulders, tucked behind his ears. He had a panty-dropping, megawatt Hollywood smile.

Who is this guy? He looks like a fucking Korean Soap star! What the hell is going on? I turn to Tari, eyes wide in horror.

"What is he saying?"

"I can't hear, the volume is turned down, but the headline reads 'Huynh Enterprises Confirms new CEO. A Mr Chen, apparently. Well, he's got my vote, woohoo!" She smiles across at me.

I feel as though the ground has fallen out from underneath me.

How is this possible? It's surely not legal? How can Tony hold a press conference without me? How can he hold a press conference about something that ISN'T TRUE?

Tari looks over at me in consternation. "You know it isn't the end of the world. Feminism will just have to wait."

I sit there mute, uncertain as to what to do next. Suddenly my handbag begins to vibrate. I apologise to Tari and dig out my phone. Jia.

"Jia?" I answer.

"Have you seen it?"

"Yes."

"Do you know what he said?"

"They've announced the new CEO."

"And your public housing fundraiser. We need to talk."

"You don't say? I need a drink."

"Why don't I meet you at the Penthouse on Beach St. Then you can drink and scream and do whatever it is you need to while I explain this to you."

"I'll be there in 20 minutes," I sigh and hang up. Looking up at Tari's face, I realise we aren't going to get to shop after all.

"I'm so sorry lovely, but I've got to go. Wanna come see my new place? I've…uh…got some explaining to do."

"Does it have anything to do with Korean Ken on the TV?" She smiles across at me knowingly.

"It might." We wave the hostess over and pay the bill.

Wandering back to the carpark I know Xi will already be there to meet us. Seal will have texted him to tell him we were on our way back to the car. Standing on the carpeted entry to the Valet Car park, Xi drives up just moments after we arrive.

"Since when can you afford a car with a driver and Valet park it?" Tari looks across at me quizzically.

"It's a very long story. Part of the explanation I owe you when we get home." I smile hesitantly across at her.

What happens if she decides she doesn't want to be friends anymore after I tell her?

I let out a sigh and climb in the door Xi opens for me. I see Seal appear out of nowhere to open Tari's door.

"Oh, hello,' she says sarcastically as she clambers in, 'and what's he? Your hire-a-007,' she stares at the back of Seal's head.

"Seal, Jia will arrive not long after we get home. Can you help get her into the building, please? Or get Shadow to? I don't care who does it." Seal nods in acknowledgement.

The ride up the elevator after we say farewell to Xi in the carpark is torture. I can feel Tari's eyes on me.

"I know I should have told you earlier,' I say quietly, staring at my feet.

"Told me what?"

"The friend of mine who died, who I came here because of…he….he…"

"Was Li Huynh,' Tari breathes as the glass elevator comes to stop at the top floor. Tari looks around, pushing the door open and staring in wonder.

"How did you know?" I can't see her face.

"This penthouse was on every major news outlet for weeks when it went on the market. When Mr Huynh finally bought it, it was all people could talk about. He spent so much time overseas, people were outraged that he dropped so much money on a property that he barely ever lived in."

I follow in her wake as she makes her way through the halls, stopping to stare out the window toward the bay.

"I don't understand what we are doing here?" Tari turns to look at me. Elation and confusion etched into her face. "I mean, this is crazy cool, to be standing in one of the biggest mega penthouses in Asia, but what are we doing here?" Before I have a chance to answer, Gladys appears carrying a basket of fresh-baked bread.

"Ah, Miss Ava you are home. And with a guest! I shall get a second plate for afternoon tea."

"Home?" Tari turns to stare at me, mouth agape.

"Uh, yes,' I mumble too embarrassed to look her in the eye.

A sudden PING announces the arrival of the elevator. Jia appears, with Seal in tow.

"Is it true that this place requires visitors to be frisked? G.I Joe here thought he'd try convincing me,' Jia stares at me a quirky smile hinting at her lips. I turn and eyeball Seal.

"You're a lawsuit just waiting to happen,' I glower.

"Good night ladies!" Seal chuckles before making a hasty retreat into the elevator.

"Ah, it"s okay, I kind of asked for it,' Jia giggles and winks at me. "So, this is the place huh?" She looks around.

I realise Tari has disappeared. I look around frantically and spot her standing out on the balcony staring out toward the Marina Bay Sands building.

"I'm sorry for not telling you. I honestly didn't know how."

"Was it some sort of legal thing? The reason you couldn't tell me?" She looks over at me as I step onto the terrace.

"No, it was an Ava thing. Can I get you a drink? There's a room in here somewhere for whisky and cocktails. I'm sure I can find it if you give me a second,' I say absentmindedly. I need to get a map for this place.

"Who's your friend?" She eyes Jia appraisingly through the window.

"She's my lawyer. She's here because she saw the announcement and we need to talk about HEH."

"I guess you need me to leave then?" Tari frowns.

"What? No, why would you say that? I want you here. This shit is getting real and you're my only friend. That is…if you still want to be my friend?" I stare at my feet.

"I guess we never really talked about it. What we were, I mean." This time Tari looks at her feet.

"I really thought we could have a girls' day today. You would show me Orchard Road and we'd get to hang out like girlfriends. I'm so sorry I've messed it all up,' I sigh and sink into the sun lounger, my head in my hands.

"Are you still the same girl who ordered cocktails and watched the gardens glow in awe, years ago?" I feel her sit down beside me.

"I still feel like me, but the world is much changed since then. Irrevocably changed, I suspect,' I sigh again. I feel her hand on my back, reassuring.

"I stand by what I said. I hope you give those assholes a run for their money,' she states fiercely.

"Do you mean that?" I look up into her face and see the determination etched there.

"I do. Now let's go find out from Singapore Kardashian in there, why some asshole is pretending to be you on TV." She stands up and offers me her hand. I giggle in shock. Singapore Kardashian is the perfect way to describe Jia. Except she also has the brains and the brawn to back it up.

We find Jia set up in the dining room. The papers the grey suits left, spread out across the surface. I can see she's noted and highlighted different points in English for me throughout them all.

"Okay. Do you want the good news or the bad news?" She asks, tapping one long red manicured finger against the table.

"Good?" I hesitate.

"Fine. The good news is you are the sole owner of HEH and you have no board to answer to. You have a team of 20 odd Executive Directors who run the company for you. The bottom line is, you're in charge."

"Okay, so what's the bad news?"

"More to the point, what the hell is Korean Ken doing on TV pretending to take Ava's job?" Tari interrupts.

"Well. That's the thing. It's called having a 'spokesperson'. Did Tony ever talk to you about that?"

"Yes? I told him in the meantime before I was ready to face the media myself that I'd be happy to have a spokesperson address them on my behalf." I looked up at her, extremely confused.

"Well, in business here that is code for "a beard"." She looks pointedly at me.

"Come again? Are you referring to…?"

"Gay men marrying women to appear straight. Yes. It is a similar practice in Business. High power women, or more realistically their companies, hire men to behave as their 'stand-in' to ensure not to upset the status quo." I sit there, mouth agape.

"That is certainly not what I meant. I only meant I needed a few weeks before it was MY FACE splashed all over the papers. Not that I needed a MAN to pretend for me!" I fume. Outrage coursing through me, I stand and begin to pace.

"Obviously this is news to you, but Ava, this is a pretty standard practice."

"What?! Are you kidding? You're telling me that there are other women out there running conglomerates who have men pretending to be them in public? How is that possible? Singapore has one of the highest statistical percentages of female CEOs in the world!" The pitch of my voice topping out into a wail.

"Yes. Businesses headed by women don't always survive in these patriarchal societies. So much business, in Asia specifically, is done where women aren't permitted. It stands to reason that a woman would go further in business if she were a man,' Jia shrugs. I stare at her, dumbfounded.

"Oh my god."

"What?" Both she and Tari stare across at me.

"Is that the reason for your office? Why I only found out about you by word of mouth and can't find you on your company registry?" Jia looked away, tossing her hair.

"That's why they gave you a shitty office even though you're a goddamn Senior Counsel?"

"It's no big deal. It's just part of the package,' Jia brushes it aside.

"Am I not allowed to take the CEO title public or is this a coverup because Tony doesn't want me to make a scene?"

"Technically, you are the CEO and you can choose to go public at any time. It may not be the best idea at this time though. HEH is going through a lot of uncertainty following Mr Huynh's death. Tony has been mighty smart about this. By announcing so publicly, he's thrown down the gauntlet. If you try to pick it up, you will end up the loser."

"How so?" Tari was eyeing her from across the table.

"HEH is already doing better on the market today-consumer confidence is increasing again. They like knowing there is someone 'in charge'."

"A man in charge." Tari and I state in unison. I look across at her and give her a weak smile.

"What the hell do I do now? I can't just let Tony win. I have never been able to shake the feeling that he's up to something. I just wish I had some way to prove it." I sat, staring up at the chandelier, rubbing my neck.

"Feeling a little tight?" Tari looks across at me.

"As a bowstring,' I laugh.

"I'm pretty sure this place comes with a masseuse,' she observes, peering around us. "You should ask, um, your housekeeper about that."

"Gladys,' I smile across at her. She nods in acknowledgement.

"I guess it's time I start looking for some of these bearded businesswomen then. I need advice and I have no idea where to start." I drop my head into my hands on the table.

"I need to get going. I have some late meetings back at the office. I'll send you my bill and analysis of these papers. I'll drop the other half back when I'm done. I may also know a few people you can talk to. Let me make some calls,' she waves a hand in the general direction of the table before turning for the door.

"Thanks, Jia. I mean it, I don't know what I'd do without you." I smile at her as I walk her to the elevator.

"Hey, do you know if your gunslinger is single?" She smiles across at me.

"Uh, I have no idea. You interested?"

"I might be."

And with a wink, she was gone. There is something about that woman.

How can so much smart and sexy all fit in the same package. I can't believe that patriarchy is the reason she isn't paid her dues at her legal firm. Oh, I should have offered for Xi to drive her home. No matter, I'm sure she'll bill me for it.

"I should get going too. I have the early shift tomorrow." Tari appears beside me. "Are you going to be okay?"

"Just days ago, I found out I was going to be in charge of a company, and today I had the choice taken away from me. Maybe I'm just being paranoid about Tony. Perhaps I should just let it go for now?" I shake my head in confusion.

"Well whatever you decide, I'll be here to help however I can." She shrugs across at me.

"Really? Oh thank you Tari!" I envelop her in a bear hug.

"I'd love to take advantage of your car though, save me the train fare or a cab home!" She laughs at me.

"Of course! I wouldn't have it any other way. Especially after I kidnapped you here,' I laugh back.

After Xi picked Tari up, Gladys made me an early dinner and I collapsed into bed. Tomorrow hasn't arrived yet and I'm already exhausted at the prospect of getting to the end of the week. How do I face this guy? Am I meant to meet him tomorrow? What do I say? Hi, I'm Ava, I didn't know you existed and I don't know why you were hired?

As it turns out, my worry was for naught. Tony and Korean Ken did not appear at the office at all on Thursday morning. Although there was much talk of it around the halls. I could tell Sasha was about to begin grilling me when my phone went.

"Hello?" I answer, the unknown number stumping me.

"Ava, its Jia."

"Oh, Hi."

"It's time you met the Invisible Women."

I found myself almost having a panic attack as Xi drove to the address Jia left me. Needless to say, Sasha was unimpressed at having to reschedule my afternoon for the second day in a row. Luckily there was only one meeting booked with the publicity team. What did Jia say - Invisible women? What is that, some kind of club? I'm not dressed for some women's country club. I look down at my attire.

Damn, I really could have done with that shopping outing yesterday. Maybe Sasha can recommend a personal shopper who can help me out.

We come to a stop out the front of a nondescript grey concrete building.

"Are you sure this is it, Xi?" I ask dubiously.

"This is the address Miss Jia gave you,' he sounded equally dubious.

"I'll take a look around, stay in the car, Miss,' Seal nods to Xi as he step out.

Why do I always forget he is there? A few minutes later he reappears, walks around to my door and offers me a hand out of the car.

"It is safe to enter Miss."

Inside the building was mind-blowingly different from the outside. The only way to describe it would be a feminine speakeasy bar. Copper and gold everywhere, bare brick, velvet and warm lighting composed the vast space. Sitting in a half-circle on velvet wingback chairs were two striking women, accompanied by Jia. Jia, as always looked like a showstopper. Long legs, airbrushed makeup and manicure.

"Ah, Ava,' she stands to air kiss my cheek.

Well that's new.

"I'd like you to meet Su, Linah and Welsh, Margot." I shake their respective hands. Linah had strong hands, just like her jawline. Sharp, clean lines shaped her face. She had a fierce black bob cropped at her cheekbones. Her suit matched, all clean lines and block colours. Margot was a little daintier, effeminate with long corn silk curls falling below her breasts. Large clear rimmed glasses adorned her face, making her look like a librarian. Her outfit however screamed woman. Her dress cut a deep V showing off her tiny waist and ample bosom.

"It's nice to meet you both. I had no idea where I was going to find female businesswomen in this city. I need some serious help." I shrug, trying to keep eye contact but feeling woefully inept standing before these women.

"I'll say. Where did you shop for that outfit? K-Mart?" Margot tutted, eyeing my blouse and skirt combination. She's certainly not as sweet as she looks.

"Ava was about to shop for new clothes on Orchard Road when the news about her CEO dropped. Unbeknownst to her,' Jia rebuts.

"Oh, a 'spokesperson' virgin. We've all been there honey." Linah smiles across at me. "Come, sit. Tell us your story."

We sat and talked, sipping soda water and lime as I recounted the story of how I got here.

"I was sitting in a restaurant when they announced the foundation for my charity ball and my 'new CEO',' I finish.

"Well, I'd love to tell you that I've never heard a story like that, but it"s far more common than you think." Linah shook her head. "I work in Banking. I closed the three biggest deals my company has ever seen and they asked my male colleague to stand in for me at the press conference. That was the first day I realised I'd become an invisible woman."

"I became an invisible woman the day my company insisted on releasing my fashion line under a pseudonym they made up. They didn't think men would by business attire from a label designed by a woman,' Margot rolls her eyes, sucking on the lime from her drink.

The three of us looked at Jia.

"What? You all know my story. I solved the two biggest court cases in business in the last 5 years and my firm insisted my junior colleague present them in court. I wrote the arguments, the rebuttals and the closing arguments. I got to present one of them in court, but he got all the credit. No one believed that a woman could have come up with it herself." She picks at her manicure.

"What did you all do? I mean, did you fight back?" I look around at them individually.

"For what? There's a reason we're invisible. It is so we remain silent,' Margot scoffs.

"I for one, know I couldn't do what I do, at the same level, if I weren't an invisible woman. I'd get laughed out of board meetings if I voiced my ideas myself. So, I have Rohan do it for me. We have a great working relationship now and he is essentially my mouthpiece,' Linah shrugs across at me.

"If you can't beat 'em, join 'em,' Jia huffs. Suddenly the gravity of what these women were saying hit me.

"For the good of my company, do I need to accept that I am an invisible woman and try to get this Chen guy on side?" I frown. I don't like how that sits with me. But I may have no choice. The raucous laughter of those businessmen the other night comes rushing back to me. Maybe a man at the helm would mean HEH might stand a better chance. It is a man's world out there after all…right?

"I'm certainly not saying it's a fix-all for everyone. But it worked for me. And if I cannot be the one calling the shots in the daylight, I'd rather be in the position I am now than still stuck where I was 10 years ago." Linah gives me a half-hearted smile.

"It's worth a shot, but damn girl. We need to update your rags. CEO or not, you can't go into a faceoff with Chen looking like that." Margot dished up yet another hard truth. The three of them eyed me critically.

"I'm open to suggestions,' I offer.

An hour later the entire building had transformed. From nowhere, Linah and Margot had mobile hair salons, beauty stations and personal shoppers with entire wardrobes arrive and set up.

"Okay. Upstairs is hair and beauty. Down here they will set up wardrobe. Asian sizes vary for Western women, so we got a combination. And for shoes, there is only one sole that should ever know those feet again." She turned and stared at piles and piles of red Christian Louboutin shoe boxes. All three ladies sighed in unison.

"First! Hair and beauty,' Linah giggles, grabbing my hand and dragging me toward the stairs. 'I could use a mani-pedi myself."

After what felt like hours of primping, colouring, cutting, waxing, massaging, painting, exfoliating and moisturising; I wasn't sure there was much more these beauticians could do to me. My refreshed hair was blow-dried and curled, my nails painted in a crisp French polish and then Jia, Margot and Linah played dress up. I don't know why they call it dress-up. I am hardly moving, these women are dressing me themselves! After another few hours of faffing around, the ladies had picked out a new wardrobe. A whole new wardrobe.

There were matching lingerie sets all the way through to evening gowns and everything in between. Complimenting my ginger locks and alabaster skin, the ladies chose navy blues, teal and emerald greens with some dark grey and black thrown in for good measure. And about 30 new pairs of Louboutin's. Flats, wedges, classic stilettos and evening heels. With a bottle of champagne decanted into long crystal glasses, Jia offered a toast.

"Wear one of these outfits tomorrow and you're going to knock Mr Chen flat on his ass,' Margot giggles.

"To knocking them dead!" Agreed Linah.
"To the Invisible Women,' I raise my glass.

On Friday morning I jumped out of bed and went for a walk down by the water to clear my head. Being a weekday, Seal was not far behind me. We wandered along the waterfront until the sun started to get warm. After returning to the penthouse and eating the omelette Gladys cooked up, I stood in front of my new wardrobe and wondered what to wear. I showered, applied a face of makeup including some of the new products the beauticians recommended yesterday and pulled on my outfit.I stood staring at myself in the mirror.

I can do this.

I had to admit, those personal shoppers knew what they were doing. I stood in front of the wall-length mirror in a teal silk jumpsuit. Fitted and sleeveless in the top and flowing down to pants that almost look like a skirt, just measuring to the floor in my new patent cream 6-inch heels.

Grabbing the matching clutch and laptop bag, I headed for the elevator, my new gold earrings catching in the light as they dangled.

I feel a million bucks. I can face the world today. I've got this. In the mirrored panel of the elevator, I check my French twist, ensuring I haven't had too many tendrils escape.

HEH was buzzing when I arrived at 8.30 am. Sasha met me at the front door and we rode the elevator up together. She was so frazzled I thought she might have zapped herself.

"Sasha, what's the matter?" I peer across at her.

"I, uh, I mean Mr Tony..." she stammers.

The elevator came to a stop at the suite floor. I stepped out, striding toward my door.

"Sasha, go down to the kitchen and get yourself a cup of herbal tea and a fruit salad. Breathe! It'll be okay." I smile at her and walk straight into my office, dragging off my coat as I go.

I head straight for the coat nook and am halfway through hanging it when I notice movement out the corner of my eye.

Spinning around I find a man sitting in my chair, his feet on my desk.

Winnie's chair.

Winnie's precious oak desk.

The desk and chair I had still been unable to bring myself to sit in. I prefer the lounges anyway.

Yeah, you keep telling yourself that Ava. Suddenly I am seeing red. How dare Chen come in here and sit in Winnie's chair!

"Get out of that chair or so help me god..." I whisper menacingly.

Wide eyes catch mine. The most astounding shade of blue. Like Winnie's. I stalk closer to the desk, my heels keeping time on the marble. Ever so slowly, Chen pushes the chair back and places his feet on the floor. Slowly raising his arms in the air as though someone's training a gun on him, he begins to laugh. A deep, rich sound.

"Tony mentioned you had spirit. I see what he means." He slowly stands and bows. "I'm Mr Samuel Chen, but you may call me, Chen." He straightens, tucking the black silky tresses of his hair behind his ears. Smiling that Korean Ken panty-dropping grin.

Ugh, I'm going to be sick.

"What else did Tony tell you, Chen?" I almost spit his name. "I'm very curious to know exactly what you think is in this for you? Because so far as I can see you're nothing but a pretty boy who is willing to sell his face for a piece of the HEH pie.

'I've got news for you, you are not going to see shit. I'll have my lawyer review your employment contract and you'll be out on your ass before close of business. Mark my words." I scathe at him.

"Whoa, Miss Elias, I assure you I have no ill intent here. Mr Tony hired me into the CEO role because quite frankly you seem to lack the skills and education to run a conglomerate. Believe it or not, it takes much more than fancy shoes and elaborate hairstyles to run companies like HEH." He eyes me critically, the snarl evident in his voice.

"How dare you come in here, sit at Winnie's desk and criticise me! You don't know the first thing about me!"

He holds an invisible phone up to his ear. "Uh? Hello? Pot? It's Kettle calling!" I take another step closer. We're just feet away from each other.

"One more word out of you and I'll have security throw you out,' I hiss. I'm raging, breathing like I've just run a marathon.

He steps in, closing the gap until there are just centimetres between us.

"I'd like to see you try,' he whispers, his minty breath hitting my face.

Oh god he smells good. What is that?! Georgio Armani?

"If you think I'm going to fall for your Korean Ken act...'

Then you might be right...

"Korean Ken!' He laughs in my face. 'Where on earth did you come up with that one?"

Suddenly Seal walks in, spots Chen and I standing toe to toe, coughs awkwardly and walks out again.

"Looks like we caused your PSO to blush! Perhaps we should give him something worth gossiping about..." Chen leans into the space between us.

I close the gap and whisper into his ear, "The first thing I'm going to do is file a harassment suit against you." He steps back as though he's been slapped.

"If Tony thought he could hire some glorified prostitute to come in here and lure me into signing over the company, he's got another thing coming. You can go back and tell Tony that I'm not falling for it. I will find a way to be rid of you both and I will not sink this company in the process.

'This may just be some payoff for you Mr Chen, but I have tens of thousands of lives to consider and I do not take that burden lightly."

I turn on my heel and make my way to the door. As I exit I turn back to spit, "set foot in this office again and I will have PS Seal katana you off at the knees."

Sasha stands on the other side of the door, ashen-faced and mouth agape.

"Come, Sasha, we've a day full of meetings ahead of us."

Okay. So, in summary, that was not the best way to get Chen on side. I don't know what happened, I just saw him at Winnie's desk and exploded.

Fuck. I need a new game plan.

The conference room is full of the Executive Directors when we walk in.

"Good Morning everyone, happy Friday,' I start, hoping to achieve 'cheery' after my spray off with Chen. Moments later Tony and Chen enter the room.

"Gentlemen, I do not believe we require your presence at this meeting." I smile across at them before they have a chance to sit.

"Miss Elias, perhaps we should have a word outside,' Tony gestures toward the door.

"I'm quite certain you can have nothing to say to me, Mr Tony."

The EDs look around awkwardly. Clearly, this is a first.

Tony stares at me, mouth slightly agape.

"Miss Elias, this behaviour is petulant and entirely inappropriate,' Tony chastises. He stops short of shaking his finger at me.

"Mr Tony, if you refuse to leave I will ask Security to escort you from the room."

"You cannot do that! I'm General Counsel,' he sputters.

"Yes Mr Tony, and this is a meeting of Executive Directors. I will see you later today at the Legal Review session." Spitting chips, Tony turns and storms out of the room. I spot Chen sitting in the back row quietly, a smirk playing across his lips.

Oh, game on.

Following another two meetings requiring tossing Tony out for attending unnecessarily, I begin to wonder what on earth he gets paid to do all day. God I hope Sasha gets Tony's employment records to Jia today. I need her to review them ASAP. I want him gone.

By the time 5 pm rolls around I am thanking the gods it is Friday. I tell Sasha to send an email to the staff advising them if what they're working on isn't urgent, to pack up and go home to their families.

After saying goodnight to Sasha, I wander around Winnie's office watching the city light up before me. Kicking my shoes off and rubbing my aching feet, I pad across to Winnie's whisky trolley. Rows and rows of crystal decanters glimmer up at me. Pouring myself two fingers from the first decanter I get my hands on, I slump into one of the large leather armchairs. I send Xi a quick message telling him to go home and have one of the afterhours guys come get me in 45 minutes.

After receiving a message back in the affirmative, I sip in silence.

"What on earth were you thinking Winnie?" I ask the empty room. 'Did you really think I'd be able to stomach this? That I'd be able to compete with Tony?! He knows all the tricks in the book! I've never even seen the book!" I lay back and throw my legs over the arm of the chair.

How the hell am I going to survive this? And not hurt the employees in the process? If the company gets a bad reputation then we're done for. Having a CEO who is a -hot-headed moron is not a good look; I need to keep my cool in public.

The glass door opens quietly. I don't bother looking over to see who it is, assuming that Xi got the after-hours guy here faster than anticipated.

"Quite an interesting day for you,' Chen chuckles, scratching his jaw. I freeze. 'Seal isn't around is he, I'd rather not have my legs hacked off with a katana.'

He saunters across to the trolley, picking up a decanter. 'Do you mind if I join you?"

"I don't have it in me to fight with you tonight Chen. Just leave me be,' I sigh, not moving from my lounger. Chen sits across from me, tumbler in hand. I can feel his eyes on me. We sit and sip quietly for what feels like an eternity.

"I believe I owe you an apology,' he states quietly. My head snaps across to look at him.

"I beg your pardon?" I glower.

"Tony did not explain to me what had happened here at HEH. I was working in the USA when he called me and offered me the job, weeks ago. I had no idea what I was walking into. I suspect you and I were both caught off guard by his antics." He looks across at me, his baby blues burning a hole in my soul.

"You really expect me to believe that? That Tony didn't lure you in here with some sweet-talk about ruling the world together and taking HEH over? He never once mentioned to you that HEH had been left in its entirety to a woman?" I look up at the ceiling.

How can I possibly know if he is telling the truth? How do I know who to trust ever again?

"I'll show you the correspondence if you don't believe me. I have all of his emails. He told me Mr Huynh had passed on and that HEH would need to find a new CEO ASAP. He knew about my work in New York and my background at Harvard and pretty much begged me to take the job." He sipped his whisky quietly. "My condolences, by the way. I hadn't realised you and Mr Huynh were so... genuinely close." I look across to see him staring at the back of Winnie's chair. I sigh heavily.

"I still haven't been able to bring myself to sit in it. That desk meant so much to him."

"Ah, now I understand your reaction this morning. It was not my intention to offend you. Shock you a little perhaps, but I see now it was misguided.' He looks at me sheepishly, then his face changes. 'Do you truly know nothing about me? Did you genuinely think I was some 'escort' with no brains of my own who Tony hired to come in here and throw you off?"

"No. I saw the media reports and did a little digging of my own. I have your CV and your Harvard transcripts. I know you aren't just some pretty face for the cameras. You caught me off guard this morning and I snapped." I hear him chuckle and prop my head up to look at him.

"I came in here this morning intending to get to know you, starting things off on the right foot. But then I saw you in Winnie's chair and I..." My throat constricts.

"Snapped?" He laughs, quoting me.

"I realised you were just the same as the rest of them. Those haughty businessmen who think women incapable of running businesses like HEH successfully; who think that women should be seen and not heard. You have no respect for what Winnie did here or for his belongings. You're just another man who wants to possess things."

"Since when is striving to be 'the best' such a bad thing? Sure, I want to possess things, who doesn't? Who hasn't dreamt of owning an office like this with their name on the door? Does that make me a bad guy?" He stands and begins to pace, his hands in his hair.

If I didn't know any better, I'd say his resolve is crumbling.

"You have no idea what it is like to grow up with affluent Asian parents. The expectations, the pressures!

One wrong move and you're exiled for disgracing the family. I had no choice but to accept this job. Tony contacted me through my father. That's how he tracked me down. He knew I would have no choice but to accept." He stopped, turning to me. The look in his eyes almost pleading.

"So what you're telling me is that Tony never told you about me? He coerced you into taking the role and you had no idea I already filled it? That Winnie had left me everything?" I peer up at him dubiously.

"That is precisely what happened. It wasn't until after the press conference that he told me. And even then he painted you in a pretty awful light." He shrugs.

"Oh, I can only imagine. Let me guess? He told you that I had conned Winnie into falling in love with me or some such nonsense and that I was a scheming little pretender who stalked Winnie until his dying breath because I was after his money?" I roll my eyes.

"Essentially, yes. He said he and Mr Huynh had been close colleagues and friends for decades and suddenly he came back from a trip down-under and wanted to restructure the whole company for some 'little tramp'. Tony made it clear that Mr Huynh had always intended to leave HEH to him if something were to happen." Well that answers so many questions! Including why Tony seemed to hate me from the very beginning.

"I realised today, watching you with the EDs and listening to you with the staff; you really care about these people and although you mightn't have the business experience, you want to do right by them." He sits again, staring into his tumbler.

"I owe you an apology too. I shouldn't have called you a..."

"Prostitute?" He laughs.

"Korean Ken. I still haven't quite decided yet whether or not you're whoring yourself out here." I smirk across at him.

"You and me both. After I learned everything, I felt so dirty. But I didn't know what to do about it."

"I'm guessing this speech is your way of telling me you're not going anywhere? Because if you do then you'll risk bringing shame upon your family?"

"Exactly. I'm sorry Miss Elias but I can't afford to mess this up. I need us to find a way to work together. Maybe one day my father will respect me enough to leave me Chen Industries. Until then, I need to prove myself." I sit up and stare across at him, my silk pants cascading down to the floor.

"Chen Industries? You're one of those Chens?" I feel my eyes boggling. I hadn't stumbled across that yet. If there were ever a company in Singapore rivalling HEH for top spot it was CI.

"Do you see what I'm up against?" He implores.

"I'm starting to." I frown.

"I'm begging you. Please don't fire me. I know you think I'm just some asshole swooping in to keep you in the shadows, but the reality is, in this market, HEH does need a male CEO to tide it over until things settle down.

'The industry is shallow and people scare easily. A new CEO is one thing, but a female CEO will be too much change too quickly. I wish it weren't so, but that is the world we live in." He perched on the edge of his seat.

'But I could teach you? I could help you understand the ins and outs of business and when the world is ready, you can take back the CEO title and HEH will be yours, not just in here but also facing the public."

"And you can prove to your father that you are a strong CEO to inherit Chen Industries?"

"Exactly,' he breathes.

I stand, smoothing down my jumpsuit before extending my hand to Chen.

"We are in agreement then. Inside these walls, I am the CEO of HEH and the staff report to us together. But in the light of day, the public will see you." He stands and takes my hand, I step in closer. "But I am warning you, Chen, if I find out that you remain loyal to Tony, I will not hesitate to oust you."

"I believe you have yourself a deal, Miss Elias." Chen shakes my hand firmly. No longer in my heels, I find myself looking up at him. His face is angular and masculine, softened by his eyes. At this proximity, I can see the turmoil roiling behind them. I take a deep breath, noticing he seems to have stopped breathing all together.

The glass door slides open, followed by a throat clearing.

"Miss Elias, my sincerest apologies for interrupting. I was unaware you would have...uh...company. I'll be in reception when you're ready." Neither Chen nor I turned to look at my driver.

"I suppose I should bid you good evening Miss Elias?" Chen whispers reluctantly down to me.

"I'll see you on Monday?" I wonder to myself why it sounds more like a promise.

"Monday."

11

Arriving home that night completely exhausted, I want nothing more than to eat whatever Gladys has prepared and spend the night in the giant black bathtub. I have been curious how the sound wave vibration thing works in it anyway. The manual said it works synonymously with music playing in the bathroom.

Walking into the kitchen I find Gladys at the stove, garlic and olive oil wafting toward me.

"Hi Gladys, how was your day?" I ask, plonking myself down on a barstool.

"Hello Miss Ava, my day was lovely thank you. And yours?" She casts a suspicious eye over me.

"Do I look that bad?" I pat my hair self consciously.

"Whoa! Did you get into a physical altercation today? You look a mess!" Tari pops in suddenly from the balcony.

"Hey! What are you doing here?" I beam at her, 'aren't you working tonight?"

"I don't start until 8. Seriously though, you look like crap."

"Thanks, hun. Do you want dinner before you start work?"

"I'll grab another bowl." Gladys smiles across at us, pouring me a big glass of Shiraz.

"I met him today." I look across at Tari.

"No! Him!" She looks at me aghast. 'Was he as big a dick-" she stops short, catching the look of horror on Gladys' face.

"In the beginning. I may or may not have called him a..." I look across at Gladys' turned back and mouth "HOOKER" at Tari.

She giggles in reply, "I bet you did. You go girl! Did you fire him on the spot?"

"Turns out, he may not be the bad guy in this story. I'm not 100% sure yet, but I think he may end up being an ally in this." I sigh.

"Oh no. Hold up. I know that face." Tari points at me.

"What?" I look at her quizzically.

"You like him."

"I said he wasn't a terrible person, 'like' is probably a bit strong for the situation."

"No, I mean you *like* him."

"Don't be ridiculous. Until this morning I was certain he was trying to steal my company from me. Even now, I'm still not sure he isn't! Why on earth would I like him?"

"How'd he smell?" Tari eyes me closely.

"Uh...well..."

"I knew it! You were close enough to smell him!"

"That doesn't prove anything!" I squeal.

Luckily Gladys decided to take that as her cue to interrupt us with giant bowls of garlic prawns and spaghetti.

After Tari left for work, I said good night to Gladys and retreated to the master suite. As time melted away, I soaked in the tub for what could have been hours. I thought of the last real bath I took, back in Dinner Plain. That life feels so very far away. I should give Ivan another call to update him. My thoughts drift to my day. To Mr Chen.

He did smell good. Who does he remind me of? It is going to irritate me until I put my finger on it.

I continue to theorise until with a sudden jolt it hits me. I jump and splash water everywhere.Ryan. Chen reminds me of Ryan.

Ryan who I haven't thought of in weeks since sending that SOS text message.

Where on earth is my Australian mobile phone anyway? I never even sent him something to say I was coming here. I suppose it doesn't really matter, we don't usually stay in touch during the summer season anyway. This is fine, right?

Trying to retrace my steps and figure out where I left my other phone, I wander the penthouse ensconced in my bathrobe. I stop in each room, flip on a light switch and check major surfaces for my phone. I get to Winnie's library and imagine him sitting at this desk penning his gold letters to me. His beautiful flowing calligraphy dancing onto the page. I walk around behind his desk, my fingers tracing the timber.

"Winnie. What compelled you to do this? Surely there must have been a better choice for this than me? Why would you trust someone who has known you for five minutes with the lives of your people?"

I pull the chair from behind the desk and slowly lower myself into it. I melt all the way down until my forehead is resting on the desk. Turning my face sideways, pressing my cheek into the cold timber top, I stare blankly at the bookshelves surrounding the room. The shelves stand tall, filled with books of all shapes, sizes and colours. Some appear to be newer, others must be first editions or very well-loved verses.

The third shelf down on the right-hand side contained a full stack of books with identical spines. These books were peculiar, no names or titles on them. Just the year.

Slowly righting myself, I stand and wander toward the shelf. The years date back from last year, through to the 60s. Slowly pulling the last book from the shelf, I open it gently. The pages were covered with elegant handwritten Mandarin script.

Are these Winnie's diaries? Next time Tari is here I'll ask her if she can translate anything from them. Perhaps there might be a key to what happened with Tony somewhere in these pages.

I look up at the books again, replacing the final one in the series.

Where is this year's diary?

I look around the room but don't spot another similar looking book.

Checking the drawers of the desk I find Winnie's other fountain pens, all MontBlanc as well as the gold paper and envelopes.

It suddenly dawns on me that I won't receive another gold letter from Winnie. Here they sit, in front of me. No elegant script or metallic wax seals. Just naked paper. Suddenly I am bone tired. It has been a long day and I desperately need sleep. At least you can sleep in tomorrow. Come to think of it, Gladys did the laundry and grocery shopped today. *What do I do with myself on weekends?*

With that thought, I drag my sorry ass to bed and pray for a sound sleep.

His hands caress my face as he drops feather-light kisses across my nose and cheeks. With my eyes closed, the sensation is overwhelming. He smells like alpine and snow and Georgio Armani. He chuckles, a deep sexy sound that reverberates through me. His hands move lower as I open my eyes to catch his gaze. Ryan smiles lazily up at me, ducking his head down to plant kisses on my bare navel. He looks back up at me and his silky black hair falls across his eyes. I lift my fingers to sweep it behind his ear and crystal blue eyes capture mine.

"Chen!" I wake with a start, sitting up in bed.

Oh my god. What was that? Did I really just have a sex dream about Chen? But it started out as Ryan?

I need a shower. Dragging my grumpy ass out of bed, I run a scalding shower and stand under the water.

"Stupid men,' I grumble to myself.

Wrapped in a bathrobe, I trudge out into the kitchen to find Gladys has left me fresh crumpets and honey for breakfast.

Bless her soul.

Mashing the button on the coffee machine I stare vacantly out the window toward the bay. Suddenly the wall panel beside the fridge lights up, eliciting the most infuriatingly cheery jingle. I walk over and peer at the screen. Jia's perfectly quaffed hair appears in the monitor. I hit the 'talk' button.

"Morning Jia. Wanna come up?"

"No, I just thought I'd come past and ring your ridiculous doorbell for shits and giggles,' she grumbles.

"I'll put a coffee on for you,' I reply, hitting the elevator button to allow her inside. I watch until she disappears from view before turning back to the machine.

Less than a minute later Jia stands in my kitchen taking in the sight. My wet hair dripping into the bathrobe and bare feet. Maybe she's wondering if I'm wearing anything under this. I bet she's already run a marathon and cured cancer this morning, all before I've even had my first coffee. I hand her a cup.

'To what do I owe the pleasure, so early on a Saturday Jia?"

"We need to talk about the rest of the papers you left with me. And Tony's contract." I grab the crumpets from the toaster and slather them in butter and honey.

"Sure, hit me with it,' I utter dryly before shoving half a crumpet into my mouth.

"Do people really eat like that?" Jia looks at me horrified.

"In my house on a Saturday morning before 8 am, yes,' I garble.

"Fine, I'll try to focus on what I came here to tell you.' She pulls a face as she begins pulling stacks of paperwork from her handbag.

"These documents are all fairly standard. They relate to the ownership of the business, the accounts and funds around the world. I've finished making notes on them in English and highlighting the parts you ought to take note of. For example, this one,' She flips to a page in one of the dossiers, 'states that the public housing project can be dismantled by someone other than the CEO." She eyes me to check I'm following.

"Tony wants to have the power to execute decisions without my approval." I stare at the papers.

"Yes. I'd recommend having all the pink parts, as I've highlighted accordingly, changed back to 'CEO ONLY'. There were also a number of places that Tony has added 'or General Counsel' to the financial authorizations. I've highlighted those in green."

"That shady bastard,' I huff.

"Yes, well his contracts are a whole different matter. I checked the one he wrote up for Chen, it's pretty - watertight but we can find a way around it. I've done some digging and there are a couple of 'outs' we can use." I wave my hand whilst chewing another overzealous mouthful.

"I've spoken with Chen, for now, I'm going to see how he goes. I think it may be more beneficial for HEH to keep him, albeit on a tight leash for the time being." Jia nods and makes a note on her papers.

"Okay, to the difficult part. Tony's contract. This thing is ironclad. I've looked at it from every angle and there are very few options for us with getting rid of him. He can't be fired for any of the normal offences people can be given the pink slip for. You can't make him redundant because it's impossible to operate at your level without a General Counsel. An unfortunate issue is his salary. It is astronomical, once all the inclusions and travel are factored in, he's easily costing HEH millions each year." I stare at Jia.

"I can't fire the bastard and yet all he does is swan around the office for 8 hours a day being a pain in my ass at the bargain rate of; millions of dollars a year?"

"That about sums it up. His contract doesn't even stipulate what his role incorporates or any KPIs. You can't fire him for failing to uphold his duties because according to this, he doesn't really have any."

"Does it refer to Winnie specifically? Can we deem the contract invalid if it refers to a deceased person?"

"Great thinking Ava, but sadly no. He must have thought of that. This contract was only signed in the past few months. It must have been just before Winnie first got sick?" Jia shrugs at me.

"What if I found a way to prove that Tony coerced Winnie into signing it whilst he was sick? Is there a caveat that the contract reverts to whichever was most recently held prior?"

"As a matter of fact, no. I don't recall it including anything like that. Which would mean if you can prove that Winnie was not of sound mind when he signed off on this, Tony would be out of a job."

"I have to find out what killed Winnie."

Come to think of it, I still don't even know where his body ended up. I know I decided to respect his wishes, but this could be really important.

"There is one other way to get rid of Tony, if Plan A doesn't work out. Tony falls under the same standard employment agreement as all HEH staff from an Ethical Standards perspective."

"Which means what exactly? If he's an asshole and I give him three strikes, then he's out?"

"At the risk of oversimplifying it, yes. If you can prove that he is in breach of HEH Ethical Standards & Code of Conduct then he can be fired."

"Jia, he's like Teflon. Wait, that's offensive to Teflon, he's like an eel. He's slippery, nothing sticks.

And no one will 'out him' for fear of their employment."

"Then you need to ensure the staff trust and respect you more." Jia leans across and nabs the last quarter of my sliced crumpet.

"Trust and Respect. Looks like I've got my work cut out for me, huh?"

"Yes ma'am. You should know, the Invisible Women are meeting on Monday evening; have Xi drop you off at 5.30 pm and we'll eat together."

"I'm invited back?" I beam across at her.

"You're one of us now. We all must stick together." She winks across at me. 'I've been meaning to ask you, has your Navy Seal asked about me?' Suddenly fascinated by her coffee mug.

"To be honest Jia, he doesn't say much to me at all. I don't even know if he's available." I shrug. 'I can ask though, if you'd like?"

"Don't be ridiculous! Women like us don't do the chasing darling. We let them come to us." She pats my hand. Standing and picking up her much lighter bag she turns toward the elevator. "I shall see you on Monday. If you need anything, I'm only a phone call away."

"Thank you for this Jia. I suspect I'll be in the office most of the weekend based on this! I can't focus here. I don't know what I would do without you, you have been an absolute lifesaver." I walk her to the elevator.

"Oh darling, nothing in this world is free. You'll be getting my bill at the office next week. I must admit, I'd be lying if I didn't tell you I'm rather enjoying helping you stick it to Tony." She air kisses me on each cheek, shuts the door and the lift disappears.

I wander back to the kitchen and place the dishes in the dishwasher. I text my after-hours guy and tell him we'll be leaving for the office within the hour.

After applying a little makeup I throw on a black cotton wrap dress and wedges. I stare at myself in the mirror. I look like a ballet teacher. I should put my hair in a chignon on the top of my head and dance around with a ribbon.

Sighing, I shove the papers Jia returned into my bag on the way to the elevator.

In the car, I drag out my diary to check my schedule for the week. I pencil in Monday's dinner with the Invisible Women.

I am looking forward to Monday night. I have so much to learn from these women and so much to tell them! My thoughts drift to Chen. I ponder his life, surrounded by wealth and what it must be like to have a family with such suffocating expectations. I wonder if he has a wife or children. I didn't come across anything in my research but that probably isn't surprising considering I hadn't connected the dots on his family. I now know the Chen family are notoriously private. From what I gather, they rarely give interviews or speak publicly about anything other than the business. I found a couple of photographs of Chen's parents at charity Galas and the like but not much else. I couldn't find any other social media for Chen or his family.

That's one thing we have in common I suppose.

I did stumble across a couple of publicity shots of Chen accepting awards at Harvard Business School. His hair was a little longer, pulled back in a low ponytail as he smiled broadly holding large framed certificates.

As we pull into the return at the front of HEH I notice a black motorcycle parked out front.

What on earth is that doing here? Maybe one of the weekend Security guards rides?

I take the elevator up to the restaurant floor. I need more coffee before I can face today. I wonder what kind of food they put on over the weekend. Maybe I'll grab a bagel or danish or something. Stepping into the restaurant, I freeze. The space is filled with people milling around, eating and talking.

How did I not know that this many people work the weekend? I'm so glad I put clothes on to come in here.

Making a beeline for the counter, I place my coffee order and select an apple and cinnamon muffin from the cake stand. The barista returns, handing me a large glass double-walled enviro cup.

"Uh, this isn't mine?" I look down at the fancy cup. Some poor sod is waiting for their coffee and their cup is being mistakenly given away.

"We keep a supply of them here Miss Ava. In case the staff forget to bring their own. The cleaning staff bring them back up from the building and we wash them up." The barista beams across at me. "It's much better for the environment."

My oh my Winnie. I'm betting this was your idea too.

Walking into my office with my environmentally friendly coffee warming my fingers, I smile at Winnie's chair. I think I might finally be ready to face the reality that you aren't coming back.

I step toward the large oak desk with trepidation. Running my fingers along the top of the leather chair, I pull it out from under the desk. I lean forward and place my coffee on the stamped metal coaster.

I unpack my laptop and the papers from Jia into neat stacks. Finally, I pull Winnie's pen from the breast pocket of my 3/4 jacket and place it in the stand at the top of the desk. I walk around to admire my handy work. Standing there enjoying the solitude, I hear my phone vibrate in my bag. Stepping over and digging it out, I see an unknown number flash up.

"Ava Elias,' I answer.

"Miss Elias, it's Samuel Chen. Sorry to disturb you on the weekend but I need to speak with you urgently." He sounds frazzled.

"Breathe Chen, I'm in the office. What's wrong?" I hold my breath, backing up toward Winnie's desk.

"One of our ships has been attacked."

"Attacked? What on earth...?" I stumble backward sitting on the first surface my bum finds. The glass door to my office slides open.

"Pirates,' Chen breathes from the doorway. My brain stops.

Pirates? Machete wielding sea scavengers.

Or perhaps it was the vision of him standing in my doorway. His silky hair pulled up into a bun, white collared shirt half-tucked into his black slacks. Was it Justin Timberlake who first started that trend? The half-tucked in dress shirt?

"Ava, did you hear me? One of our ships was attacked by pirates.' Chen strides toward me then stops suddenly. 'I see you finally found your place." He smiles down at me.

What? I look around to realise I am sitting in Winnie's chair.

"I suppose I did,' I smile to myself.

"I've got the team in the Conference room, they're about to brief me on what happened. I thought you might want to be here for this." He holds out his hand. I look from his extended fingers to his face and back again. Hesitantly, I take his hand and follow him, stopping only to grab Winnie's pen and the leather compendium.

The conference room is chock full of people. Both men and women, I am proud to note. Chen pulls back one of the two chairs seated at the head of the table, gesturing for me to sit.

"Mr Chen, Miss Elias. Thank you for joining us. I wish it were under better circumstances." Mr Peng, our head of security, begins from the other end of the table where he stands in front of a large screen.

"To keep everyone up to date, we had a vessel attacked by pirates overnight after leaving port in Oman. We do not yet know why the pirates were so far north of the Gulf of Aden."

"Where do we stand? Were any of the crew harmed?" I direct at Peng.

"Miss Elias, we had a couple of minor injuries but nothing the ship's medic can't handle. Our safety procedures held, and the ship is crossing the Arabian Sea as we speak."

Oh, thank god.

I drop my head into my hands. Peng and I only talked about safety measures onboard the ships last week. He told me these attacks happen very infrequently and there was nothing to worry about.

"We have contacted the family of the crew members and have arranged to transport them to the docks to meet the ship upon its return. The reason for the meeting this morning is to discuss the

'Compensation Clause' for the crewmen." Peng looks to me, then across at Chen.

"Under Mr Huynh, any crew members who suffered a traumatic event were covered by HEH insurance and given options." Peng takes a seat as a short woman with plump cheeks stands.

"Most of you know me, I am Lin Pei the head of Human Resources here at HEH. Historically, crewmen, and women,' she nods at me, 'have been given several options following the experience of a traumatic event. HEH immediately returns them to the port where they are required to undertake mandatory counselling and medical evaluation. Once we are certain there is no risk of PTSD we support them in returning to work when they are ready or offer them a severance package if they do not wish to continue under HEH employ." I suddenly feel all eyes in the room swivel to myself and Chen.

"Lin, I'm not sure I understand what you're asking. If there is already a procedure in place, why are we discussing it?" I turn to look at Chen, who shrugs just as uncertain.

"Miss Elias, forgive me. There were a significant number of crew members on board this vessel."

"What am I missing here? What does it matter how many crew members were on board?"

"Miss Elias, I think what Miss Pei is trying to say is that following the historical system may result in a large financial implication for HEH,' Chen offers, looking to Lin to confirm.

"Yes Mr Chen, that is correct. Based on the number of crew members and many of their senior positions, HEH may be looking at millions of dollars in compensation." Lin swallowed nervously. I notice she is wringing her hands. I look around the room, trying to spot my finance guy. Dang, he's not here.

"Someone correct me if I'm wrong, but doesn't our 'visual merchandising' team fill the building with thousands of fresh flowers twice weekly?" I look around into the eyes of the directors and heads of departments.

"Doesn't the HEH garage offer free car washing for Directors? The restaurant supplies eight different kinds of milk to the tea rooms on the floors? The multitude of bathrooms on every floor are filled with designer soaps and hand creams?" I feel the room shuffle awkwardly in their chairs.

"Miss Pei, I have no doubt HEH can afford to cover this, but if not, there's your millions of dollars. I see no reason why we would treat these crewmen any differently from those who have gone before them.'

'But if we find ourselves in a situation where we have to choose between Organic Goats Milk and helping the men and women who have to leave their families to keep this company in business, then I hope you'll all get used to bringing your own milk to work."

A nervous ripple of laughter breaks out across the room.

"Thank you Miss Elias!" Lin beams across at me. I start to wonder if she is more invested in this than I am aware. As the room clears out, I nod at Mr Peng to wait behind a moment.

"Miss Elias?" Peng bows briefly when we are alone, 'How can I be of service?"

"Ms Pei, does she have a relative or loved one on that vessel?"

"Ah, very astute of you Miss Elias. Her husband is one of our finest captains."

"Thank you Peng. Do me a favour and email me a list of the staff aboard the vessel. Now go home to your family and try to enjoy the weekend." Another bow and he departs.

I look around, realising Chen has disappeared. I spot him in the next conference room being primped and dressed by the Public Relations team.

Of course! How could I forget, the CEO will be expected to make a 'public statement' about this 'incident'.

I head upstairs to my office, stopping at Sasha's desk to pick up some note cards and envelopes. I trace my fingers over the embossed detail, With Compliments, CEO Huynh Enterprises Holdings. I'll only be sending these to the crew members and their families so it doesn't matter that I'm signing them. Perhaps I should get Chen to co-sign them?

I sit down at Winnie's desk and on a scrap piece of paper write out a note for the cards. It has to be something I can repeat for all the cards and then add their names on when Peng sends me the list.

After a few trials I decide I like;

(Name),

Our thoughts and gratitude to you and your families during this time.

-Ms Ava Elias   -Mr Sam Chen

It fits nicely on the card and isn't so long that if it turns out 100 crew were on board the vessel, my hand won't have fallen off by the time I'm finished writing. If I'm getting Chen to co-sign them, I should probably wait and check he is happy with it before I write them all out.

I put the cards aside and drag the first pile of paperwork from Jia toward me. I work my way through methodically checking and initialling beside every suggested change. Jia has done an amazing job with this. I'd love to have someone like her on my team. But I can't really make any changes to Legal until I am rid of Tony.

The thought of Tony gets me thinking. I open my laptop and bring up a copy of the HEH Ethical Standards & Code of Conduct.

There has to be something in here about deceit or manipulation or behaviour - like shouting at the CEO. He's already done that once in front of a room full of witnesses. I wonder if that would be enough to give him his first warning.

My stomach grumbles up at me. I check the time on my laptop.

Hm, lunchtime. I wonder how Chen's press conference is going.

I walk over to the window and peer as far down to the street as I can. I knew I wouldn't be able to see the bottom of HEH from here, unable to watch the press descend on the building in a swarm of microphones and cameras. Watch Chen smile and offer his thoughts and prayers to the families of HEH who are affected by this horrific event. Watch the reporters eat him up, hanging on his every word, photographing his Hollywood smile.

I sigh heavily and press my forehead to the glass.

I bet I've just made a giant face-print on the glass. Ugh. I need to write a reminder for the cleaners to spray and wipe this window.

My stomach gurgles up at me again. I look down and shush it.

"I'm pretty sure it is telling you something,' Chen's voice over my shoulder makes me jump.

"I didn't hear you come in,' I catch my breath.

"You did well in there today. I was impressed.' I hear him walk further into the room. 'Nice cards, a very thoughtful gesture. Do you really want me to sign them too?" I turn to look at him, his fringe falling across his face as he reaches down, elegant fingers picking up the card.

"Do you play piano?" I blurt. I'm rewarded with a sexy chuckle.

Oh man, I felt that. In places I have absolutely no right to.

"What an odd question." He smiles up at me coyly.

"You have such long fingers, with such a wide finger-span, I guess I was curious." I hold my hands up, splaying my fingers wide in explanation.

Chen holds his hands up, fingers splayed in the air mirroring mine. He saunters closer until our hands are almost touching, each fingertip matching.

"You are a most unusual woman Miss Elias." He breathes. He smells of mint and aftershave and leather.

Leather?

"It was your motorbike downstairs?" I frown up at him.

"What?" He looks just as confused as I am.

"You smell like leather."

"And your first thought was motorbike?" He smiles down at me.

"Motorbikes and saddlery are my most common associations to leather, but I'd assume you didn't ride here on a horse."

"Who says I rode here on anything at all?" He cocks one eyebrow, his fingertips feather-light brushing against mine. His eyes search my face before coming to rest at my lips.

I feel myself blushing and pray he doesn't notice.

"Do you want to go for a ride?" He whispers to my lips.

It's been so long.

Get your head out of the gutter girl, surely he's not suggesting...

A deep grumble erupts between us breaking the tension. Chen steps back, dropping his hands to his sides.

"I told you it was trying to tell you something,' He chuckles again running a hand through his hair.

"I suppose I should go and find something to eat,' I sigh, feeling bereft at his sudden distance. I walk past him to the lounge, picking up my purse and spot a leather jacket hanging over the wingback. I spin on the spot and point at him.

"I knew it!" I squeal.

"Didn't your mother ever tell you it's rude to point?" Chen takes two quick paces to close the distance, grasps my airborne finger and raises it to his lips, placing a soft kiss on the fingerprint. I stop breathing.

"Has anyone taken you to the Hawker centre to eat?" Baby blues burning a hole in my soul, once again.

"I went to the one in China Town the last time I was here. I fell in love with an amazing lime drink and tried 'carrot cake',' I wink up at him.

"Not what you were expecting?"

"It was nice, but I prefer the version with cream cheese icing."

"You Westerners and your sugary treats."

"Gotta stay sweet somehow." I shrug. He looks as though he is going to continue the flirty banter when a shadow passes over his face. He releases my hand, clearing his throat.

"Well Miss Elias, I believe I owe you a lunch. To say... thank you...for not firing me yesterday." He runs another hand through his hair. I look up at him, confused. For whatever reason he stopped, he is probably right. We shouldn't be doing this. He's technically my employee for god sake.

"I don't think that is a good idea. The outside world may not know it, but you are still my employee." I try to keep my voice even, hoping the hurt underneath isn't obvious. Chen's face falls, his hand finds his hair again.

"Listen Ava...I..." His tortured expression proof that the flirting wasn't something I'd imagined.

"You have nothing to explain Mr Chen. I am new in town and I mistook your kindness for something it wasn't. I can assure you that nothing of this nature will ever happen again." I pick up my bag, gather the papers, note cards and my laptop from the desk and make for the door.

"Ava..." He tries again, rooted on the spot.

"Good day Mr Chen." I smile unconvincingly back at him and make a hasty exit.

After clambering hurriedly into the back of the BBSUV I ask the after-hours guy to take me to the Gardens by the Bay. I remember Satay by the Bay, the outdoor eatery where I ate dumplings and drank lime juice years ago. Those were simpler times. I still don't even know if I can trust Chen. What if he is just doing this to lure me in? How do I know he isn't just a great actor and this was his plan all along? He has plenty of motivation to see it through if that is his intention.

Deep in the pit of my hungry stomach, I hope that isn't true.

I don't want to prove those men right. That I'm nothing but a silly woman who can't see what's happening in front of her and lose my company because of it.

Then again, I smile to myself.

I certainly wouldn't be the first CEO to torpedo their company over some piece of ass.

The screech of my mobile phone drags me out of my pity party. I dig around in my bag until I find my Australian phone. I smile down at it, Gladys found it under my bed. I check the caller ID and my heart stops. Ryan Murphy.

"Hello?" I answer hesitantly.

"Ava? Oh, thank god, where have you been?!" Ryan almost shouts down the phone; it sounds like he's on speaker. "I've been calling everyone in town trying to track you down!"

"Why? What's wrong?"

"What's wrong?? You sent a text message saying there was trouble at Arendelle and it took me days to understand it was an SOS message. I stupidly forgot the name of your chalet. By the time I realised, I couldn't get through to your phone because it was switched off and no one in town would tell me anything other than that you'd 'been seen with some scary looking mafia dudes' and then disappeared."

Bless Ivan and Danny, those men really do know how to keep a secret.

"Oh Ryan, I'm so sorry. I didn't mean to put you through all that. It has been the most bizarre few weeks."

"Well, I'm on my way to Dinner Plain so why don't I come to your place and you can explain it to me."

"What? Why are you driving up so early, the season's nowhere near started? It's only May."

"Because I was half-crazed with worry and mid-way through packing when the snow report came in. Haven't you heard? There's a low building that's likely to bring feet of snow, weeks before the season is due to commence."

"Oh, no...I hadn't heard. Um, Ryan, the thing is, I'm in Singapore."

Deafening silence from the other end of the line. I look at my phone, trying to see if I'd lost him.

"Ryan?"

"Did you say Singapore? As in, Asia? That Singapore?"

"Yes. That Singapore. I had some business to attend to and I had to travel here at short notice." A bark of laughter comes down the phone, 'Business? Ava, you work at the ski school. What could possibly take you to Asia? You're not in any kind of trouble, are you?"

Ryan really is the sweetest man alive.

"No Ryan, I'm not in trouble. I promise. I just had to come over here to sort some things out."

"If you're sure. Then when are you coming home? Are you going to be back for the season?" I can almost hear the hope in his voice.

I thought he wasn't interested in anything with me? Maybe he's just looking for someone to warm his bed in this 'snap' blizzard.

I shut down those thoughts.

"Ava?"

"Ryan, I'm sorry. I don't know when I'll be back. I have no idea how long this is going to take."

"Did you...uh...meet someone?" He hesitates.

"No Ryan, I haven't met anyone." Saying it out loud feels like a lie, but I know Chen can never be anything more.

"Good. I mean...good." He sighs with relief.

Well, who would have thought?

"Maybe if you're not back before the season ends, I could come over to visit? I've never been to Singapore." I can hear the smile in his voice.

"I'd like that,' I smile down at my lap, "I'd really like that."

"If it's okay with you, do you mind if I Skype you later? You can tell me all about the mafia guys and how Singapore has been treating you?"

"It's a date."

"I look forward to it, I'll talk to you then."

"Ryan..."

"Yeah?"

"Thanks for looking out for me."

"Always, Ava. Catch ya later."

I hang up the phone and stare at it in my hands. A feeling of elation washes over me. Ryan is someone real. Someone who knew me before all this. Someone I can see a life with. Lord knows we've got chemistry and enough in common to keep us going if we got together.

A thought occurs to me. If I knew I could trust him, perhaps I could leave Chen here in charge of HEH and go back to Dinner Plain. He could do what he needed to here and I wouldn't be causing trouble or getting in the way. Maybe it would be better that way, for everyone.

On Sunday afternoon Tari came over to look at Winnie's journals.

"This is so exciting! It's like being a detective!" She hollers as she bounds into Winnie's library with me. "Whoa." I too find myself taken by surprise every time I enter this room. I direct her to a lounge and pass her last year's journal. I still haven't managed to find this year's book. Where on earth would he have put it? Somewhere safe that Tony couldn't find it, is my guess. Tari flips through the pages, admiring Winnie's calligraphy prowess.

"Drink?" I look across at Tari, already absorbed in Winnie's musings.

"Yes, please." She doesn't look up.

Wandering into the kitchen I find the bottle of Shiraz Gladys opened last night and a couple of glasses. Deciding that drinking on an empty stomach is not a great plan, I dig through the fridge to look for afternoon snacks. Nothing appeals in particular. Gladys will grocery shop this afternoon. Turning to collect the wine, I notice a basket of savoury muffins on the counter.

These will do nicely.

Joining Tari in the library I find her deep in concentration.

"As much as I am enjoying these, there really isn't much of interest in here. It is all about business and random bits of poetry or lyrics or something?" Tari looks up at me, accepting her glass of wine.

'I've flipped through quite a few pages. Nothing is really standing out. I haven't even found a mention of Tony and I've flipped halfway through this one." She holds the book up to show me.

"Well, we knew it was a long shot. I just thought perhaps there might have been something in there to help me figure out what Tony's deal is."

"It sounds like he only lost the plot when Winnie was dying. We need to find his final journal."

"I've looked everywhere for it. Everywhere I can think of anyway. Maybe I need to go to extremes and check all his aircraft. He was in New York in his final email to me. Maybe I need to fly to NYC and retrace his steps?"

"I'm just going to say it - I feel like that's just an excuse to go to New York." Tari giggles across at me, putting her wine down and reaching for a savoury muffin.

"You're right, that was a stretch too far,' I sigh.

"I'm not saying we shouldn't go to NYC, I'm just saying perhaps that shouldn't be the reason." She garbles around a mouthful.

"We? I see, so you're in on this now too?" I laugh.

"Every heroine needs a trusty sidekick!"

"To the heroine and the sidekick!" I toast. We clink glasses and giggle. I sigh and slump back in the lounge.

"What's going on hun?" Tari looks across at me.

"You mean other than the obvious?' I laugh, 'I guess I'm kind of having boy trouble."

"No! Tell me, tell me, tell me!" She bounces up and down, an unusually girly response for her.

As we drink our way through the shiraz, I fill her in on my last encounter with Ryan. The chemistry, the fact that I can see a future with him.

"I don't see how that is confusing? Have you ever asked him if he sees anyone when he goes back to Melbourne?" Tari looks up at me from her spot on the floor.

"Well, no. Not really,' I grimace.

"Aha!" She shouts, pointing up at me.

Gladys unexpectedly pops her head around the door. "Afternoon Ladies, having a nice time, are we?" She smiles down at us. "I thought we could have homemade pizzas for dinner?"

"Oh thank goodness, I was just about to go foraging, I'm so hungry." I smile back at her.

"Did you eat lunch?" She chastises.

"No, I must have forgotten." I frown.

"Pizza will be about an hour. Why don't you both switch to spritzers until I can get some food into your stomachs." Gladys suggests as she disappears through the door.

"Did she just chastise us for day drinking?" Tari whispers up at me. We both burst out into giggles.

"Okay, so as far as I can see, if you tell Ryan the truth about how you feel, maybe he'll be honest with you too? I don't see how that is so complicated?"

"You see, that's the thing. It wasn't complicated. Until I got here and now it just feels like everything is different."

"It is an 8-hour flight back and you have YOUR OWN JET now. How is that complicated? You can quite literally 'pop across' to see him whenever you like." Tari eyeballs me. 'Unless there is something else going on that you aren't telling me."

"Well, there is one thing. Oh god, saying it out loud makes it more real!" I feel my chest constricting.

"Spit it out!"

"I'm attracted to Chen." I squeal, hiding my face in the cushions on the lounge.

"No!" Tari grabs my arm, tugging. "Tell me you're joking! Chen? Chen who you're still not sure isn't trying to steal your company? That Chen?" I peek up at her and nod.

"I knew it! I asked you if he smelled good! And to be honest, half of Asia is crazy in love with him so don't beat yourself up. You were bound to fall under his spell at some point."

"Tari, what do I do??" I whine.

"Has anything happened? Do you know for sure you like him or is it just chemistry? Because quite frankly that man exudes so much sexual energy I'm sure he'd make a panda horny."

"Tari..."

"See, it's funny because pandas are only interested in sexy time like, once a year..."

"Tari, I know panda's rarely mate. I honestly don't know. I mean sure, he has a great smile and yes, he smells divine. But there's something so gentlemanly and respectful about the way he treats me at HEH. I feel like maybe he really respects me?"

"Are you confusing good manners and courtesy with interest? Maybe he's like that with everyone?" Tari raises her eyebrow, reaching for her empty wine glass. 'I don't care what 'Mother Gothel' says, if we are going to solve your boy problems, we need more drinks."

I follow her to the kitchen where she points me out toward the deck. I meander through the silk curtains, enjoying the warm timber under my feet, the afternoon sun kissing my face as my hair catches in the breeze.

Singapore really is a beautiful city.

I look across to the Singapore Flyer, imagining how romantic it must be at night. Maybe I'll take Ryan up it when he comes to visit. Or across to Sentosa Island, or maybe to the night zoo.

Tari joins me on the deck, expertly balancing a tray with two cocktails covered in fruit, on one hand.

"I had to pretend they were virgin!" She snickers sitting down and handing me one. 'Okay, so we just have to figure out if you and Chen have a snowflake's chance in hell or if it's just sexual tension. How long has it been?"

"How long has what been? I only saw him yesterday, and I haven't seen Ryan in months." I sip the fruity concoction and choke. 'Good lord, is there anything virgin about this cocktail?' I splutter.

"Sorry, mighta been a little heavy-handed there. What I meant was, how long has it been since you've, you know, had sex?" She looks at me sideways, patting me on the back.

"Uh, I have no idea." I stop to think.

I know it was Ryan, but I can't recall how long ago that was now.

"Well honey perhaps that's your problem. It's been so long that you're mistaking Chen's good manners for interest. And so what if he smells good, I'm sure he's terrible in bed." Tari grins at me.

'You're probably right. I'm just starved for attention." I roll my eyes and laugh.

"You should send your fancy plane and helicopter to collect Ryan, bring him here to break your drought!" She cackles. 'Forget UBER-EATS, HEH-DELIVERS!" She winks at me.

"The crazy thing is, other than his CV I don't really know anything about Chen,' I sigh.

"Wait, are you telling me you've been his boss for over a week now and haven't cyberstalked him yet?" Tari shoots daggers at me, dragging her phone from her back pocket.

"What? It seemed like an invasion of privacy. I did a little google but nothing more. Besides, of what little I had heard about Chen Industries, I knew they were extremely private people." I shrug, sucking on the decorative wedge of pineapple.

"Okay. What do they say in America? 'Are you ready for the 4-1-1?' She laughs and begins to read. I sit back and prop my feet up on the lounger beside me.

'Samuel Chen, firstborn son of the Chen Empire. Currently, 35 years of age, considered quite young for his success in the business world thus far. Graduated top of his class from Harvard Business School..."

"I know all of this Tari!"

"Wait, wait! I'm just getting to the good stuff. 'Considered betrothed from birth to Lin Mei Yang of the Yang Family, Heiress to the Yang Family fortune. Oh, there's even a picture of them together.' She turns the phone to show me. 'I think you could take her." A stunning black and white photo, straight out of Old Hollywood. She wore a silk gown with a fur bolero, he wore a tuxedo with a bow tie and cumber bun. They stand staring deep into each other's eyes, toasting with champagne glasses straight out of the 1920s.

"Ava Elias-Huynh might, but plain old Ava certainly couldn't compete with that,' I sigh, 'I guess that explains his hesitation. He's already promised to someone else."

"Are you thinking about changing your name? Come to think of it, I love the sound of that. Ava Elias-Huynh. It sounds...powerful."

"I haven't thought about changing it, but I just feel like since all of this happened with Winnie, that there are two sides to me now. Ava before Winnie and Ava after Winnie. Ryan liked me before I ever met Winnie or his money, whereas Chen has only known me because of it. He wouldn't have looked at me twice if he'd met me in the street." I look out to the bay, twisting my ponytail around my fingers. "Did I ever tell you how Ryan and I first met?" Tari shakes her head, sipping her cocktail.

"It was on the slopes at the ski school. Late one afternoon, at the very beginning of the season. My first season in Dinner Plain. I'd barely learned how to walk on the ice and snow, let alone how to help kids skiing on it. That's why I usually only work inside, not on the slopes.

'This little girl came down hard, hit another kid before coming to a stop. She started turning blue and other than first aid, I couldn't think of what else to do so I called the ambulance prematurely.

'By the time Ryan and his partner showed up, she was busting to get back onto the slopes. I poured Ryan and his partner a hot chocolate for the road back to Hotham to apologise for the inconvenience.

'Ryan was the only person in town who didn't tease me for calling an ambulance for a kid who had winded herself." I smile fondly at the memory.

"He sounds like a nice guy. Why didn't you guys get together properly?" Tari frowns.

"I knew he wasn't staying in town for long and didn't want to get hurt,' I admit. 'You know, I don't know that I've ever said that out loud before. Thank you." I lean over and place my head on Tari's leg. We sat there in the breeze, watching the sky slowly darken until goosebumps began to sprout on my arms.

Funny how even as the CEO, I still don't love getting out of bed on a Monday morning. But today is going to be different. Today I talk to Lin about Tony. And I have dinner with the Invisible Women!

As Xi parks the BBSUV in the return in front of HEH, I am struck by the number of news vans parked in the lot.

"Xi, did I miss something? What's going on?" I take off my sunglasses and peer out the window.

"I believe it is a follow-up press conference for the returning vessel, Miss."

"But it isn't due back for another week or two. It's not a Greek island yacht cruise, Oman is 3600nm from Singapore."

"I apologise, Miss Elias, I know nothing further." Xi holds his hand out to me as he opens my door.

Stepping out in my black pumps, I run my hands down the front of my midnight blue Iris and Ink belted shirt dress, sending yet another silent thank you to the Invisible Women for their fashion assistance.

Walking out from behind the car, I'm joined by Seal as I try to stand on my tippy toes to see what is going on.

"They're holding a press conference, Miss." Seal states informatively. I turn and glare at him, mouthing 'no shit Sherlock'.

Placing one hand at my waist, he guides me around the media scrum toward the side doors and a better view of the podium. Suddenly Sasha appears at my other side. "Miss Elias, I am so, so sorry. I didn't know anything about this,' she squeaks.

"Sasha, why are you apologising if you didn't know?" I pat her on the arm.

"Because it is my job to know Miss Elias,' she states sternly, facing forward.

We stand in anticipation as the PR Team usher Chen and Tony out behind the lectern.

Tony.

I see the PR staff look nervously in our direction.

Oh yes. I will most certainly be asking for an explanation after this little circus act.

"Sasha, be sure to book me a meeting with PR first up this morning." I feel Sasha swallow nervously beside me.

"Good Morning Ladies and Gentlemen; members of the press. It is my pleasure to introduce Mr Chen, CEO of Huynh Enterprises Holdings." Tony smiles broadly, shaking Chen's hand as he steps back.

Chen approaches the microphone, his bright smile just barely outshone by his crisp Hugo Boss suit, the top two buttons of his linen shirt left open at his throat. He stands there smiling at the cameras, adjusting one cufflink out in front as though posing for a modelling campaign. I hear many of the female reporters in the gathering sigh and swoon. Even Sasha fidgets uncomfortably beside me. I roll my eyes.

"Good Morning Ladies and Gentlemen. It is my honour to address you today with an update on our team in Oman. As you all know, an HEH vessel was attacked at the weekend and I am here to advise that no major injuries were sustained, with no damage to the vessel. We anticipate our crew to be home within the fortnight. We here at HEH would like to thank the men and women in Oman and here at home who assisted in the security efforts and offer our most humble gratitude.' More smiles from Chen followed by a slight bow, his hand on his heart.

I think I just saw a reporter faint.

Chen reaches up to sweep his silky fringe behind one ear. His eyes sweep over the reporters in front of him, stopping abruptly when they land on me. We lock eyes for the smallest of moments before Chen clears his throat and continues.

"In news closer to home, I have been advised to make an announcement regarding the upcoming HEH Annual Fundraising Ball."

I feel the blood drain from my face. *What on earth is he talking about? He has not been involved in ANY of the event planning.*

"HEH will be continuing the tradition of honouring the Public Housing Initiative at the ball to be hosted on July 1. At that time, HEH will be making a major announcement regarding the future direction of the initiative." More panty-dropping smiles from Chen. 'Are there any questions?" Abbie, the head of PR steps forward.

"Rhonda, go ahead,' Abbie points to a woman out of our line of sight.

"Mr Chen, firstly welcome on board,' she giggles, the audience ripples with laughter. 'I was wondering where my invitation is, to the ball I mean."

Chen chuckles into the microphone, scratching his chin contemplatively. "Abbie, I think we may need to open an investigation into missing invitations."

"I've seen enough, I need coffee,' I whisper to Sasha and Seal. Our movement catches Chen's eye. He stares at me his expression unreadable, before another megawatt smile dawns as he turns to answer another question.

As I exit the elevator on the restaurant floor, I turn back to Sasha.

"I want Abbie in my office by the time I get back. And she'd better hope they have my cream cheese cinnamon scrolls today or my mood is unlikely to improve between now and then." The mirrored doors close in front of me. I suddenly realise I am wearing the deepest scowl I've ever mustered.

It isn't fair to be this tart with the team. I'm sure they are just following Tony's orders because once again, they are afraid for their jobs. Once I've seen Lin after lunch, that all changes.

I order my coffee and then use the powder room, enjoying the solace the softly lit room offers. I reapply my lipstick out of habit, realising too late that I haven't even drunk my coffee yet or eaten my cinnamon scroll. I sigh heavily, leaning my forearms against the marble counter and hanging my head. I stare at my ginger locks tumbling forward. Watching the light play through them as I sway the curls this way and that.

"I could stand here entranced by you for all eternity." The sound of Chen's sexy chuckle hits me like a bolt of lightning. I jump back, tripping on the plush rug and falling flat on my ass. Chen bursts out laughing.

"I...I'm so sorry, I didn't mean to..." Chen mutters in between belly laughs.

"Do you know if any of the windows on this floor open?" I glare up at him.

"Do you need some fresh air?" He smiles down at me.

"I'd like you to jump out of one. Or better yet, you open it and I'll push you out."

"I don't know how well 'CEO Murderer' will work out on your CV Miss Ava."

"Right back at you Mr Chen." Trying to stand I grimace at the movement, my tailbone protesting.

"It seems I owe you yet another apology,' Chen crouches down in front of me.

"I count two."

"Oh?"

"That circus act you call a press conference downstairs, and this." I wave my hand generally referring to the situation at present.

"Impressive mathematical skills you have there. I can see now why you're the boss,' he mutters. "Tony and Abbie said..."

"Oh, yes. I'd love to hear what Tony said,' I glower.

"Tony said, that you had been over it with the PR people. When I asked Abbie if Tony had cleared it with her, she said yes! How was I supposed to know that you didn't?" He throws his hands in the air.

I drag my phone out of my pocket and dial a number.

"What...What are you doing?" Chen frowns at me. His breast pocket starts to vibrate. Pulling his phone out he sees me on his caller ID.

"These days we have these magical devices called MOBILE PHONES." I hang up and toss mine at his head. It bounces off lightly and clatters to the floor.

"Um, ow?" He looks down at me, feigning hurt as he rubs his brow. 'You know, I've never met anyone so comfortable speaking to me that way. Or physically assaulting me."

I roll my eyes, 'There's a first time for everything."

"Are they the only two things you're mad about?" He eyes me warily.

"What else would I be mad about? The press obviously loves you and you spoke well about the Pirate incident. I can't be mad about you being CEO, you're doing a great job. It seems HEH needs you." I shrug.

"I wasn't referring to..." A knock at the door derails him.

"I'll be out in a second,' I holler.

"I'll leave your coffee and cinnamon scroll here, Miss. There's extra cream cheese icing, just like you asked,' Came the muffled reply.

"What is it with you and cream cheese icing?" Chen chuckles, scratching his chin.

My phone begins to vibrate, lighting up beside Chen's feet. He picks it up, staring at the screen.

'Humph." Is all he says as he hands it over, straightens up and walks to the door.

I look down at the screen and there in beautiful high definition is Ryan. All tanned skin and beach boy hair, blowing me a kiss in the falling snow. He never knew that I used this photo as his Caller ID.

I look up as the door swings closed. I hit 'answer'.

"Hi,' I smile down at my lap.

After lunch I meet Lin from HR; to discuss Tony.

"Lin, I've reviewed his contract and considering how little value Tony adds to HEH, I think it is time we look for a new General Counsel." I look across at her, watching her eyes grow wide in horror.

"Miss Elias, I understand what you are saying, but I do not feel comfortable discussing this." Lin looks around uncomfortably.

"What am I missing here? Tony is my employee; he is woefully overpaid and underutilized. You are my head of HR. Who else am I meant to discuss this with?"

"Mr Tony told all the staff at the 'staff meeting' last week that no decisions were to be made without running them past him because you are on probation." She twists her hands on the table before dropping them into her lap.

"Well, luckily for you, Tony is due here any minute. So my decision will be run past him. Don't worry, you're safe. You are only required as an accessory to this discussion." I nod at her. Tony and Chen enter the room, the look on Tony's face indicating that he was not happy about being told to front up here.

"What is the meaning of this? I do not appreciate being summoned!" Tony spits. I note Chen quietly takes a seat in the corner leaving Tony to stand by himself.

"Mr Tony, thank you for joining us this afternoon. We are here to discuss your 'performance' of late." I wave my hand, gesturing for him to sit.

"My performance? MY performance?" He raises his voice, colour rising in his face.

"Yes, Mr Tony. You have been behaving inappropriately and reaching above and beyond the scope of your role." I state measuredly.

"Excuse ME? Behaving inappropriately?' He splutters, his face now a shade of puce. I wonder if his glasses will fog up.

"Last week alone, I believe you stated, 'Miss Elias, this behaviour is petulant and entirely inappropriate.' Now, Mr Tony, does that sound like the appropriate way to address your CEO in front of the entire Executive Director cohort?

'Not to mention hijacking the PR team to host your impromptu press conference this morning without my permission, or the staff meeting last week at which you allegedly told the staff I was 'on probation'." I hear Chen snort quietly from his corner, clearly this was news to him too.

"Mr Tony, do these sound like appropriate behaviours for the General Counsel of a multinational conglomerate?" I tilt my head and look up at him. Tony stands there gawking at me, his mouth opening and closing inaudibly.

Is he having a stroke?

"You will have your secretary write a retraction of your statement at the staff meeting, which I will review and have circulated internally to the Executive Directors.

'This is your first warning Mr Tony. Keep this up and you will be out of a job. As of today, you are officially on notice." I stare him down.

"Miss Elias,' Tony finds his voice, more quietly this time.

'I am only trying to do what is best for HEH."

"As much as I am sure Mr Huynh appreciated your assistance Mr Tony, it is no longer required at this level of the company. You will return to your office and refocus your gaze to Legal matters.

'The only time I want to hear a peep out of you again is if HEH is being sued, or at legal risk. Do I make myself clear?"

"As you wish, Miss Elias." Tony bows deeply before straightening and brusquely exiting the room.

Quietly, I release the breath I didn't realise I was holding.

"Ms Lin, if you could please make a note of this in Mr Tony's file, I'd be greatly appreciative." She nods at me quietly before scampering out the door.

I look up to see Chen sitting eyeing me contemplatively. His chin resting on his hands, long index fingers steepled at his lips.

"No smart quip Mr Chen?" I enquire across at him.

"I didn't know you had it in you." He frowns. 'Even my own father knows the wrath of Zhang Wei Tony. No man dares to cross swords with him."

"Lucky I'm no man then." I offer him a small smile as I stand, collecting my compendium and Monty.

"Perhaps, but you certainly have balls." He smiles up at me. The look on his face could almost be misconstrued for admiration.

"And then what happened?!" Jia claps her hands in anticipation.

"Wait, wait! I don't want to miss the story!!" Linah squeals, running in kicking her heels off and tucking her feet up underneath her on the sofa.

"Go on, Ava what did you do next? Tar and feather him?" Margot giggles into her cocktail.

"I walked confidently into my office, waited for the door to close and profusely vomited in the ensuite." I look down sheepishly.

I was so confident and strong and then I think the adrenaline wore off and hit me like a train.

"Oh, don't feel bad about that! Do you know how many years it took me of fronting up in court before I stopped running to the bathroom the second we were dismissed?" Jia pats me on the shoulder, 'It gets easier."

"Does it?" Margot scoffs from her cushion on the floor, pointing her toes like a ballet dancer. "I wasn't a vomiter, but I was a drinker. I'd get out of a new design viewing and drive straight to the bottle shop."

"Past tense, see?" Linah smiles across at me.

"Ha! Uh, no. I just started to have the good sense to buy online and have it delivered." Margot laughs, her golden ringlets bouncing.

"Well, all that aside. I am so proud of you Ava. You have done something no man has ever done before. You made the decision not to be pushed around by Tony." Linah raises her glass and clinks it against mine.

"Thanks. I suppose now I am just waiting for the other shoe to drop, you know?" I look around at their elated faces. "For him to pull the rug out from underneath me with some swift maneuver I never see coming." I take a long sip of my Canadian club and ginger ale.

"You're earning the trust of your employees and it sounds like you are starting to get on the same page as Chen. I think you might surprise yourself, Ava." Jia tilts her head, appraising me.

"What?" I laugh.

"Are you wearing the Iris and Ink dress I picked out?"

"Yes! I have to say, I am loving the new wardrobe you ladies picked out for me. It makes me feel so empowered when I get dressed each morning."

"You can thank Mr Christian Louboutin for that! You're killing it in those heels girl!" Margot points to the pile of red soles we each kicked off onto the carpet between us.

"What is it about a good pair of shoes?" I shake my head.

"Not just a good pair my dear, the right pair." Linah beams. "There's a reason they are referred to as 'power pumps.'"

"Isn't that because we tower over little men all across Asia when we wear them?" Jia sniggers. The four of us burst out laughing, Margot flopping over on the floor in hysterics.

Another few cocktails later and our dinner arrives. I look around confused as the delivery drivers unpack Michelin star Italian onto the square dining table.

"Doesn't this place have a kitchen? It is a bar isn't it?" I lean over to Margot.

"Ha! Not quite, I bought this place as a warehouse to design my own couture from. I needed somewhere away from my workplace and it kind of became our secret hideout." She smiles, looking fondly around at the space.

"I love it, the speakeasy vibe is perfect. I also love that I can just be myself here." I lean back against the sofa and watch the twinkly copper pendants above.

"Grub's up,' calls Linah.

"What are you, a truck driver?" Jia hollers from the bar, mixing up some concoction in a copper shaker.

"You all still have to work tomorrow, right?" I look around at each of them. "I mean, cocktails and a girls' night on a Monday?"

The three of them stop, look at one another and back at me.

"I just mean, it's a weeknight..." I shrug, embarrassed.

"Ava! You're the youngest of us all and you're uncomfortable being out on a school night?" Linah giggles dragging me toward the table.

"This is the only place we can let loose. Invisible women are meant to be softly spoken and timid. In the real world, we can't wear ostentatious outfits or shout at the top of our lungs! Awoo!" Margot howls like a wolf.

"We meet here every Monday night to prepare for the week, as we are forced back into our little boxes." Linah hands me a set of tongs.

"Which is more literal for Jia, in her itty bitty office,' Margot hoots, pushing her glasses up her nose.

"Ha. ha." Jia quips, returning with a tray of martinis.

"I suppose I've been really lucky that Chen has been so good about me taking the reins inside HEH." I look around at their faces, wondering if that might have been the wrong thing to say.

"Speaking of your ventriloquist dummy, how is Mr Chen?" Jia asks, piling her plate with lasagne.

"As insufferable as his father? You know I once had to sit in on a finance merger he was party to and the man barely looked up from his phone the whole time,' Linah huffs, stabbing at the salad aggressively with a fork.

"Surprisingly, no. He has been very civil,' I state matter-of-factly.

"Hold up. Say what now?" Margot turns to stare at me. 'If I didn't know any better, I'd say..." She gasps, one hand frozen on the garlic bread.

"What?!" Linah squeals leaning in further.

"You like him." Margot points the garlic loaf at me accusatorially.

"Ooh! Juicier and juicier!!" Jia chuckles. "Leave the woman alone. I know the two of you are both happily married, but neither of you would have said 'no' to that face if it had have presented itself to you prior to matrimony.'

"Or that ass." Linah smirks. I stop and look between Linah and Margot. I had never considered that these women would be married.

"You both have husbands?" I look down at the salad quizzically. 'How?'

"You get all dressed up, stand in front of a Minister and say 'I DO'!" Margot laughs.

"Where did you meet men in Singapore who aren't intimidated by what you do?" Linah rolls her eyes at me.

"I mean what you really do? Do they know?"

"Know what? That we're secretly some of the most powerful people in Asia? No,' Margot sighs. 'My Riley just wouldn't get it."

"Neither would Chip." Linah shakes her head.

"Riley, Chip? What? Did you both marry Mid-Western American cattle farmers?" I stare at them.

"No silly, Riley is an ex-pat from England and Chip is..." Margot trials off.

"Well, he sort of is a cattle rancher from the US." Linah shrugs. "We met on a cruise around Alaska. It was his first time leaving mainland USA."

"Riley and I met at a football game in London." I try to envision Margot in a soccer team jersey and scarf.

"You both just married regular men. Normal people, who aren't caught up in this megalomaniac business world?" I sit down at the table, thoroughly thrown.

"Sometimes it's better spending your downtime with the Pauper than the Prince." Linah smiles at me reassuringly.

"I for one do not agree with that in the slightest. I am more than happy to date the prince and fly to Paris in his private jet for the weekend." Jia winks, taking her seat and handing out the martinis.

"To the Princes and the paupers!" Margot raises her glass.

12

By the time June arrived, I finally felt as though I was finding my feet in Singapore.

After putting Tony on notice, he has kept his head down and ruffled very few feathers in the last few weeks. Ryan and I have figured out a groove with Skype and phone dates and I'm starting to feel connected to him again. And Chen is winning the hearts of the people of Singapore after several well-received public appearances.

Standing in the crowd after one such appearance, I am joined by Abbie from PR.

"Wasn't he great? Did he tell you he wrote that speech himself?" She beams, adjusting her blonde ponytail.

"I hadn't heard. He is multi-talented 'that's for certain." I smile, looking up at Chen waving down at the crowd like he's the President.

"Now Ava, I've been meaning to catch you at a good time. It's about the ball.' Abbie looks across at me nervously.

"What about it Abbie? It is in four weeks. And we only had a meeting yesterday, so why the secrecy?" I turn to face her.

"Uh, this is awkward. As it is an event being held in a public space, I am uncertain as to who to list you as on the guest lists,' she whispers.

I stare at her. "I don't understand?" I frown.

"Well, Mr Chen is the CEO. You're not listed on any public record and the event is supposed to be for VIPs only." She stares down at her knotted hands.

"Surely I can just attend without having to be 'on the list'? Why does it have to be a big deal?" I look back up to see Chen has disappeared off the stage.

"It is a security issue, Miss Elias. Not only are we contending with HEH's usual security protocols but also the Chen family protocols,' she whispers even more softly.

"The Chen family are coming to the ball?" I whisper back. Abbie nods profusely.

Well, fuck.

"What are you two whispering about over here? You look like a pair of old gossips in the market." Chen stalks over.

"Why didn't you tell me your family are coming to the ball?" I hiss at him.

"I didn't think it mattered? Besides, it's more publicity for HEH right?" He looks from me to Abbie and back again. "Right?"

I look at Abbie, 'Just put me down as a member of the PR team.' She stares at me, eyes wide.

"What's this about?" Chen frowns.

"I apparently need a 'title' on the guest list to get into the ball because of your family's security protocols."

"What? That's ridiculous. You're the...uh...I see." He scratches his chin.

"Miss Elias, surely we can find someone you can be a plus one for?" Abbie offers. Chen's face scrunches up into a cringe.

I'm glad he also sees that as inappropriate. Me, the CEO, needing to be listed as SOMEONE ELSE'S date to get into my own ball.

"I'm sure we can find a way to get Miss Elias on the list without having to reduce her to being someone's tag-along guest. Let us think on it Abbie, we'll get back to you." Chen smiles down at her with such force she blinks, bobs a curtsey and disappears.

"A plus one? Is she kidding? It's your ball for god's sake." He hisses in my ear.

"Thanks for the support, Chen. I appreciate it. Once again it seems we are reduced to nothing but the labels we carry." I smile up at him .half-heartedly

"Speaking of labels, have you decided who you are going to wear? Four weeks until the big event!" He shrugs off his jacket as we head toward the cars.

"Who I'm wearing? What do you mean?" I look across at him confused.

"You know, how you see actors and actresses talking about their suits and gowns on the red carpet? HEH's annual ball is one of the 'events of the year' in Singapore. You've got to have a killer dress picked out." He stops to shake hands with a man and take a photo with a woman and her baby.

"You really have become a man of the people,' I observe, Xi opening the door to the car for me.

"You're avoiding the question. Do you not have a dress picked out yet?" He frowns across the back seat at me. I suddenly realise he is in my car.

"What are you doing?! Where's your car?" I sputter.

"We are all going to the same place, does it matter which car we are in?" He laughs relaxing back into the seat.

"What if the media catch us? They'll think..." I shake my head.

"Think what? That we're together?" He cocks an eyebrow at me. "And what's so wrong with that? I'll have you know that there are queues of women who'd love to be in your position right now." His smile falters when he realises what he's saying.

"Queues of women would love to be the heiress to several hundred million in fortune and unable to be publicly recognised for her efforts?"

"That came out wrong,' he sighs. I feel Xi chuckling quietly to himself in the front seat.

"Or that my faux-CEO is such a mega dreamboat that I can't be seen riding in the same car as him because it isn't possible for us to WORK together, no, I'd have to be your girlfriend,' I huff.

"I take it that's a 'no' to the dress for the ball then,' he mumbles, looking out the window.

"I'm sorry Chen. The PR, Events and Marketing teams have been working tirelessly with me to get this ball off the ground and the guest list thing is just salt in the wound." I dig around in my bag for my aluminum water bottle.

"Dreamboat,' Chen chuckles to himself.

"I beg your pardon?" I glower at him, having heard him perfectly clearly.

"Do you really think I'm a dreamboat?" He smirks across at me.

"I believe I said 'mega dreamboat'. If you're going to quote me in your diary, make sure to document it accurately,' I snark back.

"I don't believe you've ever been so complimentary toward my appearance, Miss Elias."

"Don't get used to it,' I state, deadpan.

"One could be forgiven for thinking you might be starting to warm up to me,' He peers at me sideways.

I try to keep my focus on the back of Xi's headrest.

"You know that's never been an issue,' I whisper, mostly to myself.

"You've barely looked at me or spoken to me in weeks,' he whispers back.

"I've been busy. Besides, it's not like you've gone out of your way to talk to me either. Not since..." I look down at my phone in my hands.

"Is he your husband? The uh...snow...man...guy?" Chen runs his hands through his hair.

"Ryan? No, he's no one. Well, he's not no one but he's untitled." I shrug.

"Untitled." Chen scratches his cheek contemplatively.

"We've dated on and off over the past few years, but he is currently just a friend who wants to come to Singapore to visit."

Why does that seem to just barely cover it? Also, why am I telling Chen any of this?

"Visit,' Chen chuckles to himself. "If he's coming all the way here, he's not just coming to 'visit'."

"Believe it or not Chen, my sex life is none of your concern. I highly doubt your fiancée would appreciate knowing you hijacked my car to interrogate me on my love life." I stare out the window.

"Fiancée?' Chen sputters. 'Seems no one remembered to fill me in on that little detail. Last I checked, I don't remember putting a ring on anything."

Hm, not the reaction I was expecting.

"So Lin Mei Yang is not your date to the ball?" I peer at him innocently.

"I...uh...I...about that.' Chen's hands find his hair again. "Yes." He sighs in defeat. "Mei is my date to the ball."

"And who is she wearing?" I ask conversationally.

"Vintage Valentino, I believe."

"Ah." I feign interest. "I'll be sure to steer clear of Valentino, wouldn't want to risk matching outfits on the CEO's Fiancée and...whoever I'm...meant to be."

"Ava..." Chen reaches toward me.

"Don't Chen. It's not appropriate,' I snap.

"Why are you building this wall? What happened to make you hate me? I thought we were working really well together and...I don't know...it felt like..."

"I don't hate you, Chen. How could I? After all you've done for me, for HEH. You heard the finance guys this morning, HEH is in the best position it's ever been in and that is all thanks to you."

"All I do is kiss babies in public. You're the one running the show behind closed doors. And someday you'll be running it in the light of day. Where everyone will see how brilliant you are." He reaches for my hand again, entwining his fingers through mine. "Stop this silliness, let's go back to how things were in the beginning. Can't you see what an amazing team we make?" He stares down at our fingers.

"So you're not promised to Mei?" I look up into his eyes. A sea of blue, adrift far beyond the shore.

"It's a little more complicated than that. Why can't you just let us be in this moment?" He pleads.

"Because Chen, when you have someone who believes they're 'in something' with you, you can't have 'moments' with other people." I move to pull my hand away as Chen tightens his grasp.

"If I ...If I knew that you would be 'in something' with me, then I'd make it happen." He stares at me with such determination.

"Chen, I'm not about to become a homewrecker. I don't care what the deal is with you and Mei, until you can stand in front of me and tell me you have no obligations elsewhere, I can't pretend something like this is okay." I implore him. "That is not even taking into consideration how wrong it is from the perspective of the company!"

"The company?" Chen frowns.

"I am still your boss. And you are still my beard so long as I am an invisible woman." I feel my heart become heavy.

"You want me to step down? You want me to tell the world right now? Because I will! I will call a press conference and announce to the world that none of this was my doing and that you were the brains behind it all!" He waves his free arm around like a lunatic. I can't help but laugh at his enthusiasm.

"Chen. It still doesn't change what you explained to me. The world isn't ready for HEH to have a female CEO just yet and I agree with you on that." I sigh. "Please don't make this harder than it is. Go back to the life you have planned with Mei and I will go back to mine." I look down at our entwined fingers and gently pry his off mine, one by one.

"Ava,' Chen breathes, leaning toward me.

"We're HERE!" Xi hollers from the drivers seat, breaking sharply causing Chen and I to lurch apart.

Xi, you are a lifesaver. With the tension broken, Xi raced to my door in record time ushering me into HEH, leaving Chen sitting in the car bewildered.

Walking into the lobby with Xi, I smile across at him in thanks. With a slight bow, he turns and heads back toward the car. As I turn toward the fountain and the executive elevator, Tony's voice catches my attention. I look across to see him bowing formally with another gentleman, then shaking hands and smiling broadly at one another. Tony ushers him into a public elevator and upstairs, presumably to Tony's office.

Walking into the lobby on the executive floor, I nod at Sasha as I hit her desk.

"Hi Ava, how was the speech?" Sasha smiles at me.

"It was great, same as always. Sasha, can you do me a favour? Call Tony's secretary and find out who he is meeting with right now." I smile at her in thanks and head through my door.

A few minutes later Sasha returns with a latte in hand. She places it on my coaster.

"Millie, Tony's assistant said he has a 'private appointment' booked and she is unaware of who Tony is meeting."

"Do you trust her?" I ask, wondering if Millie is covering for Tony.

"I do. She has never lied to me."

"Any chance you could go see if you can spot Tony and his guest and see if you recognise him?"

"Sure thing, I'll just go get my moustache and trench coat,' she laughs. "I'll go see Millie and see if I can identify the guy through the office window."

"You are amazing Sasha, thank you!"

Opening my calendar, I notice that one of my afternoon appointments has disappeared. I make a note in my compendium to ask Sasha where it went.

I spend the next half hour checking through my emails, answering questions related to what feels like every possible topic under the sun. From flower arrangements for the ball to signing off on compensation packages for our returned crewmen from Oman. By the time Sasha returns I feel like my brain is going to pop.

I can't even remember the last time I was left uninterrupted for 45 minutes straight.

"I have some news,' Sasha hesitates, waiting for me to look up at her. 'The man Mr Tony is meeting with is the head of the Public Housing Foundation."

"I thought the foundation was a subsidiary of HEH?" I frown.

"It is,' Sasha confirms.

"Then why haven't I met this man? Especially since we are arranging the ball in honour of the foundation?"

"That's the news. You were booked to meet with him this afternoon, but his staff called to cancel. They said he was unwell."

"Did he look unwell to you? Because he looked perfectly healthy from across the lobby." I grumble.

What on earth is going on? I don't trust Tony.

"No Miss. Oh, that was probably rhetorical wasn't it?" Sasha shrugs.

"Did they rebook with us?"

"No."

"The ball is in four weeks and they won't rebook to meet with me?"

"I can try and call them again to see if anything has opened up?" Sasha offers.

"Don't worry about it. I'll talk to Chen, see if he can find out what Tony is up to." I thank her and send her on her way.

What are you up to with the Foundation Tony? It can't be good. Maybe it has something to do with the 'announcement' Tony had Chen mention at the press conference a few weeks ago.

"Has he met with anyone else suspicious?" Tari asks, passing me a tall cocktail from across the bar.

"Not that I know of, but I also haven't been watching him too closely either. He has been flying under the radar these past few weeks,' I sigh, sipping my cocktail. 'I shouldn't have taken my eye off him."

"You're running a giant company. You can't be everywhere at once." She snaps her tea towel at me, causing me to jump.

I laugh, "I guess you are right. It doesn't change the fact that I am certain he is up to no good." I look around, suddenly noticing that it is extremely quiet around us for a Thursday afternoon. I spot Seal stretched out on a lounger by the balcony.

"Not a bad life they have, is it?" Tari chuckles following my gaze.

"I suppose not. Especially when I am highly doubtful anyone will ever try anything when it comes to me!" I laugh.

"Who'd wanna hurt you? Besides, it's not like many people even know who you are anyway." Her smile falters, 'Sorry, that came out wrong."

"Don't worry about it, it's not like it isn't the truth." I smile across at her.

"Excuse me!!" An American accent, followed by what sounded like clapping came from the direction of the infinity pool. I see Tari peering past me toward the gate. I turn to follow her gaze, spotting a tall bikini-clad blonde waving her arms over at us, "Can I have a cocktail?"

"Is the talking to us?" I ask.

"Uh, yup. Clearly she can't read." Tari nods toward the nearby sign No Glass in the Pool. 'I'll be right back."

I sit in peace enjoying the quiet afternoon breeze sipping my passionfruit cocktail. I started the morning so early, I decided I deserved the afternoon off.

A pair of businessmen arrive at the bar, taking a seat on the opposite corner. One of the male bartenders who had been floating around comes across to serve them.

"Ladies, first." One man nods in my direction.

"Oh, I've been tended, thank you,' I smile back, picking up my drink to clarify. I feel rather than see, Seal observing closely from the lounger.

"What brings you into town, Miss?" The other asks, loosening his tie and unbuttoning his shirt collar. *South African?*

"Business. And yourself?" I reply politely, wondering how long Tari is going to be occupied by Malibu Barbie.

"Business? Is that so? What kind of business would that be?" He leans toward me, down the bar. His friend watching us with deep curiosity.

Crap, probably should have just said I was on vacation.

"The personal kind."

"Ah, don't be coy! A lovely lady who is able to spend her afternoons in an upmarket bar must have quite the story." He winks at me, his mouth hanging open slightly.

Good lord. These two must have been drinking before they got here.

A warm presence appears behind me, a hand gently resting at my waist.

I didn't even see Seal move! Man, he is good.

"My apologies darling, I got caught up. How was your day?" Chen's voice drips like warm honey, just loud enough for my new friends to overhear.

"It's no trouble,' I turn and simper up at him in surprise, "I was just making some new acquaintances." I wave my hand generally toward the other end of the bar. Swirling blue eyes ensnare mine. His closeness, his hand at my waist, the way he smells. I feel the blush rising in my cheeks. He reaches down, brushing the backs of his fingers across my cheek.

"You're flushed- too warm or too much cocktail?" He cocks an eyebrow, a cheeky grin spreading across his face.

"You're Mr Chen, of Huynh Enterprises Holdings and Chen Industries!" Mr Wink sputters from the other end of the bar.

"The one and only,' Chen replies, his megawatt smile dawning across at the men.

"It is an honour. What you have done with Huynh EH has been nothing short of genius! We just came from a conference in the USA where your revenue to profits ratio was discussed. Under your leadership, it has grown exp...onentially,' he burps out.

"We were all getting ready for a hostile takeover when we heard the rumours about a woman in charge!" The other slaps his knee, howling with laughter.

"Thank you, gentlemen, enjoy your afternoon,' Chen nods toward them, catching Tari's eye as she returns to the bar.

"What can I get for you?" She asks when she stops in front of us eyeing Chen curiously before turning her gaze on me.

"I don't mind, whatever you feel like making." I smile across at her. 'Chen? Also, how did you know where to find me?" I turn to look at him.

"Water." He waves dismissively at Tari. "I got your message saying you needed to talk and so I asked Sasha." I roll my eyes.

"What did you want to discuss?" He takes a seat beside me, our knees touching.

"Tony. I think he's up to something,' I state.

"Tony isn't up to anything,' Chen says flatly.

"How do you know? I haven't even told you what I know yet?" I frown across at him.

"I've had someone keeping tabs on him. He hasn't met with anyone who isn't a genuine business associate since I started here. Tony isn't up to anything." He levels his gaze at me.

Why do I feel like I'm being told off?

"How can you be sure he isn't up to anything though? Just because he's meeting with real people doesn't mean he isn't being shady,' I state quietly.

"You sound like a conspiracy theorist. I would tell you if there is something going on and there isn't. You haven't been in the game as long as I have, you don't know what you're looking for or what you're seeing."

Tari hands over our drinks and takes up her usual post opposite me, wiping glasses. I'm about to introduce her to Chen when he interrupts.

"Can we help you?" He states flatly. "We are having a private conversation here."

I look around confused.

Who is he talking to? I realise he is glaring at Tari.

"Chen..." I frown.

"It's okay Ava, I'm used to it. After all I'm just the help, right?" Tari shrugs, turning to step away.

"How dare you address her so informally. She is Miss Elias to you,' Chen glowers.

Tari turns to stare at him.

"You know what, you were right Ava, he is a jerk,' She smiles at me.

"Tari!" I choke. I can't believe she just said that to his face.

"I beg your pardon?" Chen thunders across at her standing up and towering over her, even from across the bar. I put my hand on his chest, trying fruitlessly to push him back into his seat.

"Chen, Tari. Enough." I bang my glass back onto the bar top so hard I worry momentarily it is going to shatter in my hand. Eyes around the bar and neighbouring restaurant watch our trio curiously.

"Tari, be nice. Chen, stop being such a brat." I admonish them both.

"You frequent this bar so often that you are on first name terms with the waitress?" Chen leers.

"Bar. Tender,' Tari corrects, standing her ground.

"Do you have a drinking problem?" Chen turns to glare at me.

"Excuse me? What is wrong with you? No, I do not have a drinking problem.' I hiss, 'Tari is my friend. I come here so we can catch up when we're both too busy with work."

"I'm sure she is extremely busy what with slicing limes and refilling ice trays. Did she mysteriously become your friend before or after Winnie's fortune appeared?" Chen smirks, dropping his voice.

"Why don't you say that to my face?" Tari arcs up, throwing her tea towel down on the bench.

"Chen!" I glare at him. "How dare you imply--"

"It's okay Ava, this guy is just another one on a long list of assholes who think they are far too good to be seen fraternising with the help. For your information, Sir, I've known Ava for years. If you'll excuse me, I have ice trays to refill." She turns on her heel and stalks down the staff hall.

"So much for 'the man of the people',' I spit. Launching myself from my stool, I follow Tari down the hall. I spot her near a trolley stacked with napkins and utensils.

"Tari I am so, so sorry. I had no idea he would treat someone like that. I've never seen that side of him before." I bow my head. ashamed.

"What are you apologising for? You didn't do anything wrong. Silver spooners often are First Class assholes.' She smiles at me reassuringly. 'I promise not to take it to heart.' I give her a big hug. 'Why don't you come over for dinner this weekend? You said you have Sunday off, right?"

"I wish I could, but I'm supposed to be taking my girlfriend out. We are trying to 'work through' our differences." She cringes. I scrunch up my face in mock disgust. "Ugh, then I guess I'll see you here on Saturday for Alcoholics Not-So-Anonymous." We walk back down the hall, arm in arm laughing like lunatics. I air kiss her on each cheek and nod at Seal, heading for the elevators. Seal and I stand awkwardly waiting for the doors to close when a hand grabs one door from the outside. Chen.

Ugh. Go away asshole.

"Okay Navy Pup, you can get the next one,' Chen steps into the lift. Suddenly the space feels very crowded. Seal looks to me and back at Chen. I nod and hold my arm out to keep the door open for him to exit. The elevator descends 10 floors before Chen speaks.

"I'm sure you're keeping count." His hands find his hair.

"I don't know what you're talking about."

"How many apologies I've been responsible for,' he sighs. I turn to look at him, his eyes yet another sea of turmoil.

"Chen, I thought you were better than that?" I huff looking down at my feet.

"I didn't realise you knew each other."

"Until you did, and even then, you continued to insult not only Tari but my intelligence for having her as a friend."

"I am not used to people of our calibre being 'friends' with the staff."

"Our calibre? What the fuck Chen? You never knew me before Winnie. Tari did. The only Ava you've ever known is Ava Elias-Huynh, with the manicures, labels and the $2000 shoes." I'm so angry I feel the heat rising in my face. 'How dare you come in and ruin my afternoon of peace, insult my friend and make out like you have my best interests at heart."

"Ava..." Chen implores. He tries to lift my chin to look at him, his fingers burning my skin. I pull my face away.

"Just leave me alone Chen. We are two completely different people from completely different worlds. I just never realised you were this big a snob." To enunciate my point, I bend down and pull off my heels standing in the elevator in bare feet.

Oh god, that feels good. I've been dying to do that all day.

"I don't know what you want from me, Chen. If you had met me by chance in the street, or back in Australia before I was your boss you wouldn't have taken a second look. You and I both know that is true. So why is it any different now that I have money?"

"I want you to meet my family,' Chen blurts.

"What?" I stare at him deadpan.

"Then maybe you will understand what this is like for me? My life has always been planned out before me, without any say on what I want. You might be right, perhaps I mightn't have taken notice of you when you were no-one but that's only because I would never have been permitted to marry someone of such inferior birth." He reaches for my hand.

"Marry? Inferior birth?" I step back as far away from him as the elevator will allow.

Good lord, this elevator ride has never felt this long before.

"Yes, but you aren't inferior anymore. With HEH in your hands, you would now be considered suitable in the eyes of my family!" He smiles across at me reassuringly.

"Have you lost your mind?" I stare at him feeling like my eyes are about to boggle out of my skull.

"Think of the empire we could build together, with HEH and CI between us, we'd be unstoppable!"

"You need to stop before I vomit." I hold my hand up. 'We are not having this conversation. You did not honestly just use HEH as a bargaining chip for why we should be in a relationship. Not only that, but I would never, ever date someone who is rude to waitstaff."

The elevator blessedly hits the ground floor where Seal is already waiting for us.

The man is etherial.

Not giving Chen a second look, I stalk out of the elevator and across the lobby, skyscraper Louboutins in hand.

"Turns out everyone's expectations were right. Chen is nothing but a giant elitist snob,' I garble down at Ryan's face on my laptop.

"Ava, don't you have to work tomorrow?" Ryan smiles up at me from my lap.

"Yah,' I sigh, mashing another oven-roasted potato gem into my mouth.

"Perhaps you should get some rest then? And hydrate!" He chuckles.

"I s'pose you're right. But Ryan, what do I do? Everyone is so in love with him and he won't listen to me about Tony." I pout.

"Look, I've got to go, my shift is about to start. Why don't we talk about it over the weekend? I've been meaning to ask you if there are some dates that might work for me to come and visit you?"

"Really!?" I beam.

"Really. I've got to go, I'll talk to you soon!" He blows me a kiss and disappears.

I shut the laptop and look around aimlessly. Brushing crumbs of fried potato out of my lap and onto a plate, I stand and wander to the kitchen. Deciding I need a cup of tea, brownie and a long soak in the tub, I go about settling into my evening at home alone.

After dragging off my potato oil-stained sweatpants and tank top, I dip my toes into the water.

Hm. This is exactly what I need for the evening. A drama-free space to unwind and think about where to take Ryan when he comes to visit.

Without warning, the panel beside the bathtub flashes in the candlelight, throwing off the ambience.

What the hell is that?

There on the screen appeared a man wearing a hooded jumper and giant 'I'm a celebrity' sunglasses. I hit the 'entry' button.

It is 9 pm. Are you kidding me?

I step onto the bathmat and wipe off my legs, drag my bathrobe on and stomp out to the elevator bay. The elevator ascends painstakingly slowly. I pace around the space, my bare feet cold on the marble. Eventually the elevator arrives, a dishevelled looking Korean pop star standing before me.

"Chen. What the hell are you doing here?" I huff at him.

"Why are you shouting?" He holds up his hand and shields his eyes from the hallway lights.

"You're wearing sunglasses at 9 pm. What are you doing at my apartment at 9 pm? And what on earth are you wearing?" I eye his ripped denim jeans and grey hoodie more closely. Abercrombie and Fitch.

"I came to see you. I told my family 'I'm out!'" He shouts, imitating a mike drop between us.

"I beg your pardon?"

"I had a couple of drinks for dutch courage and I told my parents that I don't love Mei and that I'm out. Out of the family business and I want the family out of mine." He beams across at me, swaying slightly.

"Chen. Sit. Before you fall over and break something." I point to the floor. Like an obedient puppy, he leans down and sits crossed-legged on the floor leaning against the external elevator door.

He looks up at me, his hair falling down to frame his face from under his hood, glasses askew on his nose.

"Why is it so bright in here?" He whines.

"Don't move a muscle." I turn toward the kitchen, stopping only at the control panel to dim the lights in the elevator bay.

Returning to Chen, I find him studying his hands, hood back, sunglasses clearly having fallen off and slid across the floor. His long silky tresses catching the light. I hand him a big glass of Hydralyte and a cucumber. I think I read somewhere cucumber is supposed to be good for hangovers.

"Eat this and drink that." I pass him one into each hand.

"It's pink,' he sniffs it suspiciously.

When the Hydralyte was gone and he'd eaten half the cucumber, Chen eyed me warily.

"I'm sorry for barging into your home. I know it is rather unbecoming." He shrugged.

"That's a big word for a guy who stumbled in here half an hour ago looking like a drunken K-Pop star." I roll my eyes, sitting down on the tiles opposite him. "What's really going on with you? We both have to be

at the 8 am meeting tomorrow, we have to be sharp."
I roll my eyes.

"How come you get to drink cocktails on a
Thursday night and I don't?" He whines.

"Uh, because I was about to take a bath and go to
bed, not stay out until last call." I suddenly remember
I'm wearing a bathrobe and adjust to double-check
nothing is peeping out. I feel a blush rise in my cheeks.

"Chen, what are you doing here?" I implore him.
'I'm dead tired and I just want this day to end."

"I've never met anyone like you. The way you
challenge me and push me to be better, not just at
HEH but in the real world too.

'I don't know what came over me today, I'm not
usually that jerk-off who is rude to waitstaff." He hangs
his head, staring at the cucumber. As though realising
he hadn't finished eating it, he starts munching on it
again.

"Chen, I'm sorry for pushing you away. But I have
explained myself as clearly as I believe is possible. Are
you sure you're not just drawn to me because I'm the
first woman to say 'no' to you?"

"You can't tell me you don't feel it too." He looks
across at me with deep intensity. "That you don't feel
the crackle between us, that you don't notice how well
we work together?" A hint of a smile at the corner of
his lips.

"Are you really telling me you stepped away from
the Chen family for good tonight? That you're
renouncing your right to Chen Industries and a future
with Mei?" I frown, finding it hard to believe.

"I left a voicemail on my dad's phone." He nods
confidently.

"A voicemail?" I stare at him.

"Yup, now I can't take it back. Not for anything, I can't change my mind. It's too late now."

"Chen, if you were that uncertain about it, then why did you do it?" I shake my head.

"Because I needed to do it, so I would know how it feels."

"And how do you feel? Free? Invincible?" I offer.

"Stupid. I realised it was a mistake the second I hung up." He mutters begrudgingly.

"Then why are you here and not at your parents" house explaining that it was a drunken prank or something and trying to get out of it?" I look across at him wondering where the man I first met went. Confident, strong, capable.

"You've turned my world upside down Ava. I go into the office each day with the hope that I'll see you. That I'll watch you laugh or hear you shout at me. I don't attend every meeting you host because I'm interested, I'm there because you are, and I want to be there for you." He smiles glumly across at me.

"I had no idea,' I breathe.

"You wouldn't let me tell you,' he chuckles under his breath.

"That aside, Chen, you can't throw your whole life away for this. It isn't worth it."

"How can you say that? Here I am telling you I believe you are worth it and you're still saying no?" He shakes his head, flabbergasted.

"Despite the money and the labels and the shoes, Chen, the sun rises and I am still a nobody. That is never going to change. Do you really want to throw away the life you have worked for, to become a social pariah?" I lean across the hall to pat his hand. "You and your family deserve better than that."

"So how we feel doesn't matter?" He grabs my hand, stroking my palm with his thumb. I've gotta hand it to him, he's got amazing reflexes for someone who smells like a brewery.

"Chen, what you're asking for; what you're offering is impossible. You can't just give up your family.

'Can you imagine what kind of heat I'd cop from the world for being the wench who caused you to do that? On top of one day being the woman who usurps you of the CEO gig at HEH?"

"I suppose I hadn't thought of what it would mean for you." He draws my hand to his lips, grazing his them across my knuckles. "I was so caught up in what our world would look like, I didn't stop to think about how the world would look at us. At you." He sighs, his warm breath tickling the hairs on the back of my hand. I lean forward and run my fingers through his silky hair.

"Black as a raven,' I whisper, feeling the surprising softness between my fingers. I gently tuck it behind his ear, Chen nuzzling his face into my hand. "You don't know the real me Chen. Only this corporate personification of Ava." I whisper, feeling his eyes once again burning into my soul.

"Then let me meet the real Ava. It's only fair." He inches closer until we are only centimeters apart. I can't decide if I want to kiss him or run away and hide. Kissing him wouldn't be so bad, would it? He's here, in Winnie's apartment. Anything could happen if I wanted it to. Right?

"You're overthinking this,' Chen chuckles a rich sexy sound, he lifts his hand and touches a fingertip to the frown between my brows. "It's getting late, I should probably go anyway." He smiles across at me, his megawatt panty-dropping smile. I momentarily forget how to breathe. Staring at his lips, I'm entranced.

"Have lunch with me?' Chen whispers, his fingers sweeping my hair behind my shoulder. "I'll take you to my favourite hawker centre and show you the real me."

"The real you?" I breathe, he is so close- his body heat and scent a heady combination.

"Just Ava and Chen. Eating the cheapest food available in Singapore. No gimmicks, no fine dining, you can even go barefoot if you like." His eyes grow wide, imploring me. I giggle across at him.

"Isn't that rather unbecoming?" I smirk, quoting him from earlier.

"I'd do just about anything right now if it meant watching you smile." I see my sadness and longing reflected in his face.

"Okay,' I breathe, a mix of excitement and relief flooding through me.

"Okay?' Chen's smile dawns slowly, 'Really?"

"Really,' I smile back shyly.

"Then I guess my job here is done. I should let you get your beauty sleep,' Chen sighs without moving. Knowing I may never have another chance, I reach up and stroke his face, drawing a finger from his brow down his sharp cheekbone to his jaw. I feel the muscle in his jaw tense as my hand lingers. Dropping my hand to his chest I gently push him away.

"It is time you go,' I whisper staring at my hand on his sternum.

Chen reaches down and picks up my hand, reaching it up to his lips, he plants a gentle kiss on the inside of my palm.

"Sweet dreams, Miss Elias,' he whispers against my palm

13

The last few weeks before the ball became a blur of party planning, menu tasting, attempted dress shopping and floral arrangements.

Sitting in the conference room one Monday for what felt like the 8th hour in a row, staring at tablecloth selection and china patterns was making my eyes hurt.

Sasha ducks in and hands me a latte, disappearing just as quickly as she arrived.

"So, Ava, what do you think?" the umpteenth person from the events team looks encouragingly at me.

"I like it just as much as I liked the last 'setup' you showed me." I smile. 'What was wrong with the last four options?"

"We just want this year's ball to be extra-special." She nods enthusiastically whilst clapping her hands.

Someone needs to switch her to decaf.

"Okay, well I am happy with any of them. As long as there is somewhere for people to sit, eat, dance and drink I think it'll be okay. Just make sure to keep the cost of throwing the party as low as possible so we have a sizable donation for the Foundation.

'No point hosting a fundraiser if all the raised funds go into paying for solid gold cutlery." I laugh, noticing the slightly nauseated looks on the faces around me.

"No. Don't tell me that we aren't raising any funds because of the cost of the event itself?" I stare around the room horrified.

"Miss Elias, the kind of people who attend fundraisers have a certain expectation of what they are going to get for their money', one woman states, hidden from sight by a large floral centrepiece.

"Not to worry, even if we don't raise funds from the tickets, the real funds are raised when the attendees arrive and place their donation cheques into the box." Nods another, earrings dangling furiously.

"Okay, well you are the experts,' I sigh, watching them packing up the samples and ushering out the door. I lean forward, resting my head on my arms.

"Have you found a dress yet?" Sasha asks hesitantly from the door.

"No." I huff. 'I have tried every major store in town and no one will sell me anything because they 'are already dressing someone going to the ball'." I look up to see Sasha's horrified look.

"Ava, the ball is in two weeks! You need to find a dress, pronto!" She walks in and sits down beside me. 'If you can't find someone to buy one from why don't you get a dressmaker to go to the Penthouse and dress you?"

"A dressmaker?" I frown at her.

"Yes! I read somewhere when the penthouse was for sale that there is some kind of dressing room or tailor room or something in your house where you can have someone come in and sew a unique creation just for you!"

"Huh. You might be onto something." I smile across at her.

"I don't want to hurry you, but if you want to get to the IW dinner on time, you need to leave with Xi in the next 15 minutes." She looks down at her watch.

"Ah crap,' I sigh as I scramble out the door.

"Ava, we have decided you need to host a pre-ball party! We can come and help you get ready and enjoy a couple of glasses of champagne before you head off, then we can all enjoy watching your red-carpet arrival on TV!" Margot kicks her heels off and flops down on the lounge beside me.

"Why does this ball feel more like a wedding?' I laugh, accepting a cosmopolitan from Jia, 'today I had to confirm the final place settings and floral centrepieces."

"Who have you picked to do your hair and makeup?" Linah pipes up from the futon.

"I haven't even found a dress yet, I'm nowhere near thinking about hair and makeup!" I chuckle before taking nervous gulps of my cosmo.

"What?!" Jia and Linah exclaim in unison.

"What?" I look around innocently. 'I've still got two weeks to find something." I shrug.

"Ava. You cannot be serious. The kind of people who will be attending this thing will wear designer couture,' Jia states, unable to keep the horror from her face.

"Think the Met Gala extravagance, but less NYC chic and more Trooping the Colour,' Linah adds.

"Hun, you really have to find a dress to that ball. Take it from someone in the industry, it is all anyone will ever remember about the day Ava Elias-Huynh was launched on society." Margot nods gravely.

"You are absolutely right." I turn to stare at Margot. "You are in the industry. Except I'm not being 'launched' remember."

I've got an idea.

"You should dress me,' I state confidently.

"What!?" Margot dribbles cosmo down her chin. 'No."

"What do you mean no? It is the perfect way to launch your label! You said so yourself, the people you work for will never do it, so why not design a couture gown for all the world to see?" I smile at her, passing across a polkadot napkin.

"Two weeks to come up with a show-stopping Foundation ballgown? Are you crazy?" Margot shouts, standing up and storming up the stairs to the loft.

"Well, that went about as well as I'd expect." Linah sighs, Jia nodding.

"Why wouldn't she want to design something for the ball? It could be a major launching point for Margot?" I look at the others, frowning.

"Sometimes Ava, when you've been invisible so long, it is hard to imagine walking out into the spotlight again." Linah smiles reassuringly at me.

"I'll be right back,' I excuse myself and follow in Margot's wake.

The loft space had the same ambience as downstairs. All copper tones and warm lighting with dizzyingly high vaulted ceilings. The only difference was instead of a bar, there sat rows and rows of shelving with spools of fabric stacked on top of one another. Four different size and gender dressmaker's mannequins sat on a podium in the centre of the room, each in a different state of undress. The far wall stood covered in drawings, sketches and fabric samples. I wander over to take a closer look. Some elegant evening gowns, men's suits and vests.

"They aren't finished concepts,' Margot sighs as she comes to stand beside me.

"Margot these are incredible,' I state in awe.

"Ava, I can't do what you're asking me to. The complexity and level of expectation in these gowns are far beyond anything I've ever made for a paying client before." She looks down at her drink.

"But you've made gowns before, just not for sale?" I ask curiously.

"Sure, who doesn't dream of dressing a princess! I may design suits all day, but I have quite the collection of costumes for hire. I just don't make things to order,' she shrugs.

"Maybe I could hire one of your costume gowns?" I smile across at her.

"Oh no, they are either medieval or flappers and gangsters. You couldn't wear any of those to the ball,' she giggles.

"I don't want anything extravagant. I just want something simple, elegant and the littlest bit sexy." I shrug, 'Would that be something you might do?"

"I don't know. Two weeks! I wouldn't know where to start." She sits back against the edge of the table beside us.

"I think I found the shoes I might wear if I find the right dress. Wanna see?" I smile, bumping her with my shoulder.

"I'd love to,' she giggles.

I pull out my phone and open the photo reel. I took a few pictures after I got them home from the store. They were just far too pretty to leave there. The Krystal Du Desert heels by Christian Louboutin stood proudly, with silver studding across the strappy toe and black silk-satin ankle ties knotted into beautiful big bows.

"Ava, these are stunning,' Margot gasps. She takes the phone, swiping through the images, looking at the shoes from this way and that.

"You know what, I think I've got an idea." She smiles broadly across at me. Handing me back the phone, she reaches across the table and picks up a measuring tape. 'But first, I need to know what I'm working with."

On Tuesday morning Sasha meets me outside the elevator, latte in hand.

"I've shortlisted the best candidates who I can find and who are still available for hair and makeup for the ball." She passes me the latte. "I'll email them through with links to their work and websites. You should also probably find a back-up dress in case yours isn't ready in time,' she adds quietly.

"My dress will be fine, I have hope. Thanks for this Sasha." I nod, raising my latte in thanks.

"Also, one other thing. Um. Mr Chen came past and told me you had an urgent lunch meeting and that I had to cancel any plans you had over lunch today or for the afternoon." She looks down at her shoes.

"No problem Sasha, I appreciate you letting me know."

"Wait, you really don't mind?" She smiles up at me.

"I can't say no to him, he's the CEO." I roll my eyes.

We giggle for a moment by her desk when the elevator pings. Millie from Tony's office appears.

"Sasha, you ready for brunch?" Millie smiles at Sasha.

"Oh, um." Sasha looks across at me.

"Don't worry, I'll be fine! As long as Tony won't miss you?" I smile across at Millie.

"Oh no, he's in a meeting with Mr White from DWD and trust me when those two get to talking there is no separating them! I should know, it's their third meeting in as many days." She loops her arm through Sasha's and heads for the elevator.

Third meeting in as many days. Well, well. Who is this Mr White from DWD?

As soon as I get my laptop fired up at Winnie's desk, I open the web browser. I type in "White, DWD Singapore" and wait for the results to populate. I hang my jacket in the closet nook and grab a bottle of sparkling water from the mini-fridge.

Returning to the computer, I sit down and scroll through the results. One news headline catches my eye; "DWD Singapore announce $10bn deal in luxury housing". I click on the link. A large picture of a white-haired man standing before scaled models of extravagant looking buildings appears. I skim through the article. It essentially states that this DW Developers is looking to make a significant land purchase on which to build these insanely unaffordable luxury condos.

How peculiar. I wonder if this is the same Mr White, Millie was talking about.

I email myself a copy of the link and open it on my phone. With the photo of this Mr White in hand, I stalk out of my office determined to catch a glimpse of Tony's visitor.

Having 'casually' strolled past Tony's door twice, unable to get a look at anyone inside, I decide to find an alternate approach. I catch the elevator to the restaurant floor and find Sasha and Millie.

"Oh, Ava. Sorry, have we been gone too long?" Sasha asks worriedly, checking her watch.

"Not at all! I just wanted to ask Millie if she has seen this 'Mr White'? Or if she knows the nature of his business with Mr Tony." I look between them.

"Oh, Miss Elias I am sorry, Tony hasn't introduced me to Mr White yet. He always meets him and takes him to the conference rooms downstairs. They have only been acquaintances since sometime last year?" She looks at me quizzically.

"Just before Winnie became ill?"

"Uh, I guess so?" She offers.

"Thank you ladies, enjoy your brunch." I smile at them in turn before heading to the counter to order another latte and a cinnamon scroll. Millie has never met the guy and Tony's been meeting with him more frequently, in private. That sounds suspicious. Why is Tony meeting with a Developer?

Maybe he's buying an apartment off the plan.

I return to my office and busy myself with writing notes for Chen's speech for the Ball. The PR team will review it, but I wanted to add some more personal touches. Tari had been reading through more of Winnie's journals and sent me a few tidbits as she stumbled across them. She decided to commence them chronologically, reading from the first book through to the missing one that I was still unable to lay my hands on. One note she sent me from Winnie's early journals included an anecdote about why he decided to form the Foundation. I transcribe the story from Tari's text message into the document.

"...and from that day on, I realised I could change people's lives for the better." I finish, reading the final sentence aloud.

"Planning on global domination?" Chen's chuckle draws my attention back to the doorway.

"How do you always manage to do that?" I ask smiling up at him.

"Do what?" He asks, sauntering closer to my desk.

"Sneak up on me?" I shake my head.

"Perhaps because your chair is facing the wrong way." He points toward the window.

"I like it this way. Perhaps I just need to get you a bell so I can hear you coming." I giggle.

"Are you ready for lunch?" He stops as he reaches the desk.

"I am, seems my schedule has been cleared for the day,' I smirk up at him.

"Are you smirking at me, Miss Elias?" He grins back.

"Certainly not, that would be rude." I giggle.

We ride in Xi's BBSUV in peaceful silence. The hawker centre Chen likes is apparently a 10-minute drive out from the centre of town. I kick my heels off and swap into ballet flats, relishing the blood flow returning to my toes.

"Why do women wear those? They don't look particularly comfortable." Chen observes.

"'It hurts to be beautiful',' I quote my grandfather. "Besides I like how they make me feel."

"Like your toes are going to fall off?" Chen grins.

"Like I can conquer the world,' I state confidently.

We come to a stop outside a garden filled with palm fronds.

"Welcome to Newton Circus." Chen smiles across at me as we climb out of the car. "I had a nanny who used to bring me here as a child. She said it was important for me to learn what life is like for people 'not born into ivory towers'." He pushes his large sunglasses up his nose and takes my hand. I follow him jovially through the marketplace. The sights and smells overwhelming me. Chilli crab, peanut satay, that strange fried carrot dish they call 'carrot cake'. I smile at the locals as I pass by, used to the stares I attract by now.

"You're quite the spectacle, Miss Elias,' Chen whispers, his warm breath tickling my ear.

"This happened the last time I was in Singapore too. I had so many people stop me and ask for photos because of my white skin and red hair." I laugh, remembering it like it was yesterday. "I was so confused to start with because I thought they wanted me to take a photo of them!"

"Because it couldn't possibly be your radiant beauty that attracts them?" He chuckles. I roll my eyes up at him.

"I do recall you mentioning you enjoy this beverage?" He leads me toward a stall selling just one product, bright green lime juice.

"Yes! I've been dreaming of this for weeks! The last one I had was at Satay by the Bay." I look down at the rows and rows of cups filled to the brim. Chen converses with the lady in the stall, passing over cash in exchange for two cups.

"Was that Mandarin?" I ask him, taking the paper cover off the straw.

"A somewhat bastardised version I suppose. The dialects change depending on where in Singapore you are." He shrugs, taking a sip of his drink.

We wander in the tranquility, observing the stalls, watching their occupants frying, stirring and chopping their goods. I sip my lime drink with satisfaction. It tastes like Singapore to me. Sweet and a little tangy, it is unlike any lime I have ever found in Australia.

"Are you hungry yet?" Chen smiles down at me, taking my hand again.

"I think I am." I smile back, squeezing his hand.

Is it wrong to be holding his hand? Is it more wrong how much I am enjoying it? I haven't seen Ryan in person for almost a year, but is our relationship kind of implied at this point?

"You're overthinking again." Chen reaches up with our joined hands and pokes my frown with his index finger.

"Sorry. What do you recommend first? Or do you want to grab a whole bunch of things and have a picnic?" I place a chaste kiss on the back of his hand before dropping them back to our side. I pray that will be enough to stop him asking what I'm thinking about.

We order a few dishes from different vendors before our hands are full. Finding a table, we lay everything out before us. Satay skewers and peanut sauce, chicken in garlic and soy, duck pancake rolls, white pepper crab, steamed lemongrass rice and a jug of lime juice.

Chen jumps up to grab napkins and chopsticks from a nearby vendor. I smile at him fondly, watching him converse easily with the locals.

Why can't he be this guy all the time? This considerate, thoughtful, regular guy? I haven't seen an ounce of snob in him today.

Is it possible for the Prince to also play the pauper?

I sip on my iced lime drink, watching Chen contemplatively when he turns and catches me staring at him.

"Didn't your mother ever tell you it's rude to stare?" He grins at me, tucking a wayward strand of hair behind his ear.

"Must have missed that lesson." I tease. 'This smells incredible. I could eat in the Hawker centres for the rest of my life; this food is so good."

We eat in companionable silence, sharing our dishes and observing the locals going about their day. The lunch rush begins to pack in around us and within half an hour the place is standing room only.

I look around at our table with guilt, realising it could seat six but it is just us spread out greedily.

"Should we pack up and let someone else have the table?" I smile across at Chen. He picks up the lime jug and empties it into our cups.

"Miss Elias, I do believe you might be right." He begins packing away the plates and containers before us, when a short greying woman stomps over flapping her apron at us. Chen holds his hands up in defeat, the woman grouching in some kind of Mandarin tirade. Chen offers me his free hand as we leave the table, sipping our juice.

"Was she unhappy we were tidying?" I laugh up at Chen quizzically.

"She said we would do it wrong and to get out of her way." He chuckles down at me, placing a kiss on my hair.

"I love how different the culture is here. So unique. By the way, how much was all of that?"

"About SG$25. Why? Are you going to go all 'Miss Independence' on me and insist on paying half?"

I laugh up at him, 'No, I think you're good for it. I am always surprised at how affordable food is in this city. That's all."

We stroll lazily around the markets, hand in hand, looking at different handmade wares for sale. Candles, trinkets, scarves, jewellery. The occasional faux designer stall with sunglasses and handbags. Out of the blue, my phone begins to ring, I drop Chen's hand to dig around in my purse. The office number appears on the screen.

"Sasha?" I answer.

"Ava, sorry to disturb, I just thought you should know Mr White just left the conference room where he was meeting Mr Tony." She whispers down the phone.

"Why are you whispering?" I whisper back.

"It just felt necessary. I'll see you tomorrow." She hangs up. I stare at my phone in my hand; 3.15 pm.

White was with Tony for almost 5 hours. Good lord, what are they up to? Are they designing Tony a condo from the ground up?

I frown down at my phone. Chen's voice drags me back to the present.

"Who was whispering down the phone at you?" He smiles curiously.

"Sasha, she was just updating me on...something." I frown again.

"Care to share?' Chen asks, moving to poke my frown line again. I duck out of his reach and chew my lip hesitantly. 'It clearly has you frustrated, why don't you tell me what's going on?"

"I don't want you to get mad. You've already told me to drop it once." I chew my lip harder.

"So I guess it's about Tony then?" He shakes his head, his hands finding his hair. "I told you he isn't up to anything."

"But this is new, it only happened this morning." I look across at him, feeling the tension rolling off him in waves.

I'm never going to convince him otherwise. He will never believe my gut over his PI who has been essentially stalking Tony for months.

"You know what, never mind. I'm just being silly." I smile up at him cautiously. Chen seems to nod to himself before taking my hand again.

We spent the rest of the afternoon discussing our lives, childhoods, hopes, dreams. All that normal first date talk. I didn't broach the topic of Tony again and we steered strongly clear of any discussion related to Huynh or HEH.

As the sun began to dip toward the horizon, we decided to call it a day. Xi and I dropped Chen back at the office before returning home.

Turning to open his door, Chen pauses one hand on the door handle. He turns back and looks earnestly at me. For the longest moment I think he is going to lean over and kiss me. He raises his hand, tucks my hair gently behind my ear and whispers, "Until tomorrow."

And then he was gone.

"How was your uh...lunch Miss Ava?" Xi asks conversationally from the drivers seat. I hear Seal snort from the passenger side.

"It was very pleasant." I offer.

That was neutral right?

"Did you tell him about Tony's shady meetings?" Seal chuckles, earning himself an ear cuff from Xi.

"Chen reiterated to me that he has had someone watching Tony and he does not believe there is anything untoward going on,' I state evenly.

"We all know that man's a weasel. Why is Chen protecting him?" Seal snaps, ducking under Xi's hand the second time.

"It is not our place to have opinions on the goings-on within HEH, Mr Seal. You would do well to remember that." Xi chastises him.

"But you would tell me wouldn't you, Xi? If you knew something was going on? I mean, if you were talking to the other drivers and picked up anything that might help me?" I frown toward the back of Xi's seat. "Right?"

"Miss it is not our place to interfere." Xi clears his throat.

"I understand. You all have reputations to protect right?" I sigh, "I mean, if something were to happen to me, you'd all need to be able to get jobs and no one will hire a snitch."

"It is not that Miss. It does not look good for 'the help' to be getting involved in the business affairs of our employers."

"Well, I don't care what you think. I will happily tell Miss Ava I think Tony is a weasel. And if I had any dirt on him, I'd want to help you bury him with it." Seal states cockily.

"Well Seal that is very amiable of you,' I laugh.

After eating dinner with Gladys I sit on the balcony watching a thunderstorm rolling across the sky toward the bay. Nursing a glass of Shiraz, I think back over the events of the day, the warm breeze playing with my hair. A familiar beeping sound draws my attention to my phone. Ryan is calling me on FaceTime.

I answer and smile at his handsome face. His blonde locks poke out from underneath a navy beanie, his nose and cheeks slightly pink.

"Ava!" Ryan calls, waving at the camera.

"Hi! How was your day?" I giggle at the spectacle. He appears to be walking whilst trying to talk into the phone.

"I wanted to bring you a little piece of home!" He steps out into the open air and suddenly little white puffs of snowfall gracefully over his beanie and jacket. He fiddles with the phone, turning the camera around to face my chalet, covered in snow, long icicles hanging from the front stoop.

"Ryan! It's beautiful!" I smile, feeling my eyes prickle. I miss that place so much. Who would have thought I'd be so homesick for my tiny little run-down chalet when I'm living in such luxury here?

"Oh, Ryan thank you! What are you doing in Dinner Plain tonight?"

"Ivan invited me to join him for a beer!' He smiles into the camera, righting it onto his face again. 'Don't mind me, I'm already late so I'll talk to you as I hike up to the Hotel!"

"Ivan is the sweetest. How was your day?" I ask again.

"It was good! Ivan did his best to remove a finger today, that's when he invited me to drinks." He chuckles. "How was yours? Get up to anything interesting?" He can't know what I did today, surely. My hand burns with guilt where Chen held it all afternoon.

I can hear the snow crunching beneath his feet, and almost smell the log fireplaces burning.

"It was fine, Chen took me to lunch. I thought it would be the perfect time to tell him about Tony but..."

"But he wouldn't listen? Because he's an arrogant jerk?" Ryan offers.

"You are correct. He would not listen. But I had new information! Ryan, listen to this! Tony met with a building developer today." I stare at him on the phone, eyes wide.

"A building developer? But he's general counsel. Are you negotiating contracts on anything?" Ryan frowns into the camera, disappearing in and out of view - clearly trying to climb over something.

"Not that I know of, and everyone has been really good at running things by me. He has reportedly met with this guy a bunch of times since Winnie got sick."

"Sounds like he's up to something shady to me. Unless this guy is building him a house or something? Could that be possible?" Ryan huffs, big puffs of condensation diffusing into the air.

"I guess. But would you need the OWNER of the Development Company to meet with you for that?" I shake my head. 'I don't know Ryan, it has me worried."

"And Chen refusing to hear you out isn't helping. Grrr." Ryan shakes his fist at the camera, in mock outrage.

"God I miss you." I laugh.

"I meant to ask you, 'how's the fancy ball coming? It"s only like a week away now right?" He smiles, wiping his nose on his sleeve, the cold making his nose run.

"Yup! The 1st July. Counting down the days. I think I've finally got hair and makeup sorted, I'm having a pre-drinks party with the Invisible Women and Margot has assured me she is nearly finished with my dress." I smile broadly at him.

"I'm so glad you're enjoying one aspect of being so far from home. Seems the party planning celebrity lifestyle might suit you after all." He laughs. "I wish I could see you all dressed up in your fancy shoes and custom gown!"

"I wish you could be there too. You could come as...an...um..." I stop short. I'm meant to be a member of the PR team. In this hypothetical scenario, I have no idea what Ryan could pretend to be if we were to sneak him in.

"Lighting support? A waiter?' Ryan chuckles. 'I don't even own a fancy penguin suit anyhow. I'd have to go hire something stupid with a train and a bow tie."

"A tuxedo with tails, I think you mean! And I'm sure you'd look dashing in a bowtie."

"Tails. Maybe a top hat? Like Hugh Jackman wore in that circus movie you made me watch in Bright that time." I can't help but giggle. Even joking, the idea of Ryan at the ball has me elated.

"I'd so love to have a friend with me when I go into the shark tank." I shake my head.

"You're gonna knock their socks off honey. I have no doubt of that." He stops, a bright light illuminating his face. The sound of drinking revellers in the background.

'I'm sorry but I'm at the Hotel and I can see Ivan at the bar waiting for me. I'll try to call you again before the big day okay!" He blows me kisses and disappears..

14

With just days until the ball, I start to feel the pressure building. Not just at HEH but in Singapore in general. Banners begin to fly in the streets advertising the event, news reports on the television. Most mornings for the past week there have been TV news crews parked in the HEH lot awaiting to catch a glimpse of Chen or other high profile guests to add to their package about the ball.

At my final dinner with the Invisible Women before the ball, we sit barefoot once again with cocktails in Margot's warehouse, plates of sushi scattered around us.

"I don't care what the media say, there is no way Chen would show his face at the ball with Mei after the way he's been behaving toward you." Linah points her chopsticks at me.

"I concur, but I don't necessarily think that is how it is going to 'go down'. I think he'll take Mei because he's a spineless little so-and-so who won't risk offending his parents." Jia adds, squeezing an eye-watering amount of wasabi onto her plate.

"Sorry I'm late,' Margot hollers as she descends the stairs from the loft, 'I was putting the finishing touches on Ava's dress!" She smiles triumphantly. The room erupts with applause, squeals of delight and childish giggles.

"I can't wait to see it!" I smile up at her, handing her a plate as she kicks off her shoes.

"Wait, you haven't seen it yet?" Jia's mouth falls open.

"You know I don't much like 'see-food'!" Margot teases, closing Jia's jaw with her chopsticks.

"How do you know you'll like it?" Linah looks at me, wide eyes full of consternation.

"Because I trust Margot with my life." I reach across to pat her arm. 'Now, onto more important matters! On the afternoon of the 1st I will arrive here with the hair and makeup team. They'll get me red-carpet ready and then it's makeover time for anyone who wants one!" I clap my hands, bouncing up and down on the lounge.

"Oh thank god, I desperately need my eyebrows done." Jia taps her burgeoning mono-brow with a frown.

"And then we will watch the entire event unfold on the tv!" Linah smiles across at me.

After finishing another roll of sushi, Jia turns toward me. "I meant to ask you, what happened with Tony and the developer? Or the foundation guy for that matter? Did you end up figuring out what he was up to?"

"Nope.' I sigh, 'I have no idea what that was about. I haven't really seen Tony around the past few days. I still can't shake this feeling he's up to something though."

"Chin up hun, I'm sure it'll all come into the light eventually." Margot nudges me.

"I'm just so afraid that whatever his dastardly plan is, it'll be too late for me to rectify by then. It's eating away at me." I hide my face in my hands.

"Ava, you are doing everything you can for that company. What else are you meant to do? Drag Chen in, launch him at Tony and demand to know what he is up to?" Linah smiles. "You can't do any more than you already are."

"I haven't slept properly in days. Do you remember Tony made Chen announce months ago that 'a big announcement was coming' at the ball?" I shake my head, tears pricking my eyes. 'I still haven't figured out what that was about yet. And on top of it all, the head of the Foundation never agreed to book another meeting with me."

Silence surrounds me. For the first time, none of the invisible women know what to do either. I feel like I'm in a rowboat out to sea without a paddle. If these women don't have any answers, I'm well and truly screwed.

The next day, things only get worse. Tari calls me before I'm even in the car to the office.

"Hi hun, what's up?" I answer, trying to sound cheery.

"Ava, I need to talk to you, at the penthouse. It's important,' Tari states matter of factly.

"Uh, okay. I pretty much have bookings back to back between now and the ball. You can come over tomorrow in the afternoon before you start work?" I think through the schedule.

Yes, that would still leave me a few hours to get prepped and have a glass of wine with the ladies before I head in.

"Okay, I'll be there,' Tari sighs, 'I've gotta go, my girlfriend is awake and she'll expect breakfast." The call disconnects.

Well, clearly I'm not the only one who woke up on the wrong side of the bed this morning.

Entering the office, Sasha is nowhere to be seen. After trying to call her and leaving a voicemail on her phone to check she is okay, I head up to the restaurant to get my coffee and cinnamon scroll. Arriving at the floor, I spot a group of people crowded around a booth. Walking a little closer I notice the group are huddled around Sasha.

"Sasha!" I cry, a little louder than I intended. She looks up at me, red-rimmed eyes wide, running nose, blotchy cheeks.

Oh no, what if she and her boyfriend broke up? They were only painting their new apartment a few weeks ago.

"Are you okay?" I look down at her, fishing a packet of tissues from my handbag. The group silently disperses; ghosts into the wind.

"Ava. I'm sorry I wasn't at my desk to greet you." Sasha mumbles.

"Don't be silly. Tell me what is going on?" I sit down beside her, putting an arm around her shoulder.

"Tony,' She mumbles.

"What?" I snap.

"Mr Tony came past and told me he was about to fire Millie for eavesdropping on his private conversations and that as soon as she was gone, I'd be next." She wails, burying her face in her tissues.

Oh no, he doesn't.

I stand up, snatch my purse from the table and storm toward the elevator. Mashing the 'up' button, I wait impatiently for the elevator to arrive. In my impatience to enter the lift, I almost collide with Chen.

Excellent. Just what I need.

"Miss Elias, you are in quite a hurry?" Chen smiles down at me, spotting the rage on my face. 'Uh, and in quite a state I see."

"Get out of my way Chen."

"Does this have something to do with Tony?" He tilts his head, stepping back into the elevator with me.

"He threatened to fire staff for 'eavesdropping.' That's it, Chen, he's gone. I want him out!" I mash the 'close' button.

"You know, pressing it more than once makes no difference.' Chen admonishes me.

"Do you want me to be looking at you like this, because I assure you, I'm more than happy to share the love." I snarl. Stepping out onto the legal floor, I storm down the corridor toward Millie's desk and Tony's door. Luckily Lin from HR is already there, presumably to tell Millie she has been fired.

"Lin, this is outrageous. Millie cannot be fired for this. It's unlawful." I state flatly, trying to keep my rage in check.

"Uh, Miss Elias, technically Mr Tony has the right to select his administrative staffer and he has decided to let Millie go." Lin looks down at her hands.

"And where is Tony?" I ask, peering around to see his office empty.

"I believe he left immediately after telling Millie to pack her belongings,' Lin mutters quietly.

"Right. Then do me a favour Lin, write Millie up another contract to join me in the Exec Suite. It would appear that my EA is not likely to return anytime soon since she took Winnie's passing so hard. Millie can back-fill. Please also instruct someone to place packing boxes in Mr Tony's office. I want him gone."

Chen admonishes me again, more sternly this time. "Ava, you can't behave this irrationally. Just because he made some girl cry? You can't fire your general counsel for that."

"Excuse me?" I turn to glare up at him, realising we have gained an audience.

"This is inappropriate and admittedly a little hysterical. You can't stomp around yelling at people because they made a secretary cry." He peers down his nose disapprovingly at me.

"Hysterical?" I whisper, my hands shaking with fury.

"You cannot be seen to behave like this in front of the staff Miss Elias." He continues to scold me like an errant child. I look up to see Millie reappearing from the direction of the bathrooms.

"Millie, I am so, terribly sorry about Tony's behaviour. Lin will write you a new contract to move to the Executive Suite floor. Your first job is to find Mr Tony packing boxes. He will be clearing out his desk by the end of the week." I turn to glare at Chen as I stalk back to the elevator.

I swipe to lock the office door behind me before proceeding into the ensuite to vomit profusely.

The adrenaline wearing off, my hands begin to shake as I try to sip water after washing out my mouth.

I lean heavily against the counter, my feet tucked underneath me.

I can't do this. Maybe Chen is right, I'm too emotional to be in charge of a company this big. I've worked for men before who wouldn't look twice at a crying secretary. I too had been admonished by a man once for being seen crying at work.

Why do I take it so personally when the people who work for me are upset?

I know why. Because Millie and Sasha weren't just upset, they were attacked, verbally by Tony. I've been on the end of a tongue lashing from Tony. He isn't just mean, he's vile. I dig out my phone, desperate to hear the voice of someone kind and loving. I find Ryan's number and listen to the call ring out. I think about calling one of the invisible women, but then again, they did warn me about taking on Tony.

I hear a muffled knocking from the main office. I slowly peel myself off the floor, check my makeup hasn't run too badly and walk out into the office, swiping the door open.

Before me stands Lin, Chen and Tony. I immediately see red.

I don't care who hears me. Fuck this guy.

"Zhang Wei Tony. I warned you what would happen if you meddled in HEH affairs again. You are fired." I look from Tony to Lin, who is looking anywhere but at me. Tony's chilling laugh breaks the silence.

It's like something out of a horror movie. Where is his chainsaw?

"You stupid woman. Do you truly think you can fire me over something as trivial as making a snivelling little secretary cry?" Tony sneers at me.

"You will return your pass to security and clear your office by the end of the day." I try to keep my voice even and stand my ground.

"No." Tony spits at me. He turns and stalks to the elevator, disappearing before my eyes.

"Lin. I don't understand. We talked about this?" I look at Lin, barely containing my volcanic anger.

"Miss Ava, Mr Tony said he would sue HEH for unfair dismissal if you were to proceed. Also..." She looks up from her fingers to Chen.

"Also...?" I look at Chen. "Mr Chen, please explain?"

"I advised Lin not to proceed with your request. Ms Lin, you may go." Chen smiles sympathetically down at her.

Once the doors close on the elevator behind Lin, it's as though the spell is broken. I pick my jaw up off the floor, stalk into the ensuite locking the door and proceed to vomit until I can barely sit up. I could have been in there for hours. By the time I try to move again, my knees are stiff from the cold marble, my throat scratchy and my head aching.

I'm so angry I want to cry and scream and punch something.

The man is a tumour! And I can't find a single surgeon willing to attempt to slice him out. I'd settle for a hack job at this point. Deal with whatever scars HEH bare afterwards and sign up for rehab.

When my stomach finally begins to rumble from hunger, I stand feeling like a baby giraffe. All knobby knees and unsteady.

I dig my phone out and text Xi.
I'm going home.

Trying to remain upright, I gingerly make my way back out to the office. Standing in the doorway I stop dead.

"The. Fuck. Are. You. Doing. In. Here. Chen?" I growl through clenched teeth.

"Did you think I could let you get away with that embarrassing charade downstairs?" He stands there, exuding power.

"I want Tony gone,' I leer.

"That is not happening,' Chen states. "Perhaps it is best for you to go home, until you find a way to calm down?"

"Seal!" I scream, watching a shadow through the glass.

"Yes, Miss." Seal appears prostrate in the doorway his suit jacket unbuttoned.

Chen interrupts, his voice strikes razor-sharp.

"You might also want to rethink whether or not your attendance at the ball is appropriate. Considering your rather scathing feelings for Mr Tony, it would not be a good look for HEH to have you screaming at him at a black-tie gala."

"Seal. If Mr Chen opens his mouth again...you know what to do." I pick up my handbag and make my way to the private elevator. Feeling even less steady than in the bathroom, I bend down and remove my shoes.

"I'll be right behind you Miss,' Seal hollers from the office.

"Did you raise your voice?" Tari winces across at me, passing over a tumbler of whiskey.

I nod sullenly.

"Did you flap your arms around?" She looks like she is in pain every time I answer her.

"I do not recall".

"Did you cry?" She leans backward.

"No, I didn't cry. I vomited. But no one 'saw' that per se,' I whisper across to her.

"Oh, Ava. I'm so sorry. I don't know what to say." Tari pats my hand.

"I can't believe I lashed out. I was trying so hard not to be the 'hysterical female' everyone was afraid would rear her ugly head, and now look what I've done." I wail.

"Oh honey, after all the shit Tony has done, I don't think there is a single person on this earth who wouldn't have done the same thing. You stood up to a bully." She squeezes my hand encouragingly.

"Except that they wouldn't have let their emotion get in the way." I feel the hot tears threatening to fall.

"What is the deal with people insisting we live our professional lives without emotion? Do you think Martin Luther King could have rallied people the way he did if he lived without emotion?" I look up at her, my head resting on my arms on the black bar top.

"Did you just compare me to Martin Luther King?" I sniffle.

"You know what I mean girl! Why does the world insist that people run better businesses without involving emotion? Personally, I think it is all a scheme made up by men because they are terrible at it.

'They made sure the foundations of business were built without it so they couldn't be toppled by people with sound, emotional intelligence who won't consent to assholes bullying their staff." She concludes by banging her fist against the bar top. A kitchen hand appears suddenly with Seal by their side, carrying an enormous steel ice-cream tub like the kind you see at commercial ice-creameries. Seal directs him to place it down in front of me on a tea towel before handing me a large spoon.

"You know you'll have to buy the whole batch..." the kitchen hand says timidly. The withering look Seal gives him is enough for him to choke and back away quietly.

"Thanks Seal." I look across at him as he takes a seat beside me.

"Hit me." He says to Tari. She looks across at me, one quizzical eyebrow raised.

"Can he drink on the job?"

"Give him whatever he wants." I muster him a halfhearted smile and look down at what must be 5 litres of bright green mint choc chip.

"For the record Miss, it took everything I had not to smash the smug look off both Tony and Chen's faces today." He looked down at his balled fist, sunglasses still in place.

"I'm glad you didn't Seal. It would have meant that not only did I behave like a hysterical female but that I was chicken enough to 'set my dog on them'." I pat his hand, then dig a huge scoop out of the tub.

"That wasn't hysterical Ava.' Seal hoots with laughter, 'I've watched grown men beat the shit out of each other over puss...uh...women they were interested in..." He coughs. Tari and I look at one another and burst out laughing.

"What else have they come to blows over?" Tari hands Seal a highball tumbler.

"You name it. 'He bought the car I wanted.' 'He was making eyes at my girl.' 'He bought the condo I planned to buy.' 'He undermined me in the pitch.' 'He stole my season pass to the baseball.' Trust me. Men are far more hysterical and petty than they let on. The only difference is, they'll deck each other once, dust themselves off and move on. Women aren't allowed to punch men because it isn't 'ladylike' so they are forced to use other tactics. " He shrugs, sipping his whisky.

"Are you telling me that if Ava had just punched Tony in the face today instead of shouting at him, she would not be labelled a hysterical woman?" Tari asks inquisitively.

"Oh no, you'd still be labelled hysterical. And likely a violent crazy person to boot." He nods to himself. Tari and I look at one another, shaking our heads.

"So there's no winning." Tari tosses her tea towel down in disgust.

"Women, unfortunately tend to have to wait it out in the trenches until the men fall out amongst themselves. There is one tactic that I've seen work well for women." Seal offers, sipping his whisky thoughtfully.

"Are you going to share or leave us hanging?" Tari leans in, curious.

"The 'Rise Above the Animosity'. I suppose in Hollywood it would be something like 'Sexy Revenge.'" He shrugs.

"Rise above,' I sigh, 'the 'Take the high road, don't let it get to you, don't let them see they've upset you?' type plan?" I drop my head back against my arms.

"Uh, well a bit late for that I suppose." Tari concedes.

"I'd say it would be like you showing up at that ball tomorrow and blowing their socks off. Strong, confident, undeterred." Seal states. He checks his watch, downs his drink and turns to me, 'That's my shift over and seeing as tomorrow is a long day, I'll be turning in. I'll leave you in Xi's hands. See you in the morning, Miss." He offers a slight bow and departs.

"Did Mr 'Looks Dumber than a Box of Hair' just make a logical, well thought out point?" Tari frowns across at me.

"I think he just might have." I frown back.

15

The day of the ball arrived. I roll over in bed having hardly slept the night before. When I left Spago, Tari reminded me she was coming over today to show me something she found in Winnie's diary. I was so overwhelmed with everything that had gone on I didn't have it in me to press her about it last night.

Dragging my feet out of bed, I stumble toward the shower.

I'm going to work from home today. I can't risk seeing Chen's stupid face; or Tony's. I still can't believe Chen didn't back me up yesterday. After everything he said, I thought he'd changed.

I stood under the hot spray as the entire bathroom fogged up. A knocking at the door meant Gladys had finished making breakfast.

"Miss Ava?" She calls. I shut off the water and stand there, unable to move.

"Miss Ava, I have bacon, pancakes and scrambled eggs in the kitchen when you're ready,' She calls again.

"Thank you,' I holler back, hoping it sounded cheery.

Stepping out of the shower and wrapping myself in a large fluffy towel I stand in front of the mirror. My puffy eyes, with dark circles beneath, look too big for my face. I try to smile and break the pouty look reflected there but it only makes me look worse. Swapping my towel for my bathrobe, I make my way toward the kitchen.

I must admit, it smells divine. Ooohh, coffee.

Rounding the corner, I spot Gladys pouring me a glass of orange juice. She looks up, catching sight of my dark circles and patchy complexion.

"Uh, Miss Ava, why don't I mix you up a face mask to help with your...uh...glowing complexion for the ball." She tries to smile. 'Just something simple, green tea, avocado. Lots of antioxidants." She nods, busying herself behind the counter.

I sit down and commence shovelling food into my face. I barely ate last night, other than about a litre of mint choc chip.

"Good Morning Miss Ava, are we heading into the office this morning?" Seal whistles on his way in from the elevator before stopping dead. "Good god, what happened to your face?" He stares, mouth agape.

"Oh I don't know, seems crying and vomiting for half the day yesterday paired with about 2 hours sleep left me with this Hollywood glow." I glare at him. He steps over to me gingerly and quietly removes my coffee from the bench, sitting down beside me to drink it himself. I shrug and continue eating my pancakes. I watch with curiosity as I see Gladys place another plate of food in front of Seal.

Did I somehow completely miss the fact that she feeds him? Or is this a new thing?

"They don't call it beauty sleep for nothing....' Seal mutters into his eggs.

"Do you remember the conversation we had yesterday about punching people?" I turn to glare at him.

"Yes but you're still a lady."

"Not in my own home I'm not,' I grumble.

Half an hour later Gladys insists I take a bath and soak, being sure to use a floaty head pillow in case I fall asleep and drown. My protesting that I had quite literally just finished showering seemed to fall upon deaf ears. After climbing into the bubbles, Gladys follows me into the bathroom and gently pastes the avocado concoction onto my face.

"I'll come back to get you in 20 minutes. We can't have you all pruney!"

After a while, I decide I had better do some other kind of 'prep' for this evening. I grab a jar of body scrub off the shelf beside the tub and begin massaging the sugar and coffee scrub into my arms and legs. After a minute or two of scrubbing, it occurs to me that most people attending the ball probably booked themselves full days at the spa today in preparation for tonight. I guess I'll keep that in mind for next year. If I'm still here next year. Maybe I shouldn't even be going this year? What if Chen is right, what if Tony sets me off and I end up making a scene?

A knock at the door drags me back to the present, realising I'd been caught up in my thoughts and I didn't notice how hard I was scrubbing. Parts of my skin were red raw.

Oh well, nothing a litre of moisturiser won't fix.

By this point, I'd spent so much time scrubbing and fretting, I'd all but talked myself out of going tonight.

I rinse off the scrub and my avocado mask. Using very gentle pressure, I lightly scrub my face too.

After climbing out of the tub I lather a thick layer of moisturiser onto my body and then my face. Feeling a little more human I decide it is time to check my emails and do some work for the morning. I head back to the kitchen to grab another glass of juice.

Back in Winnie's office I check my schedule on my laptop and decide to pencil in a nap after lunch before Tari arrives and I have to head to Margot's for a final fitting of my dress.

Other than the basic 'mock' dress Margot had me try on, I am still completely in the dark as to what she has created for me.

I flip on the television to watch the news headlines scroll past. I answer a few emails when a familiar face appears on the television before me.

"Winnie?" I get up from behind the desk and stalk slowly toward the TV, fiddling with the volume on the remote.

The story was reported in mandarin and so finally managing to turn up the volume was entirely pointless. A series of clips flashed up onto the screen; Winnie shaking hands at a groundbreaking; I recognise it as the last foundation building that was erected; a series of incredibly suave looking men and women walking a red carpet, presumably at last year's ball and Winnie standing behind the HEH podium giving a speech. By some miracle, it was in English.

"It is my hope that the legacy of the foundation and its strong roots within HEH will live on and continue to care for those less fortunate than ourselves, long after I am gone." He bows and smiles broadly to a round of applause. Those beautiful veneers sparkling in the spotlight as his smile crinkles the corner of his eyes.

I feel my eyes start to prickle.

I will never live up to this man's legacy.

It hit me like a freight train. The harsh, cold realisation.

I will never be good enough. Winnie was wrong to choose me.

The story concludes with a shot of Chen's angular Hollywood face smiling and waving at the cameras. I can only imagine the story is explaining that as HEH's new CEO, Chen will give the address at this years' ball. The first time in the history of HEH that Winnie will not give the address himself.

I stand before the TV dumbfounded. I cling to the remote control like a life raft, feeling the world falling apart beneath me.

I can't do this.

I should just leave Chen here to manage this himself. I have brought nothing but trouble and turmoil to HEH.

Feeling a sense of utter despair, I dig my phone out of my pocket and try to call Ryan again. It goes straight to voicemail. Again.

Where is Ryan when I need him?

There I go again, selfishly only thinking about myself. What if something has happened to him?

I send him a quick text to ask him to let me know he is okay. I notice the clock on the phone and realise it is already lunchtime.

I sat satiated at the kitchen bench having just finished Gladys' spaghetti carbonara when I see the kitchen wall panel light up. Tari's face appears on the screen. I see her disappear in the front door, Seal must have let her in.

She's early. I guess I'm not getting my nap after all.

"Hey,' I smile grimly across at her as she enters the kitchen. She's wearing her regular uniform, black pants and white long-sleeved shirt; her vest is missing.

"Is this about the news this morning? I saw the thing about Winnie and the ball." She grimaces at me pointing to my face before giving me a one-armed hug.

"I shouldn't be here Tari. I'm not doing anyone any favours, I'm only making things worse for people." She levels a gaze of false sympathy at me, nodding with a pout.

"I'm serious Tari, I don't think I'm going to go tonight. It will only cause more trouble. I'll only be an embarrassment to Winnie's legacy."

"What are you talking about? Is this about yesterday? That shit Chen said was so out of line." She frowns at me.

"It isn't just about yesterday, I'm just not cut out for this. I'm too passionate, I care too much. I can't play in business at this level with these sharks." I drop my face into my hands, "I should just go back to Australia and leave this to the people who know what they are doing. I'm only getting in the way here."

"Winnie picked you for a reason." She pulls my hands away, nodding enthusiastically. "Listen, that's why I wanted to come over. There's something I want to show you." She digs around in her oversized satchel and pulls out one of Winnie's diaries. I notice this one is from over a decade ago.

"Tari, what on earth could possibly have happened 10 years ago that meant Winnie picked me now?" I frown looking at her sceptically.

"Where is that fancy-ass pen?" She rolls her eyes and holds out her other hand, palm up.

"I left it in Winnie's office. Why?"

She drops her bag on the floor and makes her way to the office. I follow in her wake, incredibly curious but very confused.

"Tari, what is going on?" I huff at her. 'I'm really not in the mood today, I'm sorry. I am also running out of time to cancel everything for tonight. Hair, makeup. Oh god, I'll have to tell Margot. After I basically bullied her into making me a dress."

"You didn't bully her. Now sit your bum down. It's storytime." She points to the lounge as she picks up Monty from the desk. She looks at it, this way and that.

"Tari, you've seen and held it a dozen times now. What is the deal? Does it contain a hidden treasure map? Is it a secret key to some underground bunker?" I roll my eyes, taking a seat begrudgingly in the centre of the couch. Tari clears her throat, opens the diary to a bookmarked page and begins to read dramatically.

"Today I was contacted by an old business associate who believes he has come across an excellent investment opportunity.' She looks at me to check I'm listening before continuing.

'Personally, I think he is a little bit on the crazy side, but I agreed to discuss it with him over drinks. We met at our old haunt and he explained the proposal. It was a small Swiss family-owned company who had this idea for creating diamonds from carbon.

'It is better on the environment and the diamonds can be given a GIA rating, just the same as diamonds dug from the ground. I must admit, it was interesting to discuss by way of conversation, but I was rather sceptical about it as a business venture.

'He told me this family were only seeking a few hundred thousand in cash funding to get their business off the ground. It is 'revolutionary' my colleague said. I shared my scepticism with him when he explained the selling point." Tari stopped again, this time I suspect for dramatic effect.

"Tari, please,' I sigh. I must admit, I am a little curious myself.

Suddenly I hear the front door go. I frown and look at Tari.

"Are you expecting anyone else today?" She turns to look toward the door.

"I'll just go check, don't move. I'll come back to finish storytime." I roll my eyes at her as I head out into the hallway.

I'm met halfway to the kitchen by Gladys carrying a shoebox sized package.

"Sorry to disturb Miss Ava but this just arrived for you by private courier." She looks down at the box and passes it across to me.

How odd, I don't recall ordering anything from overseas lately.

I eye the Swiss stamps suspiciously. I walk back into the office to find Tari sitting down on the lounge.

"A package?" She looks over curiously.

"Did you say something about a Swiss family?" I frown down at her.

"What?"

"In Winnie's diary, did you say something about a Swiss Family?"

"Yes, they were the people his business partner was talking about. What does that have to do with the price of oil? Can I finish the story now?" She smiles up at me, patting the couch beside her.

"Sure." I frown, placing the box down on Winnie's desk and moving across to sit back beside her.

"Okay, where was I?" She opens the journal again.

"I shared my scepticism with him when he explained the selling point. He said he didn't understand the exact science but that the diamonds were created from superheating and pressurising carbon. Carbon which can be sourced, for example from human hair or cremated ashes."

Tari stops and looks up at me expectantly.

"Um okay, that's creepy,' I state bluntly.

Where is she going with this?

She giggles and turns back to the book.

"He told me he could understand my hesitation, but asked if I'd consider investing if he could prove the quality of their product."

She stops and stares at me again.

"Am I being incredibly thick here? Why do you keep staring at me like that?" I ask bewildered. She continues to read.

"He withdrew a handkerchief from his pocket and told me to lop off a lock of hair. Naturally, I was not carrying scissors and we made the waitress rather uncomfortable when we asked to borrow a pair; thus resorting to yanking out a small chunk. I gave him the hair and departed the bar feeling a little silly. Upon reflection now I am wondering if I have just fallen foul of a joke. As I sit here rubbing the small bald patch on the side of my head, I feel rather silly wondering if it will ever grow back."

Tari smiles at me again, stopping to turn the pages toward the very end of the diary where another bookmark sat.

"Today I received a most unusual package in the mail; from Switzerland of all places. It contained a notecard from my old colleague, "Winnie, I hope this is enough to allay your cynicism. If not, just know there will forever be a part of you in your pocket from this day forth. Also, the lab advised that you provided more hair than necessary and therefore asked it be returned."

'Upon opening the box, I was met with a small glass vial containing a few strands of my hair and a fountain pen box. The box contained a MontBlanc pen with a star-shaped diamond embedded in the lid. I realise as I sit holding this pen, that it feels like an extension of me. Perhaps that is today's whisky speaking, but for some strange reason I feel connected to it.' Tari looks up at me once again before continuing.

"I will reply to my colleague and advise him that sadly I will not be participating in the investment of the start-up but that I will forever cherish this most unique item for the rest of my days." I feel my eyes begin to prickle.

"A part of me will always be with you,' I whisper, the hot tears threatening to overflow.

"Hm?" Tari frowns taking my hand.

"In the letter Winnie sent with the pen, he said, 'Remember: a part of me will always be with you,' I sniffle. I pick up the pen and look down at it with a fresh new perspective. It wasn't just a writing implement to him. This diamond was forged 'of him'.

"Where is the letter? I'd love to read it if you wouldn't mind sharing something so private?" Tari squeezes my hand.

"I left it in the box." I frown down at myself.

"Where is the box?" She raises an eyebrow.

"In a safety deposit box back home." I shrug. "I freaked out because of the value of the pen, but when I put the box in the wall, I just couldn't leave the pen behind."

Tari pats my hand gently.

Wait a second.

I stand up slowly and walk toward the desk.

"Did he ever mention in the journals, what the name of the company was?" I ask Tari over my shoulder.

"Uh, yes. Wait, I'll find it...I think it was-" She flips through the diary.

"Lonite,' I cut her off.

"Yes, how'd you know..." She stops.

I stare down at the package on Winnie's desk.

"Carbon which can be sourced, from human hair or cremated ashes,' I whisper as I reach for the box, Lonite printed in grand silver text across the top. I turn and sit back down beside Tari, speechless.

"Lonite." She reads off the box. "Oh my god. You don't think he...that he..." She looks from the box to me and back again.

"I never found out where his body went. It was stipulated in his will and I decided it was none of my business. I assumed it was a 'donation to science' thing and I couldn't bear to think about that." My voice quakes as I look up at Tari. She checks her watch, hesitating.

"I can go if you'd like to do this alone?" She squeezes my hand again.

"The last thing I want right now is to be alone." I feel the hot tears swim again. I look down at the box with blurry eyes and pull open the tab. Inside the box sits two small jewellery boxes, a book, a few envelopes I recognise as the certificate of authentication; and a gold envelope. Hot tears spill over onto my cheeks. One, two, suddenly a torrent of emotion hits me like a tidal wave.

It's a gold envelope. Could it truly be a letter from Winnie?

I pick up the envelope, my hands shaking. Turning it over, I see the familiar metallic wax stamp. I run my finger under the inside, popping the seal in one piece and lifting out the matching gold parchment.

My Dearest Ava,

I cannot apologise enough for writing to you under these circumstances. I imagine by the time you receive this you will have been notified of my passing and faced with many, many challenges that I cannot begin to comprehend.

I hope you can forgive me for not contacting you in these my final days. Many questions will go unanswered, however, those that can lie in my journal. I am hoping by now that my 'thank you' gift has arrived and you will now understand the meaning of the multiple contents of the box.

This letter and this box are in strictest confidence to you. I had my private lawyer ensure that neither this letter nor my journal Part II becomes common knowledge.

Ava, I must apologise for the trouble I will have landed you in. I have no proof and perhaps I am simply an old man who is losing his sanity, but two weeks ago I was perfectly healthy, and doctors cannot tell me what is wrong. I have grown more and more suspicious of Tony, in these my final days.

I write, knowing in my heart that this is my deathbed and I wish for you to know that I am thinking of you and the joy you have brought me this past year.

I do not know what choice you will have made regarding Huynh Enterprises Holdings, or how Tony will have treated you following my passing.

I know that the woman I met that fortuitous winters day, has the strength inside her to fight for what is right. I entrusted the people of HEH into your hands and I know you will have made a decision you believe to be best for everyone involved.

If you decided to continue my legacy and take up the mantel as CEO of HEH, I know my people will be in good hands.

Your kindness, compassion, courage and strength were the reason I knew you were the right choice. Any man can rule with logic and reason, but that is not what makes a great leader. It is the ability to hear the unheard, to see the unseen and to love the unloved that makes a true leader.

Ava my darling, if you decided you did not wish to wade into the politics and scandal that business attracts, I will not be disappointed. I could not rest peacefully if I felt you were unhappy with this outcome and the future for your life.

Regardless of your decision, I hope you will take these pieces and think of me fondly. I put a lot of thought into what I wanted to happen after my passing, and I must say you gave me quite the inspiration. I cannot pretend to believe in the 'science' behind it, but I hope having them with you brings you some sense of peace.

In this my final letter, I wish you a most joyous and wondrous life my darling Ava.

-Winnie

I can hardly finish the letter, wracking sobs bursting out with such force.

"He had so much faith in me Tari,' I cry.

"He was right to." She whispers to me, patting my hair.

With shaking hands, I lift the first jewellery box from the packaging.

Lifting the lid back, I stare down at the silver text printed into the black fabric underside.

"The Huyhn-ston Legacy Diamond."

Before me sparkled a platinum ring beset with a large pink emerald-cut diamond, nestled between two pentagonal colourless diamonds. Tari lets out a low whistle from beside me.

"He said you inspired this?" She whispers.

"It's based off the Harry Winston Pink Legacy Diamond." I sob even harder. The second box contained a matching pair of emerald-cut pink diamond studs.

"All I can say is, I hope they go with whatever Margot has made for you,' Tari whispers into my hair at the top of my head.

"I still don't think I can go." I feel the sobs subsiding, hot tears stinging my cheeks.

"You can't tell me that you're going to deny taking Winnie to the ball tonight?" She waves her hand in the direction of the jewellery boxes.

"I suppose I hadn't thought of it like that,' I laugh quietly. I lean over to the box and pick up the book.

"Winnie said this is his final diary Part-II." I frown down at it, handing it to Tari.

"He said the other was in the 'gift' he sent?" She takes the book, flipping through the pages, 'Does he mean the box with the pen?" I stop and look at her. I had never even looked at the remaining contents of the box and after Tony turned up I hadn't given it another thought.

"He said he didn't trust Tony and that the journal contained answers,' I whisper. "Tari, I have to go home and get that book."

A knock at the door makes us both jump.

"Oh, sorry my dear I wanted to let you know that Xi is here to drop Tari to work and take you to Margot's for the pre-ball preparation." Gladys frowns at the spectacle the two of us must have been. Tari picks up the delicate boxes and hands them to me. "What do you say Cinderella, are you ready to go to a ball?"

Margot's warehouse is buzzing when Xi and I pull up.

How many vehicles do a makeup artist and a hairdresser need?

I enter the main door to be greeted by a stern-looking woman with a clipboard.

"Name?" She looks down at the papers in front of her.

"Ava Elias?" I surprise myself; it sounds more like a question than an answer. Ms Stern looks up in surprise, her face transforming into a wide smile. She reaches up and talks into a headset hidden behind her hair.

"I have the package."

Um. Okay. What am I? The President of the United States today?

"Right this way Miss Elias." She almost bows, ushering me inside. She takes my duffel bag and strides into the warehouse.

The inside of the cavernous space is once again magically transformed into a beauty parlour, similar to the first day I met the Invisible Women except this time it is on steroids. Every spare surface of flooring was covered with some kind of table with products and equipment. Large massage tables had been arranged in one corner and the entire space smelled like a department store fragrance counter.

"Ava!" Jia calls from the bar. "I'm making mimosas!" She waves me over.

"Jia, what is going on? I was only supposed to be coming here for a fitting, hair and makeup?" I frown, overwhelmed by the sheer volume of bodies in the space.

"Don't be silly! We couldn't let you loose in that shark tank without a full afternoon of pampering beforehand!" She waves away my awe and hands me a tall champagne flute.

"Ava!" I turn to see Linah appear, ensconced in a fluffy bathrobe, hair piled high in a towel turban. She picks up a mimosa and clinks her flute against my own.

"How great is this! I feel like we should do this all the time!" She squeals uncharacteristically. Suddenly Ms Stern Clipboard is back.

"Now Miss Elias. We have a tight schedule to get you to the event on time. We will commence with massages, complexion clean up, manicure, pedicure, hair, makeup and final 'glam'."

"Complexion clean up?" I frown, looking at Jia and Linah.

"It isn't quite a fake tan, just more like a rejuvenation." Linah smiles at me, sipping contentedly.

"Now, where is the other one of you?" Ms Stern looks around. "We must get started." Margot appears at the top of the stairs, descending into the chaos from the tranquil sanctuary of the studio above. After joining us in a toast, Margot obliges Ms Clipboard and we process toward the massage tables.

My masseuse was incredible, other than vocalising a grumble whenever she hit a large knot, which was often. "Very tight, you very stressed Miss?"

Once that was over, every surface of me was waxed, buffed, polished and moisturised again. The team were polite enough not to mention the spots where I had 'overdone' it with my exfoliation this morning. I then had a face mask applied, along with large under-eye patches to reduce the dark circles and puffiness. The four of us were then plonked into giant lounges where we had our legs and hands massaged again before our manicures and pedicures. I realised halfway through the pampering that I had not been asked what colours I wanted on my nails.I look down to see my fingernails were being expertly painted in a crisp snow-white French tip and my toenails were a deep shimmery emerald green.

An interesting choice with the green. I like it.

Once that was over, I was ushered to a basin where my hair was washed and toned to bring out the natural vibrancy of the ginger. My hair was wrapped into a towel turban-like Linah's when it was announced that afternoon tea had been served.

Shuffling along like a geisha in my spa slippers I slowly make my way to the table. Before me sat multiple high tea-style cake stands covered in sandwiches, cakes, tarts, biscuits and scones.

"Ava, come sit!" Margot waves me over, pouring me a large black tea. "How do you take your tea? Sugar? Milk?"

"Just milk thank you, Margot." I smile across at her. "This day has been so tumultuous, I'm exhausted already."

"Don't be silly! It has barely begun!" Jia scolds as she sits down, reaching across to place scones and cake on her plate with decorative tongs. I notice her fingernails have been painted bubble-gum pink.

"I had kind of decided this morning that I wasn't going to go tonight…" I admit guiltily.

"What?" Three pairs of eyes spin around to stare at me.

"So much happened yesterday that I haven't had a chance to tell you about. There was a blow-up; Tony tried to fire staff for no reason, threatened them publicly and so I fired him. Chen didn't back me and Tony left knowing his job was secure and there was nothing I could do about it. Chen and I argued and he told me I should rethink attending tonight because of my 'volatility'." I sigh, frustrated at the thought all over again.

"Good god. Did you punch Chen? I would have." Jia states, simmering quietly.

"Ah Ava, I am so sorry. I really thought things were getting better with Chen?" Linah reaches across the table to squeeze my hand.

"There's nothing to be done about it, but I was in a really bad place. But then something bizarre happened. Winnie turned up." I reach up to tong a lemon curd tart and a chicken and mayo sandwich onto my plate. Three sets of eyes stare at me in horror.

"Winnie turned up? As in Winnie who...last year..." Margot freezes, a sandwich poised halfway to her mouth. I look around for my duffel. I jump up, grab the bag and place it on the seat beside me. I dig around past the shoebox and find my clutch. I pull out the two jewellery boxes and the certificates from Lonite and hand them to Margot and Linah who leaned over to show Jia.

"Oh!" Linah exclaims, opening the ring box.

"I've heard of these groups, Cremation diamonds they are known as. No real scientific proof that any 'DNA' is left in the diamond after the process is complete, but it makes for a nice story." Jia nods, reading the certificate.

"And a great way to make money apparently." Linah's mouth drops open eyeing the certificate Jia held. Margot sat mute. I turn to look at her to check she is okay.

"I was hoping to wear them tonight, if you think they'll go with your planned outfit?" I smile across at her. She looks at me and takes my hand between us.

"They're perfect,' she whispers. Across the table, Jia raises her glass.

"A toast, to Winnie continuing his tradition of attending the Annual HEH Ball in style!" She laughs.

"To Winnie." We all clink glasses together and dig into our afternoon tea, falling into excited chatter.

Fed and bubbly from the Champagne, I felt much more relaxed as my hair was blow-dried and curled into a cascade of red. Pushed over to one side and pinned to fall down my left shoulder, I stare at myself in the mirror.

"You look like Blake Lively!" Linah claps from her chair where her updo is taking shape.

"Except you're a ginger,' Jia laughs rolling her eyes.

"Next is makeup and we're almost ready!" Margot smiles at me in the mirror.

My chair is turned so I am facing away from the mirror. I follow along with my eyes closed as the makeup artist works on her craft. Foundation, blush, eyeshadow, eye liner, lip liner, lipstick.

"Time to get dressed!" Margot beams down at me. She, Jia and Linah are all dressed in cocktail gowns, hair and makeup looking red carpet ready.

"I do wish I could take you all with me! You look incredible!" I feel the tears begin to well. Jia looking like a Greek goddess wearing a one-shoulder number in baby pink. Margot in her classic little black dress with feathers at the hem and Linah draped in ruby red chiffon.

"No tears!" Jia scolds me.

"Don't worry Ava, there's always next year?" Linah leans down, takes my hand and leads me toward the staircase.

I hike up my robe so as not to trip and follow the three beauties before me. Making it to the top of the stairs I see the entire space has been curtained off into a glamorous dressing room. One of the assistants had brought up my bag and laid out my clutch, shoes and Winnie's jewels. A large mirror took up one end of the room, reflecting back the four of us.

"No peeking! Turn around." Margot grabs my shoulders and spins me to face the wall before I get a chance to look at myself too closely.

I hear rustling and whispers, gasps of 'ooh' and 'aah' behind me.

"Okay, close your eyes,' Linah whispers.

I feel like a mannequin being dressed in a store window. The ladies hold up the dress and guide my legs in before pulling it up and removing my robe. Slipping my arms into what feel like off the shoulder sleeves, the zipper goes up and I feel snug. The fabric hugs all the way down to my bum and thighs.

"The wait is killing me!" I cry, stamping my feet impatiently.

Holding one of my hands on each side, I feel Jia and Linah giggling at each other. Margot takes each of my feet and slips on the Louboutin heels, zipping the ankles and puffing the bows.

"Okay, let"s turn her around."

I feel each of the ladies take a step back as I turn and open my eyes. I do not recognise the woman standing before me. She has a cascade of ginger hair flowing down her shoulder, her eyes a smoky cat eye in shimmery emerald green. Her black dress of stretch knit fabric, hugs every curve to just below the knee, with taffeta trim across the bust, billowing out into puffed off the shoulder sleeves. Her legs go all the way to the floor, long and glowy.

"Margot…" I sigh, speechless.

"I got the inspiration for the sleeves from your shoes. Like one big taffeta bow." She shrugs, embarrassed.

"I couldn't have imagined anything more perfect,' I whisper, running my hands down the front of my dress. I turn and open my arms wide, embracing the three of them.

"Where would I be without you?" I sniffle, trying to keep the tears at bay.

A gentle knock at the door reminds us that my departure grows nearer.

"We need champagne!" Jia and Linah disappear downstairs. I hug Margot tightly.

"Thank you,' I whisper.

She looks at me with watery eyes. "No Ava. Thank you."

"If I manage to get onto the red carpet, who do I say I am wearing?" I look at her, tucking her hair behind one ear.

"Fuck 'em. You're wearing Margot Welsh." She smiles brightly at me from behind her oversized glasses.

"That's my girl." I give her another hug before she too departs downstairs.

I turn to take another look at myself in the mirror. I reach across to pick up my clutch and stop, seeing Winnie's jewels. Picking up the ring box I turn it this way and that, watching the light catch the giant centre diamond. It sparkles so magnificently I hardly dare touch it.

Taking a deep breath, I place the box down and pick up the earrings. One at a time, I remove the studs from the box and secure them in my ears. I look back down at the ring, lift it gently from the box and slide it onto the ring finger of my right hand.

"Well Winnie, here goes nothing!" I whisper down to him, reaching for my clutch and watching him glimmer up at me, almost like a wink.

16

"To Ava and Winnie!" The invisible women toast me one last time before I climb into the BBSUV with Xi.

He grabs my duffel and opens the car door just outside the warehouse.

"I love you all." I hug them each again before handing Jia my champagne flute and walking to the car. Xi offers me his hand as I clamber in.

"You look very lovely this evening Miss Ava." He smiles fondly at me.

"Thank you, Xi. Is that a new tie?" I smile back, noticing tonight he is wearing a bowtie and vest under his suit.

"It is Miss. Thank you for noticing."

"Did you notice my new tie?" Seal smirks from the front seat.

"Yes, and it appears to be cutting off the circulation to your brain." I chuckle back at him.

"You look good Ava." He states brusquely, turning toward the windscreen.

The procession of cars lined up outside the venue wrapped around the block. It took Xi ten minutes to get to the part of the queue where the guest list is confirmed. Winding his window down he greets the security guard.

"Name?" The guard grumbles.

"Elias, Ava,' Xi responds politely. The guard skims the list, flipping the page over twice, scanning it with his flashlight in the encroaching evening light.

"She's not on this list."

Seal turns to face me in the car, one eyebrow cocked.

"I guess because I'm listed as a member of the PR team, maybe I'm not allowed to walk the red carpet after all?" I shrug, trying to conceal my crushing disappointment.

"That doesn't seem right." Seal mutters.

"Oh wait, hold up a second." The security guard holds up his hand at us, muttering into his earpiece. "Yes, Elias. That's what he said."

Seal fidgets with his suit in the front seat. I look down at Winnie's ring, glinting in the light reflecting down from the tower beside us.

I'm sorry Winnie.

"I've found the discrepancy. Elias, Ava is listed as function staff. Please proceed to the rear entry. Another Security guard will assist you and show you where staff must report in." The man holds his arm up indicating for us to proceed. Xi nods his thanks quietly and drives on.

"You have got to be kidding me?!" Seal rages from the front seat. "Function Staff? What, like a damn cater-waiter? They expect you to skulk in through the back door?"

"Seal, I appreciate the support, but it is okay. At least I'm able to get in. That's something right?" I shrug.

"Yeah, sure. If they even let you in the back door." He huffs, sinking down into the seat. "Maybe we should go get the helicopter and drop you in via the helipad. They couldn't deny you entry then."

I must admit, he has a point. And that would be rather a fun way to 'make an entrance'.

Xi slowly makes it around the corner to where a roped door and security guard appear. Xi comes to a stop as Seal climbs out and opens my door. I lean in Xi's window and thank him. "Go get 'em." He winks at me. Seal takes my arm and walks me to the door.

"Elias, Ava." He states confidently to the guard who consults yet another clipboard.

"And who are you meant to be?" The guard eyes Seal's suit and sunglasses sardonically.

"PSO Ng,' He states confidently.

And yet, he will always be Navy Seal to me.

"PSO Ng? As in Private Security? Oh, this I've gotta hear. Why does a waitress need a private security guard?" He doubles over letting out a howl of laughter. Straightening up he adds, 'She's on the list, she gets in."

I turn to Seal, certain he is about to argue. "I'll go in, find Abbie and get her to 'update the list' okay?" I pat his arm encouragingly.

"It's my job, Ava,' He states sternly.

"I know, but the Chen family are here, everyone will be packing. There's no chance anything is going to 'go down' tonight Seal. It'll be okay." I smile up at him before disentangling my arm and walking through the door.

The room immediately inside the door is complete chaos. Men and women are racing around in different states of undress, looking for pieces of uniforms. I ease my way through trying to avoid being trampled. I spot a familiar face near the rear of the room toward the exit.

"Abbie!" I call, waving over the crowd.

"Oh, Miss Elias!? What on earth are you doing here?" She bulldozes her way through the throng to rescue me.

"I was apparently listed as 'Function staff' on the guest list. They wouldn't let me in the front door. They wouldn't let Seal in either. Can you please go out and tell the guard to let him in? He'll have an aneurism if he's left out there much longer." I chuckle.

"Oh my goodness. I have no idea how that happened, I cannot apologise enough for this. What a disgrace to treat you so." She looks as though she is about to cry.

"Abbie, I promise it is fine! Just point me in the direction of the bar and a chair and it is all forgotten." I smile at her, patting her arm. Once we emerge from the chaos she stops and looks me up and down.

"A crying shame you didn't get to walk the red carpet looking like that Miss Elias. You'd have blown the socks off the world tonight."

"Thanks, Abbie, that's very sweet of you to say." I bid her farewell and head up the corridor toward the elevator.

Three floors up I hit the lobby where the red carpet lets out. I walk through the space dodging handsomely dressed couples posing for pictures for the roving photographers. The room is a vast space with back silk covered cocktail tables and wandering waiters carrying trays stacked with champagne. Bright floral arrangements and candelabras were scattered throughout the room. I walk toward the glass façade at the front of the building, looking out toward the red carpet lined with flashing cameras and a throng of media skirmishing for the best pictures. The city outside glimmered in as the sun set.

Car after car arrives, birthing yet another Instagram ready pair who pout and pose their way up the 20m aisle. I flag down a waiter and grab a glass of bubbly. Fishing out my phone I sneak a quick selfie and send it to the invisible women, Tari and Gladys. I consider sending it to Ryan but do not. He hasn't returned my calls for days. I shake my head, trying not to let the disappointment drag down my mood. I stand peacefully taking in the room, quietly proud of what the Events team have achieved here. The space feels like a Hollywood awards night.

If I were to guess what the Oscars were like rather than watching the highlight reel in my pyjamas on the couch.

Suddenly a ruckus erupts from outside. A stretch black limousine appears at the carpet. A hat-wearing driver races to the door and out steps a suave, clean-cut, hair tied back in a sleek ponytail; Chen. He steps one long leg out of the car, followed by a second. Waves to the crowd before turning back to the open door and offering his hand. Out steps an incredibly elegant Mei. She is wearing a silk cream gown that shimmers and flows to the floor. Perched atop her head, I swear is a tiny tiara. I try with all my might not to giggle at the spectacle.

But considering I'm not technically even here and as far as anyone knows, Ava Elias is a waitress – who cares if I giggle at them?

A second vehicle of even more glamour appeared at the carpet. I can only imagine it is the arrival of Chen's parents, given the fanfare they are receiving. A stern looking man steps out, his face similarly shaped to Samuel Chen, barely recognisably aged. He turns to offer his hand to a short woman with sharp features. They stride toward the carpet, stopping only to shake hands with one man before crossing the threshold into the party. Mrs Chen's dress of midnight blue satin had a feminine boatneck and delicate beading. Mr Chen looked like he walked straight out of the 1920s with a short, sharp moustache, three piece suit and silk opera scarf.

I must not giggle, I must not giggle.

I see Chen and Mei enter further into the room, having completed their photo op at the entry. Chen stops on the precipice, before a mass of people swarm him and his date. A sea of deep bows, enthusiastic handshakes, people shoving business cards in his direction.

You'd think this man was a rock star.

I see Abbie appear at his elbow, introducing him to different guests, steering both him and Mei through the crowd before racing back to all but curtsey to Mr & Mrs Chen and complete the circuit again.

Out of nowhere, I am suddenly reminded of what it feels like to be the last person picked for a team in P.E. I look down at Winnie's ring, taking a deep breath. I am not alone. Winnie is with me in this. Hell, he's the one who threw me in here! I place my champagne flute down on the nearest table, adjust my dress and make my way toward Chen.

He did say he wanted me to meet his parents. Except we have had several arguments since then. Oh well!

I'm merely metres away when a hand grabs my elbow and yanks me back harshly. I turn around in shock to find Tony's bony fingers digging into my flesh.

"Not so fast. You're no one to these people. It would be the most dishonourable impertinence for you to approach Mr Chen yourself in a setting such as this. Especially considering you are here as a waitress." He sneers in my ear.

"You. Of course, it was you who changed my registration on the guest list." I shake my head, wrenching my elbow free of his grasp, stumbling slightly. I look up and lock eyes with Chen, realising he'd witnessed the entire exchange.

"Excuse me." I spit at Tony and leave the main space, searching for the bathroom.

The solace I sought eluded me sadly because as soon as I entered the bathroom, I could hear the giggles and whispers of women oohing and aahing over Chen and Mei.

"You know I heard they are already engaged but no one wants to confirm it until he is also in charge of CI."

"I heard Mei is pregnant!"

"I heard they just arrived!" I gasp, pointing toward the door. A mass exodus followed leaving me alone in the bathroom with only one cubicle remaining occupied. I place my clutch down on the sink, finding a dry spot and dig out my lipstick. After touching it up,

I wash my hands and check my phone. Still no messages from Ryan.

A couple of lovely messages in reply from the girls to my selfie.

I look down at my arm in the mirror, already seeing the darkening red spots where Tony's fingers gouged into my skin.

Asshole. I don't care who he thinks he is. I am officially listed as the owner of HEH on the national registry. Only a few people know how to access it, but it is still a matter of public record. I am still the goddamn CEO of this place.

I square my shoulders, pick up my clutch and yank the bathroom door open. Stepping out into the hall I almost collide with a tall male figure.

"My apologies!" I stammer embarrassed, trying to sidestep the man. His scent makes me stop dead. Chen turns to smile down at me.

"Miss Elias." He bows elegantly.

"Mr Chen," I grind out. His tuxedo sits elegantly cut in all the right places. I notice at this distance that his tie has a faint silk checkered pattern on it, his cufflinks look as though they are made from solid gold.

"We have many things to discuss, you and I." He eyes me warily.

"I have nothing to say to you, Chen. You didn't back me with Tony, I can't trust you." I shake my head, moving to sidestep him again.

"Ava, he threatened to sue. What else could I do?" He implores me.

"Oh, I don't know. Spoken to me about it perhaps?"

"You were a little 'flying off the handle' at the time if I recall correctly."

"Perhaps if I felt like you had my back I wouldn't always switch to defensive mode!" I whisper angrily up at him.

"You look stunning tonight." He lifts one hand to sweep an errant curl back into place.

"What?" I stop, derailed. 'Stop it Chen. You're here with your fiancée for god's sake." I swat his hand away.

"That doesn't change anything. And I do want to talk to you about Tony, but we need a game plan. We can't just..." He stops suddenly, looking past my shoulder. I turn to see Mei standing at the end of the corridor. She stalks slowly toward us, like a predatorial cat. I notice her tiara glimmering in the light. It looks like one of those flower crown things boho women wear to their weddings.

"I take it you are the 'Ava' we all hear so much about." She states bluntly, eyeing me critically.

"I...yes..I'm Ava." I frown looking between her and Chen. "I don't understand. You know who I am?"

Mei lets out a high pitched sarcastic laugh.

"Of course we do. You're a no-good tramp who stole dear Mr Huynh's fortune,' she whispers threateningly.

"Now Mei, that's not very nice." Chen admonishes her gently.

"I don't care what the public records state, my Chen is the only CEO of HEH that I or anyone else will ever recognise." She scathes at me before stomping down the hall, the long train on her dress dragging behind her.

I feel as though I've been punched in the gut. Can today get any more fun? Why don't we have a 'throw the shoe at Ava' game too?

"She can be a little territorial,' Chen sighs, reaching up to run a hand through his hair, only to drop it back to his side when he remembers the ponytail.

"Chen. There is something really wrong with Tony. I can't explain it right now, but we need him out. As soon as possible. I still haven't figured out what he has been up to with the foundation and we are running out of time."

"Ava, please stop with the conspiracy theories. They are giving me a headache. I told you there is nothing going on. You keep asking me to have your back, when are you going to have mine?" Chen holds his hand up in my face to silence my protests, turns on his heel and walks down the hall in Mei's wake.

Ugh! Men!

I head down the hall to see the seating attendants are assisting guests to their tables.

"Miss Elias?" A lady with a clipboard approaches me.

"Yes?" I turn to see her eyeing me curiously.

"Would you like me to escort you to your table?" I am still listed as seated?

"I'd be most grateful. Thank you." I nod for her to lead the way.

The dining and ceremony space took up the majority of the meetings I attended with the Events team. The ceiling glittered with fairy lights amongst the gossamer wrapped beams. Every inch of space that wasn't covered in plates or flowers held tealight candles housed in crystal cubes. I smile wryly to myself, noting the gold cutlery on the tables. Each table setting appearing to have been measured out with perfect precision, not a fork or water glass out of place as far as the eye could see.

My attendant leads me to a table on the back row of the gargantuan room. The table accommodated eight people and sat to the left of the speakers podium. After my escort departs, I step into the middle of the room, staring up at the glass podium.

For so many years, Winnie stood here and gave the address. I wish I could have been here for just one of them and seen you in all your glory.

Turning back to face my table I notice the number. 13.

Ah, the number of death in Japanese culture and the 'sad singles' table in American Wedding planning.

I look down to find my name card.

"Eva Elias".

I roll my eyes.

Of course. Fucking, Tony.

I look up to see him entering the room deep in conversation with Chen, his parents and Mei. He looks up and smirks at me before taking a seat at the main table with the Chen family.

The dinner proceeded in relative normalcy. Having never attended one of these 'dos' before I could only assume that proceedings would follow as discussed with the PR team in planning. The emcee steps up to the podium and welcomes the guests to the event. He gives a short spiel about HEH and the history of the Foundation. He introduces Mr Ling the head of the Public Housing Foundation. My ears perk up as I watch a gentleman of Winnie's age take to the stage.

There you are. Why have you been avoiding me, Mr Ling?

A standard applause follows the conclusion of his speech before the emcee welcomes Chen to the stage.

I watch with curiosity as Mr Ling shakes hands with Tony and sits down in the vacant seat beside him.

"It is my greatest honour to be here tonight, representing Huynh Enterprises Holdings. As you all know..." Chen's enchanting voice captivates the entire audience as he smiles his megawatt Hollywood smile.

I watch with interest as Tony and Ling continue to lean over and whisper quietly to each other. Ling frowns deeply, pulling back to watch Tony's face.

'...Mr Huynh concluded '...from that day on, I realised I could change people's lives for the better' and I too hope to follow in his footsteps." Chen bowed deeply to each side of the podium before Mr Ling joined him on stage to shake hands for a photo op. Chen handing Ling a giant cardboard cheque in donation to the foundation.

After stepping down from the stage, I note with curiosity that Tony and Ling disappear out a side door. I excuse myself from the table and follow them, trying not to arouse suspicion. I step through the door with trepidation, but am unable to immediately spot Tony or Ling.

'...What do you mean you were going to tell me?"

I hear outraged whispers from the end of the corridor.

I follow the narrow walkway until I come upon a corner, peering around it quietly I see Tony and Ling standing about 5 metres away, frowning angrily at one another. I pull out my phone and switch it to silent mode, flipping on the audio recorder.

"It seemed like a minor inconvenience and I assure you I am taking care of it." Tony hisses.

"Minor inconvenience? This woman is the owner and proprietor of all of HEH and all of Winnie's assets and you didn't think it was important to mention it?" Ling almost shrieks.

"It will not get in the way of our plans. Chen is calling the shots and he is securely in my pocket. The woman is a nobody. No one will notice if she disappears and she will. I will find a way to make her go away." Tony implores Ling. I feel my mouth gape open, the blood rushing from my head.

"And what of our deal? You said you had a developer lined up to purchase the land the second you could get Winnie's signature on the papers. That was over a year ago! Now he is gone, and some bimbo is in charge of his affairs?! I've put a lot on the line here Tony and you said it would be worth my while." Ling points an accusatory finger in Tony's face. Tony begins to redden, his brow sweating profusely.

"I helped Winnie build this foundation and I am starting to regret getting into bed with you. I should never have let you talk me into selling off foundation land right from under Winnie's nose." Ling begins to pace back and forth anxiously.

Oh my god. This is even worse than I could have imagined.

I hear someone coming down the corridor and turn to look down the hallway. Seeing no one I turn back around and come face to face with Tony.

"You little bitch!" He grabs me by the wrist and drags me into the corridor with Ling. "How dare you eavesdrop on a private conversation." Out of nowhere, he backhands me across the face launching me into the side of a giant decorative vase. I feel my head crack against the carved marble.

"Zhang Wei Tony!" I shout as loud as I can muster, my head pounding. 'You are FIRED. F.I.R.E.D. As are you, Mr Ling!" I prop myself up against the vase stand.

Tony rushes toward me again, this time his hand balled into a fist. I manage to duck his fist and clock him one across the face with my right hand- Winnie's ring leaving a deep gash in his cheek.

Note to self, get Winnie's ring cleaned.

"What on earth?!" I hear Chen's voice bellowing down at us. I see him at the corner taking in the scene.

"Mr Chen, she came in and attacked Mr Ling and I like a rabid animal!" Tony wails from the floor, holding his bleeding face. Chen looks up at me, his eyes betraying his stony face.

Holy shit. He doesn't know whether or not Tony is lying.

"Tony and Ling..." I gasp, my vision beginning to spot.

"Shut up!" Tony howls from the floor.

"Tony and Ling have been negotiating the sale of Foundation land to a property developer, right out from under HEH...." I stumble away from the pot, landing on my ass on the floor, my phone clattering away from me.

"Tony, is this true?" Chen looks from me to Tony, still uncertain. Tony spots my phone and the recorder still blinking on the screen in front of me.

"You were recording a private conversation!?" He rages, lunging toward my phone. Chen reaches forward and grabs him by the collar of his jacket, just as security arrive at the corridor.

"Take Mr Tony and Mr Ling to the local police station. Miss Elias will be pressing assault charges." He hands a wailing Tony across to the security team. Ling raises his hands in the air and whilst weeping quietly, departs in a far more dignified manner.

"Ava?" Chen steps closer to me cautiously. He bends down and hits 'stop' on the recorder, passing me back my phone.

"You didn't believe me,' I mumble up at him, shock starting to set in.

"What?" He frowns at me, squatting down to my level.

"I saw your f...face. You didn't know who was telling the t...truth." I feel hot tears burning my eyes.

"Did he hurt you?" Chen peers more closely, eyeing the darkening bruise on my cheek and arm.

"Just leave me alone Chen." I spit, uncertain if I am going to vomit or pass out.

"Let's get you some air." He reaches his arms out and lifts me until we are both standing. I wobble a little as he wraps his arm around my waist and helps me to the door.

Chen leads me downstairs from the hotel to the side entry. We stand in the glow of the doorway, staring at one another.

"Are you okay?" He looks down at me, his face full of concern.

"I bumped my head when Tony hit me, but I'll be okay." I glare at him. "I think maybe I should sit down." I look around finding nowhere suitable, spotting a bush I can vomit into if need be.

"I never thought I'd see the day when anyone could slug Tony like that. Let alone a woman. Remind me never to get on your bad side.' He chuckles, picking up my hand to kiss my bruised knuckles. "I am sorry for doubting you. For all of it. Seems you were right about Tony all along."

'I knew he was up to something, but I can't believe he was trying to sell the foundation land." I feel the anger welling up inside, my hands starting to shake. "He even said something about 'getting rid of me'." I shudder. The logical half of my brain knows the adrenaline will wear off soon and I'll be in pretty rough shape. The romantic side of my brain is batting its eyelids at Chen, standing here in his arms dressed like two Hollywood stars from an old black and white film.

It's not like I have anything to feel guilty about. Ryan hasn't been returning my calls anyway.

"I've thought about what you said all those weeks ago and I've decided I'm not buying it. You can't hold it against me." Chen reaches down, sweeping a curl behind my ear with the gentlest of fingertips.

"Hold what against you?" I breathe up at him, my head throbbing.

"The fact that I didn't know you before. You don't get to dictate what might or mightn't have happened between us if we'd met under different circumstances." His body heat radiating off him, standing pressed so close together.

"Chen, I ..." I stammer.

"Because I can tell you one thing for certain. There is no way your radiant smile; your auburn mane; your infectious laugh or your incredible generosity would have passed me by unnoticed." He breathes, his minty breath fanning my face, my lips.

"I know deep down that I would have fallen for you, Ava Elias, with or without the Huynh part." He leans forward until we are just barely touching, his hand reaches up to cup my face. I reach mine up and grasp the lapels of his tuxedo, worried I might fall over.

"Chen, stop. Someone might see." I implore him, my terrified eyes meeting his. I don't see terror reflected back, but lust and longing.

"I don't care who sees. I will shout it to the world." He whispers, his lips in the hair at the crown of my head. My heart starts to hammer harder inside my chest, my hands shaking against Chen's. 'Please Ava."

I close my eyes, willing my heart to quiet.

"Ava?"

Chen and I turn embraced, toward the voice.

Please god, tell me I'm wrong. It can't be.

Standing in the glowing light of the entry, in a tuxedo and tails, bowtie and combed beach boy hair.

"Ryan,' I breathe. I feel my legs give way from underneath me.

Chen catches me and eases me down onto the sidewalk, not letting go of my arms. I feel Ryan rush to my side, ripping off his jacket to cover my shoulders.

"Ryan, it's....not what it...looked like,' I stammer, my hands shaking so hard I let go of my purse.

"Good god Ava, how much have you had to drink?" Ryan scolds, grabbing my purse off the ground and dusting it off.

Suddenly Abbie appears with a string of PR staff behind her. "Oh, Ava! We just heard about Mr Tony, are you okay? Did he hurt you?" She begins to flail about ineffectually. "We have had security escort him off the premises. Should I get a medic to come and look at you?" She suddenly seems to realise Ryan and Chen are also present.

"Who hurt you? Ava, what is going on?" Ryan squats down in front of me taking my hands. He notices my knuckles in the dim light. "Did you get into a fight?"

"It's a very long story,' Chen states monotonically down to Ryan.

"Is that so?" Ryan stands up, even at full height, he is half a head shorter than Chen.

"Stop it, all of you." I grind out through clenched teeth, trying not to vomit on Ryan's shoes. 'Abbie, can you get Xi to bring the car around. I just want to go home." I sigh, raising my hand to my head where I hit it, wincing. I pull my fingers away and see glistening blood in the dim light.

"Oh no, we are taking you for a CT. And then someone is going to tell me what the fuck is going on." Ryan growls.

"Dr Golden-boy to the rescue. But, wait. You're not a real doctor, are you? You're a paramedic,' Chen sneers.

Ryan squats down in front of me again, taking my hand. "You're right, he is a jerk." He smiles warmly at me.

"Ryan?" I mutter.

"Yeah, honey?" He pats my hair.

"I think I'm going to vomit."

The entire crowd jumps back a pace or two.

"Adrenaline spike, head trauma and vomiting. My darling, I think you may have a concussion. Let's get you to a hospital. Someone do me a favour and grab us an ice bucket."

As Ryan assists me into the car, I spot a familiar face sprinting up the sidewalk.

"Miss Ava!" Seal howls. "They wouldn't let me in because I WASN'T ON THE GUESTLIST! And now look! I have failed you."

"Seal, honey, go into the party and get drunk. Find someone to take home. Or better yet, call Jia. I'm sure she'll love that." I pat his hand absentmindedly before pushing him away from the door. "Let's go, Xi."

The hospital fluorescents are bright, making my eyes hurt.

"Ryan?" I whisper.

"Hey, I'm right here." He takes my hand, patting my hair.

"Can you turn the lights off?" I squint up at him. He laughs and leans across to flip the switch on the wall.

"Did you really come all the way to Singapore to come to my ball?" I turn to look at him, my hospital gown crinkling.

"I did." He smiles down at me.

"I thought you weren't talking to me. You never called me back." I feel my eyes begin to well.

"I wanted to keep it a surprise. I never imagined I'd get there to find you like this!" He waves a hand referring to the current situation.

"Did you like my dress?"

"Even vomiting into an ice bucket in Xi's SUV, you looked stunning." He chuckles.

"Xi is going to be so mad." I feel a tear slide down my cheek.

"It isn't like you were drunk Ava, you have a serious concussion. No one could blame you for vomiting after that ordeal." He strokes my hair softly.

"So you aren't mad at me?" I look up at him.

"Why would I be mad?" He shakes his head confused.

"Because I was standing so close to Chen and..." I can't bring myself to say it.

"Ava, you looked like you were clinging to him for dear life. It certainly didn't look romantic if that is what you are worried about." He kisses my hair softly.

'Oh, I should give you these back. You won't need another CT so you can put them back on." He pulls out a handkerchief from his inner jacket pocket and unveils Winnie's ring and earrings.

I cry even harder, lifting Winnie's ring from Ryan's hand and slipping it on.

"You'll have to tell me the story behind that one day too." He smiles at me, helping me fasten the earrings. "But for now, you need to sleep. Gladys tells me you haven't been sleeping particularly well lately."

"Gladys is here?"

"Everyone is here." He chuckles rolling his eyes. 'But the doctors will release you in the morning so they can all wait and see you at breakfast."

17

"I can't believe he hit her!"

"She said from the start she didn't like the guy.'

"Every businessman in Singapore knows he plays dirty."

Turning off the steaming shower and opening the bathroom door, I hear raised voices echoing upstairs from the kitchen. Ryan turns away from the mirror and kisses my damp hair, "Don't listen to them."

"Is everyone here?" I sigh. I refused to see anyone yesterday when I got out of the hospital. I just wanted to go home, eat pancakes and sleep in my own bed.

"Last I checked we were still waiting on Tari." He smiles at me, taking my hand and pulling me toward him. He leans back against the vanity and envelopes me in a warm hug.

"I missed you,' he whispers into my hair.

"I missed you too." I lean back, lightly dragging my fingernails through his stubble and kissing him chastely on the lips.

I lean past him to stare at my face in the mirror at the dark purple bruise blooming across my cheekbone.

"Showtime princess!" He winks at me as I turn toward the door.

Wrapped in my giant robe, I decide I don't care what I look like and walk down into the kitchen to the awaiting crowd.

I spot everyone seated around the large table on the deck and the kitchen bench covered in a smorgasbord of breakfast. Ryan joins me in the kitchen, his hand finds my waist like it is the most natural thing in the world.

"Gladys went all out!" He picks up a plate, handing it across to me. "Coffee or juice?"

"Both please!" I smile across at him.

Is this what Sunday Mornings would be like with him? Waking up, sneaky kisses in the shower and eating pancakes over the city of Singapore?

"The food isn't going to walk onto your plate." Ryan cocks an eyebrow at me, halfway through scooping scrambled eggs onto his own plate.

"I was just thinking how great this is." I smile at him shyly. He looks around us nodding.

"I mean, it is' no fry up at Ivan's but it is pretty special,' he teases.

"Come on you two! We're waiting!" Jia hollers from the balcony.

I roll my eyes and pile my plate with pancakes, bacon, eggs, fruit, mascarpone and grab the jug of maple syrup in the other hand.

Ryan and I head out and join the others, enjoying the warm morning breeze. I smile around at the table, looking into the faces of the people who have made me feel so welcome here. Jia, Margot and Linah. Xi and Seal, Sasha and Gladys.

"Where's Tari?" I frown.

"She's on the breakfast shift, she'll be around later." Gladys pats my hand reassuringly. I turn to Margot.

"I'm so sorry I didn't get to wear your dress on the red carpet. I was so excited to tell the world about your design."

"Don't you dare apologise! It was hardly your fault!" She waves her fork at me from across the table.

"I wish I could have been there to see you punch Tony in the face. I hope Winnie's ring leaves him with a dirty great scar!" Jia cackles maniacally. After seeing the shocked expressions around the table, she mutters, 'Everyone was thinking it." I laugh and lift my hand to high-five her.

"Speaking of Tony. I fired him and I expect it is going to stick this time,' I chuckle, turning to face Jia front on.

'It seems I am in the market for a new General Counsel. Do you know anyone who might be interested?" Jia's mouth falls open into a perfect 'O'.

"I think that's the first time I've ever seen her speechless." Seal quips from his end of the table. Jia throws a cube of watermelon at him.

"Ava, are you saying what I think you are saying?" Jia gushes.

"I could think of no greater honour than walking into this next phase of HEH with you at my side." I feel myself starting to choke up.

"I'll have to review the offer, but YES! You can count on me!" She hugs me tightly.

The front door goes, lighting up the panel inside the door. Gladys stands and tends to the visitor.

"That must be Tari." Sasha smiles down the table at me.

"Before you go this morning Sasha, I have a couple of things we need to go through." I smile at her as I stand and excuse myself, heading toward the elevator to greet Tari.

She has been so good to me, she sent me a bouquet of flowers and some pre-mixed cocktails. Which Ryan confiscated because I can't have alcohol for a few days.

I roll my eyes at the thought, just as the elevator comes to a halt.

"Good to see your brain injury didn't affect your eye-rolling abilities,' Chen smirks down at me. The breeze from the open door catches his fringe, making him look like a model standing before a wind machine.

"Chen!" I grimace, somewhat louder than I intended.

"Oh goodie, here come the dogs." He stares down at me as Ryan and Jia walk in from the terrace.

"What do you want Chen?" Jia stares him down. In her 6 inch wedges she comes nose to nose with him.

"I came to check that Miss Elias is in good health." He smiles wryly.

"That's gallant of you,' Ryan mutters, placing a territorial hand at my waist. It doesn't pass by Chen unnoticed. His eyes sweep back up to my face.

"May I ask for a private audience with you?"

Jia and Ryan both begin to protest as Seal enters; sunglasses in place.

"I'll supervise,' he states blandly, cutting them off. I point Chen in the direction of Winnie's study. I squeeze Ryan's hand and follow Chen and Seal into the room.

"What can I do for you, Chen?" I turn to face him after closing the door.

"I am here to offer my resignation." He states flatly.

"Wh..what? Why?" I frown, feeling the weight of his statement hit me. I look around confused and plonk down on the sofa.

"It is the right thing to do. I have dishonoured both you and HEH." He bows his head, looking at his hands. I hear Seal snort an acknowledgement behind me. Chen's head snaps up to glare at him.

"I don't understand..." I feel lost.

"I should have listened to you about Tony. It just goes to show that I am unfit to lead anyone. It also proves that you were the rightful leader of HEH all along." He looks down at me, his regret and embarrassment clear as day.

"Chen, I don't want you to resign. But I suppose if it is what you want, I can't force you to stay." I frown down at Winnie's ring, glinting up at me.

"How can you say that after all the trouble I have caused you? I have been nothing but an arrogant show pony." He chastises himself.

"Sure, you might have been a little...' I smirk up at him, 'But I certainly don't want you to leave. I have watched in awe as you have helped me transform HEH. The people and the public love you, they don't see any of the behind the scenes drama."

"Do you really not blame me for what happened with Tony?" A glimmer of hope tints his voice.

"Of course it might have been avoided had you listened to me, but no. I do not blame you for the illegal shit he was doing. You weren't to know how bad it truly was." I shrug.

'Jia looked over the properties and papers. Tony had one almost in the bag and two in the queue. Something akin to $100m in land and property."

Chen grimaces.

"Seems he was starting with the smaller plots, hoping to get them out unnoticed before moving on to the larger properties." I sigh heavily, feeling the exhaustion creeping in.

"Listen, Chen, you can do whatever makes you happy. But I have something I need to do for Winnie. I don't know how long it will take but I'd really appreciate having someone I can trust in the job while I'm gone." Chen's face contorts immediately into an unfamiliar emotion.

Fear? Worry? Sadness?

"Where are you going?"

"I need to go back to Australia and investigate something. I suspect that Winnie's death may not have been of 'natural causes' after all." I look down at his ring.

"Are you saying you think someone wanted to do him harm?" Chen drags his hands through his hair, sitting down heavily on the lounge beside me.

"I told you, I heard Tony telling Ling that he could 'get rid of me' without anyone noticing. I am starting to wonder if he did the same to Winnie,' I shudder at the thought.

"What could possibly be in Australia that can help you solve that?" He turns to look at me, an ocean of baby blue.

"You're just going to have to trust me. But for the meantime, I have made an offer to Jia as replacement General Counsel. She will work with you while I am gone."

Chen's mouth opens to protest but he seems to decide the better of it. "Very well. As you wish." He nods.

"Approximately how long will you be gone? Weeks, Months...?" He almost whispers.

"I don't know. As long as it takes, I'm afraid. This is one thing I won't let rest. But I need you to promise me you'll keep tabs on Tony, I can't have him sticking his nose in ever again." I look across at Chen and hold out my hand 'Deal?"

"Deal." He shakes it firmly, turning over my hand to inspect Winnie's ring. 'You will have to tell me the story behind this piece one day."

"It belonged to someone very special,' I whisper, feeling my eyes prickle.

A knock at the door jolts us both.

"Coming,' I call toward the door. I stand, following Seal to the door and walk Chen to the elevator.

"When will you leave?" He asks as I turn to farewell him in the lobby.

"I'll head back as soon as I am allowed to fly. Besides, I have quite a lot of explaining to do with my family and friends back home,' I shrug.

"Safe travels, until I see you again,' Chen bows deeply, taking my hand and kissing my knuckles.

"Stay safe Chen. Look after our people,' I smile up at him.

Ryan stands in the hallway watching curiously.

"Is it a cultural thing? The bowing and the hand-kissing stuff?" He scoffs.

"I think it's a Chen thing?" I shrug, grabbing his face and kissing him hard. "Is there a problem?" I smile up at him.

"None at all!" He smirks, kissing me back.

"Miss Ava! Oh..." Sasha rounds the corner. "Apologies Ava." She blushes.

"None necessary,' I chuckle, peeling myself away from Ryan.

"You mentioned you wanted to go through a few things?" She pulls out her iPad to take notes.

"Ah, yes. Where is Seal?' I look around, he usually lurks close by.

"Present." He steps forward into the hall, standing at salute.

"How'd you like to come to Australia?" I cock an eyebrow at him.

"Is Xi coming too?" He queries.

"Xi?" I holler.

"It would be an honour!" Xi steps up beside Seal.

I turn to Sasha who is scribbling on her iPad.

"Sasha, please have the Screaming Eagle ready for midday tomorrow. We're going down under."

Tari never made it to breakfast, so the next day before heading to the airport Ryan and I stopped in at Spago to say farewell.

"I promise, the second I get my hands on it I will bring it back here for you to translate!" I hug her tightly.

"That could be weeks by the time you get things sorted with your family back home!" She wails, hugging me back fiercely.

"I promise you." I lean back to look her in the face. 'I couldn't leave my main gal for much longer than that anyway." I wink at her.

"I suppose you have a plane to catch huh?" She sniffles.

"Oh, haven't you heard? When you own the jet, the jet waits for you!" We laugh together, feeling lighter for the first time in a long time.

I can't help but smile at the look on Ryan's face when he first comes face to face with Screaming Eagle.

"Wait. No. This is some kind of joke,' He stands, mouth agape with his hand in mine.

"No joke,' I giggle.

"You're telling me I paid $800 and flew economy for 8 hours to get here only days ago and this thing was sitting here at your disposal the whole time?!"

"If I knew you were coming, I would have sent it over to pick you up,' I shrug. He turns to stare at me.

"Okay, Ava honey. I saw the penthouse and I didn't say anything. And I heard you talking to Sasha about 'the jet' and 'the helicopter' but I didn't think it meant this!" He stops to face me. 'Exactly how rich was Winnie?" His eyes look as though they will boggle out at any moment.

"Winnie was very rich Ryan." I look down at our entwined hands. 'I hope that doesn't change the way you see me."

He lifts our hands to his lips and kisses my knuckles gently.

"You're still wearing the same sunglasses you scratched on the slopes last year. Somehow I don't think the money will change you." He whispers, chuckling deeply. I lean forward and kiss him tenderly.

"Thank you." I sigh, resting my forehead against his. 'Are you ready to meet the flight crew?"

"We have our own flight crew?" He stares at me before turning to look at the G650 on the tarmac.

"Shotgun!" Seal shouts, screaming past us to the stairs.

After eight hours of napping, movie watching, gourmet eating and playing board games we land back at the Melbourne Air Base.

Disembarking, our journey back to Dinner Plain was essentially my trip to Singapore in reverse. We stayed the remainder of the night at the Crown Hotel after I decided Seal and Xi deserved a little pampering.

The next morning, we climbed aboard the helicopter and flew to Hotham where the snow had been cleared for us to land. The weather was crisp and clear- not a cloud in the sky. A parked BBSUV was waiting for us with the heater running nice and toasty.

"I need to stop in at the bank to look for something,' I tell the driver, giving him directions back to Bright.

Entering the bank, I take my key out of my handbag and hand it over to the teller. After an age, they walked me through to the little room full of safety deposit boxes. I insert the key into the lock and turn it hesitantly. Pulling the door open, I stare at the handbag dustcover wrapped box inside.

Why am I surprised to find it is still here? Clearly I've seen way too many movies.

With trembling hands, I pull the box down and take a seat, placing it on the table. I gently remove the dustcover and look down at the stunning Walnut timber box. I run my fingers over the surface, Winnie's ring seeming to hum at the contact.

I lift the lid and peer into the box, realising for the first time how many other items I overlooked the last time. The one item I knew I sought, peered up at me from the side of the box. A bound book, simply labelled on the spine in gold embossment 'Part I'. I am so glad I left Part II safely secured in Singapore. Winnie had written in his final letter that I needed both halves for the 'answers I seek'.

I lift the book from the box and flip through the gold-flecked edges. As it is only a year or so old, it is in much better condition than some of his other journals. Reaching the last page containing text; about halfway through the book, I stop and stare. There in Winnie's beautiful calligraphic script stood two words.

"Be careful."

AUTHOR NOTES

I hope you have enjoyed The Invisible Woman as much as I enjoyed writing it. As someone who fell in love with both Dinner Plain and Singapore the moment I set foot there, I hope to do both communities justice through my depictions.

I ought to note very strongly that Singapore is in fact one of the most inclusive countries in the world when it comes to female inclusivity in CEO and other Board positions. For this novel, I pushed the Invisible Woman angle, as I believe it was necessary for the story and globally this narrative is still strong today. South-East Asia however is a different story and for many years has held the title of the highest percentage of Women CEOs in the world.

It must be very clearly noted that according to Deloitte (2024) "Women hold less than one-quarter (23.3%) of the world's board seats. Just 8.4% of the world's boards are chaired by women and 6% of CEOs are women. Southeast Asia sees an increase in the percentage of board seats held by women – from 17.1% in 2021 to 19.9% in 2023 – a 2.8 percentage point uptick". (*Deloitte, Women in the Boardroom A Global Perspective - 8th edition*, 2024)

I also note that I took creative licence when giving Samuel Chen blue eyes, as I know statistically and genetically the likelihood of this is near impossible.

If you enjoyed reading, please let other readers know by leaving a star rating or review on Amazon or Goodreads. As an independent author, my readers are my lifeline, and without your support I wouldn't be a writer. Thank you once again for reading, and I hope you enjoyed The Invisible Woman and are ready to dive into The Invisible Fight, where Ava's adventure continues. – Anna

www.ingramcontent.com/pod-product-compliance
Lightning Source LLC
Chambersburg PA
CBHW030021180626
46810CB00001B/157